DE[illegible] OF[illegible] EDITOR

An utterly gripping murder mystery

LESLEY GRANT-ADAMSON

A Rain Morgan Mystery Book 3

Previously published as *Wild Justice*

JOFFE
Ostara
CLASSICS

Revised edition 2023
Joffe Books, London
www.joffebooks.com

First published by Faber and Faber in
Great Britain in 1987 as *Wild Justice*

This paperback edition was first published
in Great Britain in 2023

Cover art by Dee Dee Book Covers

ISBN: 978-1-83526-316-7

For Judy Porter

CHAPTER 1

The proprietor of the *Daily Post* was found dead at his desk. He had owned the paper barely a month. He had been stabbed.

Hal MacQuillan's death went unmourned for some time because this was the day the printers walked out and the readers stormed in. It was 6 July, a Friday, at the end of a week of heatwave.

Tempers had risen in step with the temperature and the day of the murder was the hottest. There was a failure of that fragile co-operation which normally allows disparate factions to produce a newspaper together. Many people said and did regrettable things, and someone killed.

The discomfort of working with inadequate air conditioning merely exacerbated trouble. The trouble had begun when MacQuillan moved into the big office on the second floor; or it had begun months before when the previous owner announced he was selling; or it had always been there, and in every office in Fleet Street, because the interests of those disparate factions could never quite be reconciled.

Losing their first skirmish with MacQuillan, the printers seethed and turned their minds to smaller things. That inefficient air conditioning system, for instance. The fathers of the union chapels reported that their members could not be expected to work in such conditions. The management said the system would be inspected; but the contractors were overworked with similarly pressing requests and did not come. The unions said things were no better; the management said they were equally unpleasant on the second floor. The fathers demanded action; the management prayed for a thunderstorm. The printers threatened to strike; the management brought in an array of electric fans. But the printers would not allow them to be connected up, saying they wanted fresh air and not stale air swished about. The management retorted that fresh air was at a premium and if the printers could find any they could have it. The fathers marched their men out of the back door for a meeting which voted they should all go home.

While the printers were in the rear yard, nine young men with close-cropped hair and quiet shoes arrived in the front entrance hall. Their T-shirts labelled them the Patriotic Ten. They ignored the receptionist and made for the lifts. The woman called, they pretended not to hear. She went over, was grabbed and dragged into a lift by two of them. The rest ran up the adjoining stairs.

It took a few minutes for everyone in the first floor editorial office to notice them. Gradually typewriters and telephones fell silent and journalists watched the news editor being harangued. The leader of the group, Zak Smythe, was doing most damage, thrusting his jaw into the seated man's face, thumping his fist on the desk and making papers fly, giving the occasional noisy kick at a metal waste bin. He was about twenty, a big-boned bull-necked youth it appeared reckless to antagonize.

The news editor, a willowy Irishman very new to the job, put up a token resistance: he moved his wire mesh basket of copy out of the line of attack. Another of the youths swiped it to the floor. Riley never gave it a glance. He said to Zak: 'If you're not happy with our coverage, why don't you write us a letter?'

Zak sneered. Then: 'Oh dear, Tony,' he said over Riley's head, 'you've knocked all the man's papers on the floor. Don't you think you ought to pick them up?'

'Yeah,' said Tony and scooped the papers into the bin. He stamped on the mesh basket and then strolled around the desks gathering up all the pieces of paper which had stories or page plans on them or appeared in some other way important to the making of a newspaper. And he tipped them all into the bin and he waited.

Riley spoke, but Zak shouted him down. The detail was lost on those further away but the abiding impression was that no one moved to Riley's defence while the Irishman was subjected to racial abuse along with more general humiliation. The burden of it was that the youths did not approve of the *Daily Post's* reporting of the troubles in Northern Ireland and that it was no surprise to them to find the paper had an Irish news editor and that he was exactly the sort who was ruining their country and ought to be repatriated. They expressed it more crudely than that.

'And when we've finished with you, Paddy, we're going to have your editor,' snarled Tony.

'Yeah,' echoed the others.

Zak snapped his fingers and a tattooed youth tossed him a box of matches. He tipped lighter fuel into the bin and threw a match after it.

Riley leapt up, swearing. Zak blocked him, his own body shielded from the flames. He shoved Riley backwards. People sprang from their chairs, shocked at how far things were going. A sub-editor took up an identical bin, intending to drop it inside the one that was alight, but one of the youths scared him off. Zak swung a fist at Riley who was forced a shade nearer the fire. Zak jeered, jabbed at him again. But this time Riley ducked and seized the bin and hurled its contents over him.

There was a yelp of pain and surprise as hair was singed and flames licked skin. Zak recoiled and his troops recoiled from him. Riley savagely kicked the bin down the room and it lay there on its side, blackened and hot, with an acrid smell as the fire died.

It came to rest by Rain Morgan's desk. She pushed blonde hair back from her forehead and wrinkled her nose. Her deputy on the gossip column, Holly Chase, muttered that she would like to kick the bin back again. Rosie, their fashion-conscious secretary, chewed a lacquered fingernail. The two journalists who completed the team were away and Oliver West, one of the paper's cartoonists, occupied a chair.

'Who are the Patriotic Ten?' he whispered.

Rain shook her head.

Holly said: 'I don't know, but I know what they're like.' She shuddered.

Oliver put a protective hand on her arm. Holly was black. The Patriotic Ten had demonstrated their loathing of Irishmen and would probably not care for blacks, either. Oliver said: 'Why are the Ten only nine?'

Rain suggested that number ten had commandeered the switchboard. 'There haven't been any calls since the invasion.'

But Rain was wrong about the Patriotic Ten taking control of the switchboard. That had been done by the left-wing activists who were parading with placards outside the building and denouncing Oliver and that morning's cartoon. It made a cruel stab at the free speech lobby whose crazier ideas included giving readers control over the contents of magazines and newspapers. In the name of free speech they had cut off contact between the *Post* and the outside world.

After obstructing the pavement and posing for photographers from rival papers they ran inside, relieved the guard on the switchboard and headed for the newsroom. By this time the Ten had gone to find the editor.

There were fourteen free speech campaigners, advancing complicated arguments in favour of readers' control and making simple statements about Oliver. Unlike the Ten they had no leader, they were all equal and entitled to speak. They did so, simultaneously.

'Comrades!' A woman's shrill voice towered from time to time. 'We are here to . . .' The rest was hubbub.

Riley, stooping over the remains of the day's copy, looked stricken. For the second time that afternoon he made the mistake of eye contact. The most vociferous of the contingent gathered around him with demands for a right of reply to cartoons they did not like.

Oliver shrank behind the sweetheart pot plant which a grateful reader had sent Rain, a 'small token of gratitude' which had grown into a large one. Groups of invaders were stalking the room, chanting and breaking off here and there to ask where he was. Someone indicated Oliver's vacant chair. Protesters took up position by it.

'Why doesn't someone tell them I'm not in the office today?' Oliver hissed.

Rain told him. 'Because they can see your things scattered about and a half-finished drawing for tomorrow.'

'Suppose they don't like tomorrow's either and rip it up?' There came a ripping sound.

'Never mind,' said Holly, feeling it was her turn to be consoling. 'At least they don't look violent, they only want to yell at you.'

Some of the stalkers recognized Rain. 'You're Rain Morgan!'

'So I am.' She offered them a dazzling smile but steeled herself for an attack on the doubtful principles of publishing gossip. It had not gone far when five of the Ten returned to see what the noise was about. Tony was there but not Zak.

'Tell them to shut up,' Tony instructed, and his team went around telling the free speech people to shut up, and smashing placards when they didn't.

'Now you listen to me, young man . . .' The shrill woman got no further.

'No, *you* listen to *me*.' Tony was menacing. 'We're having a consultation over there.' He jerked a thumb towards the editor's office. 'We were here first and we're having our consultation first, and we'd like everything nice and quiet while we have it. Now, are you going to let us have our free speech or are we going to have to fight for it?'

'Well . . .'

'Shut up!'

She did.

Shortly after, the missing four came out of the editor's office and Zak struck off in the direction of the room where telex machines spewed out news reports from around the world. Rain feared a massive bonfire of miles of paper but as Zak neared the room she was distracted by Oliver being suddenly identified and berated. He was valiant now the moment had come.

Rain whispered to Rosie who slid from her seat and got to the editor's office without hindrance. She returned with the request that spokesmen of the group gathered about Oliver meet the editor.

'We must all go,' said a determined man with a beard.

Rain intervened. 'You four can go.' She picked out those who had been hardest on Oliver.

The bearded man said: 'That won't do, there are no leaders here, we are all equal.'

'Exactly,' said Rain, continuing to be bossy. 'You are all equal so it doesn't matter who goes.'

'You don't understand,' an intense young woman argued.

Rain shot back: 'If you don't approve of my choice, pick another four. The editor won't see more than four.'

The four she had chosen were not willing to risk losing their chance so they set off before any others were nominated.

Matters settled into a spurious order. Riley, in the absence of Zak, came to an agreement with Tony that the local government reporter, a staid and unprovocative man, should help them draft a statement. The editor would then consider it for publication, as he had promised.

The Patriotic Ten and the local government man began work. The youths formulated their arguments with his help and he typed a grammatical version. Progress was reasonably smooth until one of the free speech people plucked the paper from the typewriter, saying the reporter was using the police method of taking down statements and what he had written did not sound like the speech of any of the Ten and therefore it was hardly their statement, was it?

Coolly the reporter asked the patriots whether they might not prefer one of the free speech people to help them instead. They said yes. A volunteer, a spare desk and a typewriter were found and work started on a second version of the statement.

By now word had filtered into the newsroom that the printers had gone home and there would be no Saturday paper. Some of the tension seeped away, the degree of disruption no longer mattered. When it was announced that the editor had negotiated restoration of the switchboard, there was no dash to make calls.

The editor was a colourless man who took refuge behind bombastic ties. Whatever the deputations of protesters expected when they were led to his office, it was not Luke Eliot. He was not a man who would give fight. He would not, like Riley, lose his temper nor, like Oliver, unleash a biting wit. He had the infuriating facility for making people do the things he wanted, but making them believe they had wanted them themselves.

It was unremarkable that he had turned aside both the Patriotic Ten and the free speech activists with the promise to consider for publication the statements they had not known until then they intended to write. With both groups quietly working at their texts at opposite ends of the newsroom he had achieved a kind of victory. Peace, at any rate. It served as an illustration of the day-by-day negotiating that usually resulted in people with conflicting interests bringing out the paper.

Eliot was decisive and reticent and, some said, deadly. His journalists called him God and did not easily tear up his commandments. MacQuillan had not believed in this particular god and let it be known. While he blustered and posed, Eliot — if rumour was correct — had instigated an investigation of the MacQuillan empire.

Eliot came out of his office, insignificant as a messenger boy, and made a slight gesture to Rain. She went to his room. Dick Tavett, the features editor, was already there. He'd had a difficult time since MacQuillan came and was increasingly careworn as the days went by. His staff used to laugh at his fretfulness, but lately it had been infectious.

Eliot sat upright at his desk, making a steeple of his fingers, and began. 'As there's no hope of a paper tomorrow this gives me an opportunity to talk to you about Hal's plans for the gossip column.' He gave a wry smile. They all knew MacQuillan was not entitled to any plans. He had given promises not to interfere in editorial matters and only on such conditions was he accepted as a buyer for the paper. They also knew the promises had been broken the day he walked into the building.

He had forced his political views into the leader column and sent the paper tumbling down-market by introducing a frivolous competition. *Girlie* was an elaborate version of Snap, played with pictures of nude women: the holder of the card which matched the published photograph won a prize as over-generous as the model's curves. Before his incredulous staff grasped that he meant to do it, MacQuillan launched *Girlie* with heavy coverage in the *Post* and an expensive television promotion. 'Why bother with numbers when we've got figures?' he asked viewers, with a knock at the bingo games on which other papers had staked their futures in the circulation battle. Sadly for his journalists, who had attempted an eleventh-hour stand for news and decency, the public warmed to *Girlie*. The National Union of Journalists passed a motion deploring a decline in standards, the print chapels were disappointingly slow to echo it, and the story that the Post Office could refuse to deliver the cards because they were obscene ended up as rumour in *Private Eye*. With *Girlie*, as with all else, MacQuillan got his way.

Tavett, nervously passing a hand over his balding head as if searching for the missing hair, began to say as much. Eliot interrupted. 'Hal has let several people know of his plans. I shall oppose them, of course, but . . .' He let the sentence trail.

Rain said unruffled: 'Tell us the plans.'

'No rumours yet?'

She told him: 'Only the one which says the new broom sweeps us all out and starts from scratch.'

Eliot said: 'The plan is for the gossip column to become three pages a day.'

'*What?*' Rain and Tavett spoke together.

Eliot went on: 'And for Holly Chase to edit.'

Tavett groaned. Rain, her loyalty to Holly torn, asked: 'What becomes of me?'

Eliot said: 'He thinks you wouldn't want to stay.'

Tavett repeated the groan. Rain, who found Eliot's news neither alarming nor surprising, asked whether Holly had heard.

'I don't think so,' Eliot said, 'at least, not directly.'

'No,' said Tavett angrily, 'he never chooses the direct route if there's a sneaky sideways one, does he?' He thumped a hand on the arm of his chair and stood up.

Eliot looked up at him, unflurried. 'Sit down, Dick. There's more.'

Tavett slumped. Eliot began: 'Obviously three gossip pages would mean the whole thrust of the features department's effort changing . . .'

Tavett said: 'He's going to force me out.'

'He's talking about leaving you where you are but giving you a different deputy, someone to oversee Holly.'

Rain and Tavett looked at each other with dawning realization. Rain said: 'Maureen!'

Tavett said: 'He must be crazy. She's a disaster as a reporter on the column, she knows nothing.'

Eliot shook his head. 'She's his daughter. What does she need to know?'

Tavett leaped up. 'I'm going up there to tell him. If he thinks I'll teach her my job and let her put me out of business . . .'

Rain reached out a restraining hand. 'Dick, don't see him now.'

'This is the best time, I've got a lot to say.'

'We both have,' she said with a little laugh, 'but we must think about it first.'

He would not be distracted. 'I've done as much thinking as this needs. I've had a month of his stupid ideas and his stupid daughter and . . . It's high time somebody stood up to him.' The door crashed behind him.

Rain went after him, hoping she might still be able to stop him saying and doing all the worst things. She ran through the outer office. The deputy editor's office led off it, too, and his door was ajar. She guessed he was not there, that Eliot had checked. Whatever confidence had once existed between the two men was destroyed with MacQuillan's arrival. Simon Linley no longer saw himself as a deputy but as the next editor.

Their offices were at the front of the building so the quickest way to the second floor was to take one of the two lifts which rose from the entrance hall. One lift was already at the second floor, suggesting Tavett had reached the management suite. Rain summoned the other and when it did not come raced up the stairs.

On the landing she turned left into the office where Mona Washbrooke, MacQuillan's secretary, worked. No one was there but there was a typists' room beyond it and she made for that. The room was empty. While she was in there she heard the door linking MacQuillan's office and Mona's open. She spun round to catch the movement of a running figure. Rain moved fast but when she reached the landing she was in time only to see a lift beginning its descent.

She sighed, defeated. Then she called the other lift but it did not respond so she went into the cloakroom across the landing and splashed cold water on her face in a hopeless effort to feel cooler. The noise and the heat beat up from the street and the open window brought dust and no cooling breeze because the city had no cooling breezes.

On the landing again she found Tavett, half in and half out of a lift and looking frantic. He jumped at the sight of her, then came away from the lift. When he spoke his voice was a croak and he had to try again. 'MacQuillan,' he said. 'I think he's dead.'

CHAPTER 2

The Carton King? Is that what he was known as? Detective Superintendent Paul Wickham allowed himself a momentary flicker of amusement.

He moved away from the newsroom television set once the item ended and the screen was no longer filled with the triumphant smile of Hal MacQuillan, filmed on the day the American learned his bid to buy the *Post* had succeeded.

Rain told Wickham: 'He made his money by patenting the first milk carton which reliably opens. That allowed him to go shopping for newspapers: first one in Detroit, then this one.'

Wickham had been familiarizing himself with the layout of the building and then gone, in a deceptively casual way, to discover Rain behind her pot plant. 'I'd like you to come upstairs now, if you can leave all this for a while.'

Of course she could leave it. They were not getting a paper out and most of the staff could have gone home, except that Wickham had said no one was to leave the building.

They went upstairs without speaking, Rain holding back a stream of questions. She could imagine how much Wickham had to cope with: so many bits of information to absorb, so many strangers to get to know. Wickham was actually considering the atmosphere in the newsroom. He had been into other offices where there had been murder and he had found shock and fear. At the *Post* there were already black jokes, MacQuillan's killing was just another news story. More than that, Wickham's firm impression was that his death was welcomed.

Mona Washbrooke, a tall angular woman ashen beneath newly waved hair, was in position outside MacQuillan's office. Carrier bags slid into view behind her desk. The door to MacQuillan's room was open and the body had been removed. Rain did not want to go in there. She could not grieve for MacQuillan and with a tinge of self-disgust noted that it was really rather exciting to be marginally involved in such an event as murder. But even so, she did not want to go in there. Wickham ushered her in.

Several other police officers were there. Wickham introduced Detective Sergeant Marshall, a young man with fluffy fair hair above a round face. Rain assumed he was older and brighter than he looked.

Wickham asked her to show him what she had done when she went to the room with Tavett. 'Don't touch anything, just show me what happened.'

'Very well.' She retraced her steps to the door, turned and took a couple of short paces. 'I stopped about here.'

'And what did you see?'

Marshall was writing it all down. Rain said: 'MacQuillan was in his chair but he'd fallen forward over the desk. I stopped as soon as I saw him.'

'You didn't go up to him at all?'

'No.'

'Did Dick Tavett?'

'No. I remember looking around and seeing him in the doorway, clutching the frame with one hand.'

Wickham suggested that MacQuillan had looked as though he were asleep. Again she said no. 'The position was wrong. If he'd meant to sleep he'd probably have put his arms on the desk to cradle his head, and if he'd dozed off upright and fallen forward he'd have woken himself when he hit the desk.'

'What did you do next?'

She said: 'I dashed into the circulation department across the landing and asked the manager to telephone for help.'

'But there are telephones on MacQuillan's desk. There are telephones on Miss Washbrooke's desk and in the typists' room. Why didn't you use any of those?'

She looked uncomfortable. 'I wanted somebody else to decide how to go about it. Offices run on procedure and I didn't know the procedure for calling in a doctor.'

'The circulation manager did, though?' Amusement rekindled in his eyes.

'He coped, I didn't.'

Wickham said: 'You'd better discover what he did, in case it happens again.' Then, the smile vanishing: 'What became of Dick Tavett while you were in the circulation department?'

'He didn't come with me and when I returned he was in Mona's room, walking about looking worried.' She laughed. 'Actually, he was running his hand over his head where the hair used to be. It's what he always does when he's anxious.'

Then she explained that she had stayed in Mona's room to prevent anyone going near MacQuillan. Tavett, who was busier, had gone to the newsroom. Nobody else had come, except the circulation manager who reported that the doctor was on his way.

Wickham looked at his reflection in the broad oak desk, his eyes moving from the clutch of telephones to the neat stack of papers. Then he walked around the desk slowly, taking in the leather chair, the closed drawers and the empty waste bin. He went to stand near Rain, thinking it a pity she had not ventured further because she could not have seen the drawers or the bin, nor known that MacQuillan lay with his right hand dropping down as though he had been reaching for something when he was struck.

He stepped out of the way of colleagues going through their routine of checking for fingerprints and traces of fibres or substances that might eventually prove who else had been at that desk with MacQuillan when he died. They were finding little: so far only a short thread of cotton and a fragment of old newsprint.

The room was in the corner of the building with windows along one side. Anti-glare glass was supposed to reduce the heat, but the benefit was minimal and totally cancelled if the windows were swung up to let in air. Wickham's men had opened them, found the traffic noise troublesome and shut them again. Like everyone else they were suffering from the inadequate air conditioning.

Dominating the room was a boardroom table where meetings of directors or senior staff used to take place before the paper changed hands. MacQuillan had taken his decisions alone. His desk was towards the back of the room, facing the windows. It was about halfway along a wall from which two doors opened. Wickham walked as far as the first door, called over to Rain: 'Did you notice whether this was closed?'

She shook her head. He asked: 'Have you ever come into the office through it?'

'Quite often.' She preferred to go nearer to him to explain and was aware of Marshall bobbing like a cork in her wake. She said: 'Martin Ayling, the previous owner, used to have meetings in here. There are stairs which lead down from the lobby behind this door and it was quite normal for some of us to come up from the newsroom that way.'

The only other door off the lobby led to a men's cloakroom which had been reserved for MacQuillan's private use. The stairs did not go any higher than the second floor although the building had four storeys. When the top floor was leased to another company a wall was built and the final flight taken out.

Wickham asked Rain whether she knew the other door opening into MacQuillan's office was only the entrance to a cupboard.

'Yes, but I didn't notice whether it was open or shut.' She gave a wary glance at the chair which Ayling and then MacQuillan had used and no one would want to use again. Then she and Wickham and the trailing Marshall had to get out of the way of one of the other officers and they retreated to the wall of windows. Wickham spoke to Marshall who closed his notebook and walked off, fanning himself with it.

Rain pushed open a window. The street sounds rose so that only Wickham heard as the first of her questions bubbled out: 'Paul, what happened in here today?'

'Someone stabbed MacQuillan.'

'*Stabbed* him?'

'Until we get the pathologist's report the official word can only be that he was found dead.' He did not disguise that she was being comical, bursting with passionate curiosity one moment, then capable only of echoing him.

She remonstrated: 'But you can't expect a man of his prominence to die violently in Fleet Street and keep the details to yourself.'

'I don't have many details.' He reached forward to close the window but she stuck out her arm to prevent that.

Recovering her determination she said: 'Promise you'll tell me about the case.'

He spoke with sham formality. 'We shall be making the usual statements to the press.'

'Exactly, and I want you to tell me *first*.'

He laughed. 'I'm sure you do.'

'Paul, you're being maddening. Think how dreadful it would be if the staff of the *Post* had to read about it in another paper!'

His expression showed that he had already thought of that and would enjoy it. Rain groaned. 'How can I persuade you?'

'That could take some time,' he said and could either have meant he was too busy to bother with her or else that he wanted to.

He took hold of the window and although she did not release it she let him gently close it as he said: 'You could have saved some time if you'd noticed the knife stuck in MacQuillan's back.'

She was open-mouthed in astonishment. He went on: 'Isn't that the usual office procedure for getting rid of colleagues? Or shall we ask the circulation manager?'

CHAPTER 3

'Stabbed in the back!' roared John Wainfleet and rocked on his bar stool. His laughter startled the few non-journalists in the pub but the rest were familiar with his antics and did not flinch. '*Literally* stabbed in the back?'

He appealed to Rain. She demurred. 'I didn't see . . .' He was the gossip columnist of one of the brasher daily tabloids, a short overweight boisterous man who loved his own jokes. There was no reason to add to his sum of knowledge.

'What did your chum Paul Wickham tell you?' he asked. 'My spies say you were closeted with him for half an hour.'

She gave a teasing grin over her fruit juice. Wainfleet jerked his stool a few inches nearer to her. 'Now come on, Rain, the *Post* can't publish anything before Monday so why not do an old friend a favour?'

'An old friend?' She looked around, as if puzzled.

Wainfleet beckoned Sean, the barman, and ordered another scotch for himself and a glass of wine for Rain. She protested but he over-ruled her. Then: 'Did Wickham drop any hints who the suspects are?'

'Ask your crime reporter, John.' She was enjoying herself, tantalizing this benign rival as Wickham had tantalized her.

'No, that would be official. I'm after the tittle-tattle just as you'd be in my place. Except that you'd have the immeasurable advantage of having once been a — how shall I put it? — a close companion of the superintendent in charge of the investigation.'

She said he would find that hard to prove and he replied: 'So what? How many of the stories you run could you prove?'

Rain pretended to take offence. 'Are you threatening me? It wouldn't be a good way to get any help, would it?'

He yawned. 'I'm tired of asking nicely.'

A hand dropped on Rain's shoulder and a reporter from one of the more upmarket papers spun her round. More questions, more evasion; but at least he did not rib her about Wickham. Wainfleet was cut out of the conversation. He swivelled round and latched on to Tavett instead.

Tavett and several colleagues were suffering the torture of showing off how much they knew about the big story of the day without giving away anything to the opposition. 'What was MacQuillan stabbed with?' Wainfleet began.

Tavett waffled. Wainfleet roared again. 'Well, you're supposed to have found the corpse, you must have noticed.'

'Well actually I . . . I mean it was all rather . . . You see, I didn't really . . .'

'Are you telling me you didn't find him? I thought that was the only thing you all agreed on.'

'It wasn't quite like that,' said Tavett.

'Oh, wasn't it? Perhaps you put the knife between the shoulder blades? Is this some sort of confession, Dick?'

Riley, paying for a round, said: 'Give it up, Wainfleet. Our lips are sealed.' He had a plaster on a finger burned when he threw the waste bin at Zak. He used the hand gingerly.

Wainfleet crowed. 'It's the best bit of chat you've had for years and you're all afraid to speak up.' He pushed his empty glass on to the bar but Riley ignored it and turned away. 'Don't go,' said Wainfleet. 'You haven't told me yet how you single-handedly felled the combined forces of the Patriotic Ten.'

Riley gave him a withering look. 'That's about as accurate as your column is most days.' Wainfleet pulled a face behind Riley's back before signalling the barman for another drink. With his fresh glass in his hand he cast about for his next victim, then flung up an arm and shouted to a man coming in from the street. 'Frank! Over here!'

Frank Shildon's appearance was summed up by the word average, and the reward for being so nondescript ought to have been the ability to avoid notice. This time he was unlucky.

Whether he realized it or not, he had attracted interest in the office, too, because he was rumoured to be the reporter conducting Eliot's clandestine investigation into MacQuillan's business affairs. Any other reporter would have been asked outright for the truth of such a story, but Shildon was the quiet type who hugged to himself whatever secrets he held. Expecting to be rebuffed, nobody bothered to question him.

Shildon had no choice about joining Wainfleet if he wanted a drink. It was notorious the way Wainfleet parked himself by the bar. 'What'll it be, Frank? A cool lager for the heatwave or spirits to help you over the shock of bereavement?'

He got a wan smile. Shildon asked for a lager. Wainfleet peered at him. 'Feeling all right? You look a bit . . . er . . .'

'I'm fine, but hanging around waiting to be what the police call eliminated makes me jumpy.' He spoke with a trace of northern accent.

Wainfleet chuckled. 'No need to worry, Dick Tavett's virtually confessed to the murder and there's a nice little story about Rain Morgan and Detective Superintendent Paul Wickham.'

Shildon did not look impressed. 'What else have you heard, John?'

Wainfleet prattled on with his nonsense, all of it loud enough to irritate the people it featured. Suddenly he broke off and when he next spoke it was in a whisper. 'What's going on over there?'

Shildon looked over his shoulder. 'Rain and Tavett conferring over the dry peanuts?'

'Quite so. I'd heard they weren't the best of friends.'

'I hadn't heard that.'

Wainfleet tossed back his whisky. 'I'll bet you say you hadn't heard MacQuillan was easing them out, either.'

Shildon remarked that there had been many rumours. And Wainfleet said: 'Come on, Frank, you know more about it than that. A chap like you with his ear to the ground . . .'

'I work for the business section these days.' Shildon was bitter.

Wainfleet shook him by the shoulder. 'Yes, I know. The rising sun set all too soon, the high flier crash-landed on the dullest pages in the street . . . God, I can't keep this up.'

'Thank heaven for that.' But he was not mollified by Wainfleet's jokey tone.

Wainfleet spelled out his sympathy. 'You had a rough deal, and you had it from Hal MacQuillan. I was there, remember?'

Shildon did not want this either. He tried to change the subject but Wainfleet was reminiscing. 'Undeserved, that's what it was. And I'll never forget that day — in here, weren't we? — when I told you MacQuillan was a bidder for the *Post*. You looked as if . . . as if . . .'

Wainfleet was spared his search for a parallel because other people pushed up to the bar. By the time he leaned round them to keep contact with Shildon, he had lost his thread.

Rain was trying to shake off Tavett who believed, mistakenly, that no one was interested in their discussion. She said firmly: 'Cheer up, Dick. I doubt if we'll hear any more of three-page gossip columns.'

Tavett would not be reassured. 'But there's Maureen MacQuillan. It must have been her idea and for all we know she owns the paper now. It'll be even easier for her to get her way.' He grew more agitated. 'A few years ago people could float from one paper to another, picking up decent jobs. But now the jobs aren't there.'

'It doesn't matter, Dick, because you won't be looking for one.' Rain could not see how to break free without leaving him stranded or finding herself hooked again into interrogation by Wainfleet. The matter was solved in an alarming way. She saw Tavett's switch of attention and then heard Frank Shildon burst out angrily, shouting at Wainfleet. It was remarkable because Shildon was not a man given to fierce words.

Wainfleet pretended to duck from blows. 'Steady on, Frank. You can usually take a joke . . .'

Shildon snarled back that it was all very well for Wainfleet, sitting there day after day with a glass in his hand and a silly smile on his face, but people had enough to endure without tolerating his sniping, too. Anger intensified the north-country accent.

Wainfleet managed a mocking laugh. 'Now come on, Frank, I've been through it. I know all about it . . .'

Shildon shut him up by saying viciously: '. . . and I know how you handled it.'

The quietness that followed was deeply uncomfortable for everyone. Few people had watched and all pretended not to have heard. Then they had to sidestep rapidly as Shildon crashed his glass down on the bar so hard that it broke, and stormed out of the pub.

Wainfleet mimed plucking a dagger from his heart but the few who saw were too embarrassed to be amused. Tavett said under his breath that he must go home and did, thrusting his empty glass absent-mindedly into Rain's hands. She took it to the bar.

'Well done, John,' she said before Wainfleet could speak. 'He was supposed to be a friend of yours, wasn't he?' It was a little gibe at the way Shildon sometimes passed on to Wainfleet stories about events at the *Post*.

Wainfleet watched the barman delicately clear the pieces of Shildon's glass. 'I blame the weather, Rain. It makes the long-suffering short-tempered and the quick-tempered lethargic. You're not going, are you?'

'I want to get home.' She was imagining a cool shower, a change of clothes. The barman clattered the broken glass into a bin and began slicing a lemon.

'Oliver won't be there, he's gone to that wine bar.'

In spite of herself she raised an eyebrow. Wainfleet liked that. She had given away that he knew something she did not.

'Yes,' he continued, dabbing the sweat from his face with a frayed handkerchief, 'I expect he'll meet Linda Finch from the feminist publishers there.'

The remark was mischievous. Rain and Oliver endured an undulating relationship and it was entering another of its troughs. She said brightly: 'Lots of people use the wine bar apart from the staff of Women's Word.' Then she said a general goodbye and went out into the sultry evening.

Several men were standing outside the pub, their glasses on the windowsills and their long shadows straggling eastwards. 'Rain?' The paper's crime reporter, Alex Harbury, asked whether she was getting any more from Wickham than the police were saying officially. The sun exaggerated the redness of his hair but there was the usual alertness about his green eyes. Rain was convinced he had been waiting to question her.

She liked Harbury, one of her newer colleagues. He was quite popular in the office although he took himself and his work a shade seriously and often made her feel frivolous in comparison. He had the wary eagerness of people who have seen too many pieces of luck mature into disappointments. At the *Post* there were already ominous signs. One power struggle on the newsdesk caused the vacancy which took him to Fleet Street, another made the crime job available. The job appealed to plenty of reporters but was not highly rated by news editors. They considered carefully before uprooting, say, a local government man or a social services correspondent, but felt that crime was in their gift. A reporter who proved his worth could always be rewarded with crime.

If the timing was favourable an ousted crime reporter might slip straight into another specialist job, with the ease of a cabinet minister after a reshuffle. But if he were truly doomed he became motoring correspondent. Until

MacQuillan came Harbury believed that motoring, from which no one had been known to return to real journalism, was the worst that Fleet Street threatened.

Harbury had heard that the printers intended to get Monday's paper out. 'The air conditioning is as bad as ever but they want to hear the gossip.' His other news was that MacQuillan's position might be filled by Ron Barron, one of MacQuillan's imports from his American business. Then they talked about the plans for the gossip column, Rain asking who had told him. 'Riley,' he said, 'in the strictest confidence, the way all rumours go round the building.' He added the understatement that a lot of people would be relieved that MacQuillan had gone.

She could not disagree with that. 'But how many of them would have killed him?'

She was startled by his reply: 'I might have. When Riley said MacQuillan wanted me taken off crime and made responsible for interviewing the *Girlie* winners, I felt as though it was the least I could do.'

* * *

Rain was delayed by a brief interview for television before she met up with Oliver in the wine bar. Linda Finch was there but they were not together. Oliver was telling a humorous version of his interview with the police before he was allowed to leave the office. A wisp of a girl, tearful with laughter, leaned against Rain for support, although Rain herself could not stop laughing. The girl gasped: 'Poor Martin Ayling. He can't have dreamed what he was letting the paper in for when he sold it to MacQuillan. I wonder if he changed his mind and decided to remove him?'

'The police have hundreds of suspects,' said Oliver, switching from court jester to lecturer. 'They don't need Ayling, too. They've got almost everyone who works there, plus the Patriotic Ten and the fourteen free speech folk.'

'Anyway,' someone reasoned, 'Ayling won't have stirred from Gloucestershire. He's too busy playing farmers since he gave up the paper. I haven't seen him in town once.'

The wisp of a girl dried her eyes. 'Do you ever hear from him, Rain?'

'I had a letter today, about the charity ball next week.'

Discussion moved to the ball, to who was going and who wasn't and what a pity it clashed with someone's birthday party in Norfolk. Oliver mouthed across to Rain that they should leave. Together they walked home to Kington Square. The heat was enervating. They talked little.

Rain's flat was on the top floor of a Georgian terrace of creamy stuccoed houses where fuchsia and petunias tumbled from windowboxes. Her long white sitting room led on to a roof garden. Rain loved the flat but in the heatwave would have willingly swapped it for a shady basement.

It was suffocating inside. Oliver threw open doors and went into the garden. The chair he thought of sitting on was hot so he stood until Rain brought cushions and glasses of iced water and then inspected plants wilting in their tubs. She pottered with them for a few minutes before telling Oliver what was on her mind.

'Ayling's letter was delivered by hand.'

CHAPTER 4

Simon Linley was a languid man of thirty. He had come to the *Post* with an excellent degree, a deep knowledge of Etruscan pottery and an indelible ambition to edit the paper. In a short time he became deputy editor, his predecessor dying suddenly. If Luke Eliot had been an older man or a sicker man or a man unhappy in his job, Linley could have expected his way to be cleared. But Eliot was none of those things. Linley's dash had ended in a cul-de-sac.

The languid manner disguised his increasing frustration and made it unlikely that other papers would dangle offers. Besides, what was true for Tavett was equally so for Linley: there were precious few good jobs around. Until Martin Ayling sold to Hal MacQuillan, Simon Linley was blocked.

Linley had written a book about Etruscan pots. On the Friday MacQuillan died there was a party to celebrate publication.

'It looks rather callous, he and MacQuillan were so thick,' said Oliver as Rain drove them to Linley's Islington home.

'There wasn't time to cancel. At least it will give people something to talk about apart from his arcane book.'

She turned into Thornhill Square and parked alongside railings surrounding an open space. Children were listless in the heat, dogs panted, lovers fondled in the shade. Rain said: 'There's a suspicious lack of cars outside Simon's house.'

'Perhaps no one's come. Maybe we could slip away. Have we been seen?'

'No, we haven't and no, we can't. I promised we'd come.'

'*I* didn't.'

Beside the bell was a note saying Push Door. They followed the sounds of voices through to the back garden. There were about a dozen people there, bravely smiling and praying for reinforcements. John Wainfleet was among them, rather drunker and quieter than in the pub. Linley's voice echoed around the square: 'Sorry about the hide and seek, but we simply can't keep trudging in and out to open the front door. Emelda, come and see who's here.'

Emelda Linley was standing just a yard away with a bottle in her hand. Rain had met her briefly before, registering only that Linley's wife was short, plump and Italian. Oliver put out a hand but Emelda did not grasp it. She launched herself at him for a welcoming kiss, no, *two* welcoming kisses, one on each cheek. The bottle jogged in the confusion and red wine splashed her white skirt.

A heavy-jowled man from Linley's publishers was striving to say something interesting about *Etruscan Pots Reconsidered.* He had the field to himself because no one had read it. A police siren, wailing down Caledonian Road, interrupted him and prompted Linley to mention the owl which used to live on a tiny patch of scrubland nearby. 'Every night it flew over our garden.'

A woman, who read the paper's nature notes, asked what type of owl but Linley did not know and the subject foundered. The group stood awkwardly, unsure what to attempt next. The man from the publishers asked whether Eliot was expected. 'He's been invited,' said Linley, with a careless gesture indicating that the editor was an unreliable fellow but what could one do?

Four reinforcements arrived: Stuart Pascoe, an elderly man with round shoulders and pebble glasses who had been head of finance in Ayling's time and demoted in MacQuillan's; Cecil Hunter-Blair, a tall blond MP who looked as though his ancestors had come over with the Vikings and whom MacQuillan had commissioned to write a weekly column on Irish affairs; Alex Harbury, the young crime reporter; and Linda Finch. Pascoe's appearance was unsurprising as he shared Linley's passion for Tuscany. Hunter-Blair owed his column to Linley who had put his name forward to MacQuillan. The mysteries were Harbury and Linda but the puzzle was solved with the explanation that Linda was the Women's Word editor overseeing Emelda's attempt to write a book about the subjection of Italian women. Emelda had invited Linda, and Linda had brought Harbury.

They probably all wished they had stayed at home because things remained very flat until Linda stepped backwards into a diminutive pond and damaged a fountain. Linley assured her it was of no consequence but Emelda was anguished about the fate of her goldfish, repeating that the fountain was no mere ornament but oxygenated the water.

Linley protested: 'Honestly, darling, those fish are at more risk from neighbourhood cats than from lack of bubbles.'

Wainfleet had to be restrained from making good the loss of bubbles by tipping a bottle of sparkling wine into the pond.

Emelda told her husband: 'Simon, you are not a Chinese carp so how can you understand what they are enduring?' She ran to the kitchen for a chip pan full of water and a chip basket to sieve the fish from the pond. 'I shall put them in the bath overnight and tomorrow their oxygenator must be mended.'

'Darling, there's no need . . .'

But she felt the need and her efforts with the chip basket provided the entertainment of the evening. Guests gathered round giving encouragement, placing ridiculous bets on her chances of success and awarding her on a scale of points: high for a clean catch, low for a bad one with the fish wedged in the mesh, and none for coming up with an empty basket.

Oliver and Linda stood back, Linda barefoot while her sandal dried. Hunter-Blair trapped Rain against a sharp-thorned rose bush and demanded, in a theatrically low timbre, to know all about the MacQuillan murder.

She said: 'I thought we would have talked about nothing else tonight.'

He agreed, revealing that was mainly why he had come. 'Everyone's showing an unusual degree of delicacy. Unless, of course, it's because they know all the *Post* people suspect each other.'

'Do we?'

'Naturally. It must have been an inside job, although there was such a noise in there today because of all your intruders, anything might have happened.'

She argued that anyone could have walked through the front door and a lot of people had. He said: 'Not without being challenged by your watchdog of a receptionist. If I come in that way, she even demands to know who *I* am and what I want.'

They both considered this slight and the danger he might lose his column. He toyed with the opening bud of a rose, and asked, 'Who do you think did it?'

'I find it impossible to imagine anyone I know killing him.' Except, she added silently, that Harbury had admitted wanting to and circumstances made Tavett appear guilty.

Hunter-Blair bruised the young petals. 'Of course, he'd upset a lot of people. It wasn't easy sorting out the mess Ayling left. Getting a business to move off in a fresh direction is always tough.'

'And is that all a newspaper is — a business?' She did not doubt that most of the new breed of proprietors believed exactly that.

'Hal wasn't a man for sentiment, he knew where he was going and how to get there.'

Pascoe appeared at his elbow. 'The paper's in deeper trouble now than at any time the Ayling family owned it.'

Hunter-Blair said: 'Nonsense, Stuart. He's given it a firm editorial line, especially on foreign affairs . . .'

'. . . meaning Ireland, I presume,' Pascoe interjected.

'Certainly. That's the most important issue affecting life in these islands and it's consistently the most under-reported. Until MacQuillan bought his way into Fleet Street there was no British paper which wasn't simply printing government propaganda.'

Pascoe growled that now the paper could be accused of printing propaganda for terrorists, and Rain tried to defuse the argument by asking how they expected the circulation figures to reflect the change.

Hunter-Blair said: 'They're up and rising. Hal was very pleased with them.'

Pascoe said coldly: 'No one produces circulation figures that fast. MacQuillan was claiming a fortnight after he bought the paper that he had increased sales. It's not possible to know that soon, any newspaperman will tell you that.'

Rain murmured that all they were certain of was that MacQuillan had printed more. Hunter-Blair countered that it was equally certain that Ayling and the old guard had not made serious efforts to promote the paper. He snapped off the damaged rosebud and tossed it aside.

Pascoe bridled. 'The Ayling family ran one of the most successful papers . . .'

'History, Stuart. They've gone, there are new people at the helm now and great things will be done.'

Rain thought Hunter-Blair sounded like one of his mediocre columns, except that in those he was too wise to play down the importance of history. She asked whether he knew who was to be at the helm in future.

He smirked a knowing smile, then told them: 'Ron Barron. He told me today.' And added that no one could have taken over so effectively because Barron had worked closely with MacQuillan for a long time.

Rain thought of someone else. 'What about the Carton Princess?'

Hunter-Blair raised an eyebrow at Pascoe, inviting his opinion. Pascoe gulped his wine and said: 'Maureen MacQuillan is no match for Barron.'

At that Hunter-Blair took issue with him about MacQuillan's daughter and Rain gave up trying to prevent an argument and cast about for Harbury. She wanted to say he had been right about Barron.

Oliver and Linda were at the end of the garden. Wainfleet was with a knot from the publishers. Harbury, noticeably more relaxed now that he was away from the pressures of the office, was sitting with Emelda on the grass near the pond. Goldfish were splashing about in the chip pan while Emelda made another sortie with the basket. Her other guests congregated near the food.

Rain made a move but the rose bush had her in its grasp. She wriggled and was hooked on another thorn. Pascoe and Hunter-Blair had grown heated and were oblivious to her gyrations.

Once free she slipped away from them, filled her glass with mineral water and listened to the unhappy gaiety of people who were having a dull time but knew it was too early to escape. Standing there, she was ideally placed to hear when Pascoe accused Hunter-Blair of opportunism and Hunter-Blair flashed back that Pascoe had taken all the opportunities which had come his way and that he had been found out.

She saw Pascoe stalk away indignantly towards the house and Hunter-Blair tear to pieces another rosebud. Rain headed for the couple at the pond before he thought of joining her again.

Harbury was saying: 'Give it up, Emelda. Perhaps there were only five goldfish to start with.'

'No, no, Alex. I know there were six.' She thrashed about with the chip basket.

'Well, maybe Simon's right and the neighbourhood cats had a paw in this.'

'That's not possible. When we aren't out here there's a net over the water.'

Harbury's green eyes squinted up at Rain backlit by the evening sun. 'Don't you agree Emelda ought to retire defeated? We've got five but she wanted six.'

Rain suggested that if the missing fish was any smaller than the rest it might be falling through the mesh.

'Ah!' Emelda scrambled to her feet. 'I shall fetch a strainer.'

Harbury wanted to put his hand in and feel for the fish but Emelda gave a little cry. 'Oh, be careful, Alex. You mustn't squash the little creature.'

Harbury rolled up his sleeve. 'My hand will do less damage than that chip basket.'

Emelda said she could not bear to watch and would take the pan indoors while he tried.

'He won't have anywhere to put the fish if he catches it,' Rain pointed out.

'Then he will have to hold on to it until I come back, I must put these into the bath.' She bent and began to lift up the pan, very carefully.

Harbury plunged his hand into the opaque water of the pond, sending little waves up on to the lawn. Rain watched his face, tight in concentration. Then his expression changed to bewilderment. He withdrew his hand in a rush. It was holding a large, sharp knife.

Emelda screamed and dropped the pan. People ran forward and she shrieked for them to get back. The nearest fell to their knees to save the panicking fish. Some guests lobbed them into the empty pan, others aimed for the pond. Emelda knelt wailing, and Harbury slowly lowered the knife and put it on the grass. No one revealed any doubt that the knife was linked to the murder.

CHAPTER 5

Rain was preparing for bed when the doorbell rang. She expected Oliver on the entryphone, penitent about mislaying his key after she had left him at the party. She was taken aback to hear Wickham instead.

'I was driving home and saw your light,' he said following her into the roof garden.

'You're lucky. I haven't long been home.' She mentioned Linley's party, telling him about Pascoe and Hunter-Blair sparring, Wainfleet being subdued, most guests failing to turn up and Oliver, Harbury and Linda staying on when everyone else drifted home. Then she told him the comic tale of the knife. 'A kitchen knife. With a black handle and a smooth blade. I can show you one rather like it.' She fetched a knife. 'The one in the pond was roughly this size and shape.'

Wickham weighed it in his hand. Rain's mood shifted. There was no longer the slightest amusement in the story. She sensed a chill as he drew the blade across his palm. Then she asked a question to which her instinct had already given the answer: 'Paul, is this like the knife that killed MacQuillan?'

'Very like it.' He stroked a finger down the long thin blade. 'Did the Linleys say what a knife was doing in their pond?'

'They couldn't explain it. I'm sure everyone was convinced neither of them had seen it before.'

There was an unnerving silence while Wickham toyed with Rain's knife, its blade glinting in the lamplight. Rain broke the silence, saying brightly: 'You can't keep it. It's part of the Morgan *batterie de cuisine* and it's going straight back to the kitchen.' She leaned over and took it.

When she rejoined him she carried glasses and the remains of a bottle of white wine. He refused the drink, saying he did not count himself off duty until he got home.

Rain laughed off his refusal. 'I won't have you here officially.' It felt strange but not disagreeable to have him there at all. She put a glass down near him and pushed the bottle across.

After a moment he poured an inch or two into the glass. He said: 'I want to ask you some questions about your colleagues. That will make this official, won't it?'

'Not really. I gossip about them all the time.'

'Good.' He sipped before saying: 'It's a dangerous thing, you know, to confuse the personal with the professional.'

Rain thought he ought to get to the point. 'Whom shall we gossip about first?'

He suggested Linley as his name had already come up and as he was one of a number of people whose movements that afternoon were unclear. But before they got to Linley he talked about MacQuillan. Wickham was piecing together a wholly unflattering picture of MacQuillan as an overbearing little man who had made many people's working lives miserable. He had interfered with the running of the paper at every level, from ordering leaders to be written expressing his personal views to shunting reporters on and off stories at his whim. His spate of staff promotions and oustings had made everyone insecure and the generally happy atmosphere of the office had been destroyed because no one knew any longer who was a friend and to be trusted.

Wickham believed the picture to be incomplete. He reasoned that MacQuillan must have presented some appealing qualities, genuine or contrived, to persuade Martin Ayling he was a suitable buyer for the paper and to get the co-operation of the few staff loyal to him. Some people had found the sheer power of the man attractive, some had hoped that showing themselves willing to work with him would gain promotions they would not otherwise have earned, but no one had suggested MacQuillan was likeable. Wickham expected to learn about the redeeming characteristics over the next few days.

He said to Rain: 'We know MacQuillan was in his office all morning and went out for lunch at 1.25 p.m. The receptionist saw him go. At 2.15 p.m. he travelled up in the lift to the second floor with a tele-ad salesgirl. She's sure of the time and her colleagues confirm she got back from lunch then. She says MacQuillan went straight to his office. We haven't found anyone who admits to seeing him alive between 2.15 p.m. and the discovery of his body shortly before 4 p.m.'

'Phone calls?'

'No use. Mona Washbrooke says he told her he was not to be disturbed this afternoon come what may so at 12.30 p.m. she switched off the telephone to his room. When the switchboard tried to put calls through to either of them they got no answer because she switched off her own line, too. Can you guess why she did that?'

Rain protested. 'When you deduce something it's a solid piece of detection and when I do it it's *guesswork*!'

He laughed. 'You got it, then.'

'Of course. She'd been shopping and to the hairdresser's. The bags by her desk gave away the shopping trip and her hair was immaculate. Also it's Friday, a traditional day for taking advantage of the boss.'

'Is she well known for sloping off on Fridays?'

'Oh no, not when she worked for Eliot. But MacQuillan poached her and she loathed the man. She's worked here for years, she knows everything about the paper and that was why he snapped her up.'

Wickham got to Linley, who had been absent from his office from late morning according to Eliot and a string of

Eliot's visitors. Like Rain they had noticed his door open and his room empty. 'Linley's being vague if not entirely unhelpful, shrugging off questions by saying he was around the building all the time. Do you have any idea where he's likely to have been?'

Rain understood how Linley's dismissiveness would rankle with Wickham. She said he could have had business on any part of the premises, but emphasized: 'He's the last person to suspect because he stood to gain everything if MacQuillan prospered and nothing at all if he went.'

Wickham said, not unkindly, that he had noticed that but it could be vital to know whom Linley was with and what they talked about. 'I gather MacQuillan ran the paper on rumour and Linley was one of his channels.'

Rain mentioned that Riley was another. Wickham said: 'Riley was in the newsroom all afternoon, a score of people tell us so. Even when he wanted ointment and a plaster for the finger burned on the lighted bin a secretary fetched them.'

They talked about the levity which puzzled Wickham and she excused journalists everywhere with the plea that a daily diet of drama, with the best-selling stories always the most tragic, had an inevitable effect. Life in a newspaper office was picaresque, she added. Rogues tumbled in to tell their adventures, larger than life was the norm and the readers regarded journalism as a branch of show business. She thought he suspected her of exaggeration but that a few days spent at the *Post* would convince him, if the Patriotic Ten and the freedom of speech people had not already demonstrated her point.

Wickham showed every sign of wanting to talk longer. Rain offered coffee and switched on a filter machine. He followed as far as the sitting room and she found him there, looking at the colourful silks and paintings which turned her long room into a gallery. For a moment or two she stayed in the kitchen doorway unobserved and watched him.

He was older than her by ten years. Silver flecked his hair and weariness exaggerated lines about his eyes. He was still an attractive man. She had always thought him so, since their first meeting several years ago. They had arrived simultaneously at a viewing at an art gallery and it was mistakenly assumed they were together. All that held them together over the next few months was a shared interest in modern painting and an admiration for the work of Vanessa Kyle whose show had introduced them. They both bought pictures at the exhibition. A year after it Paul Wickham married Vanessa Kyle.

Suddenly aware of Rain he jerked round. She began: 'Paul, I'm sorry about . . .'

He made a gesture to dissuade her then said, as though neither of them had been thinking of anything but the MacQuillan murder: 'Usually we have to hunt for a weapon in a stabbing case. This time the murderer left it stuck in the body. It's an ordinary very new kitchen knife of a type sold everywhere and it has no fingerprints on it. Usually, if we are lucky, we have one or two potential suspects. This time we have hundreds. When we whittle them down, eliminating the people who had no opportunity or motive to kill, we still have a ridiculous number.'

The coffee machine gasped to a halt. By the time Rain brought the cups he was sitting on the couch, stretched out, eyes shut, fingers laced behind his head. He opened an eye and sat up as she flicked the television on to see the late news. The MacQuillan story was one of the main home news items, scant information padded out by interviews as empty as her own.

She always found it odd seeing herself on screen, looking a shade plumper than she hoped she was, and hearing her voice as others did. Usually her appearances were confined to panel games and chat shows. But here she was, inappropriately cheerful as she said what little she had to say about the discovery of the corpse.

Wickham grumbled good-naturedly that she had all too obviously enjoyed showing off on television. But she hushed him for the next contribution in which the reporter claimed in a roundabout way that the police believed the killing was a political assassination carried out by an Irish group. 'Do you?' she demanded eagerly as the reporter was replaced on screen by the latest oil price war.

Wickham gave her a look which said he expected her to know better than to believe what she heard from journalists. 'When was the last time Irish terrorists carried out assassination by kitchen knife?' he asked. Then he had some more serious questions for her. She answered as fairly as she could, wondering what her colleagues might in turn say about her.

When the questions dried she said lightly: 'Presumably I'm on your list of suspects, too? No doubt you've found out that Dick Tavett and I were about to lose our jobs because of MacQuillan?'

He nodded. She said: 'Well, surely a night-time visit to gossip with a suspect is a little questionable, superintendent?'

Before he could answer, the door of the flat crashed open and Oliver was home. He had Harbury with him. Oliver said: 'I've told Alex he can sleep on the couch tonight. Assuming it's free, of course.' He and Wickham were introduced and regarded each other with distaste. Harbury did not know whether to advance into the room or wait near the door for the all clear. Oliver waved him forward. 'I told him he shouldn't drive all that way home.'

Rain remarked quietly that Fulham was not far, and Oliver explained that Harbury did not want to risk being stopped for a breath test. Harbury's mumbled denials were ignored.

Rain asked Oliver: 'What if he'd been stopped on the way here from Islington?'

Oliver said: 'Well, I had to get home, didn't I? And anyway we didn't think about that when we set off.'

Wickham said it was time he went and Rain saw him out while Oliver, grunting a goodbye, made for the kitchen and what was left of the coffee. When Rain returned Harbury had ventured a little further into the room. He gave her a tentative smile. She wondered what had become of Linda, whether she had gone home alone as Rain had. Rain rang for a taxi and packed Harbury off to Fulham.

Oliver raged and then fell asleep as she had known he would. She lay wakeful beside him and thought how the day had been composed of vivid images: Tavett's fury, MacQuillan dead at his desk, Shildon's outburst, the Patriotic Ten's outrageous behaviour and Riley's vicious response, the free speech demonstrators parading, Emelda dredging the pond, and Harbury bringing up the knife like a gift from the Lady of the Lake. But no less memorable was the pain in Wickham's face as he discovered Vanessa's painting hanging on Rain's wall.

CHAPTER 6

Saturday morning began with the telephone ringing. Oliver pulled the sheet over his head and moaned. Rain went to the sitting room. The sun which struck across the carpet was already very hot.

'Rain?' Tavett's voice. 'I don't want you to tell Wickham what a rage I was in when I went up to MacQuillan's office yesterday. Thinking back on it I can see it looks rather suspicious.'

She smiled at his foolishness. 'It's hardly proof you killed him and the police know you found the body.'

'Yes, but only Eliot and you know what I went up for. He says he hasn't mentioned the mood I was in.'

'Dick, Wickham knows we were both threatened with losing our jobs. You don't have to be a detective superintendent to realize we were both very angry.'

Tavett cleared his throat nervously. 'Actually, Wickham's asked me to see him again today.'

'Oh?'

'Has he told you what it's about?'

'No, but you were first on the scene . . .'

'Rain, you don't think it means they . . . that they think I . . .'

'They have to consider everything.'

'Everyone. It must look as though I had a chance to do it and a reason for doing it right then. God, what a mess. I wish I'd said nothing and let somebody else find him.'

She said: 'That would have looked a lot worse.' She heard him sigh and pictured him brushing a hand across his bald head. There was nothing she could say to cheer him and she was relieved when he rang off.

The telephone sounded again. A reporter from one of the Sunday papers needed quotes about the murder. She said what he wanted her to say, knowing his sub-editors would twist it to suit their racy style. Then a similar call came, from the crime man on one of the more sedate Sundays.

She had time to set up the coffee machine before the following call. This was from a former colleague, now working for one of the papers with the biggest sales and the lowest standards. He had been notorious in his *Post* days for his cheek and had apparently grown worse. 'I've written something out so if you'll OK this I won't take up any more of your time,' he said.

Rain heard: 'It was horrible. There was blood everywhere. Hal was lying across his desk with a huge carving knife sticking out of his back. I screamed and ran towards him but something told me it was too late. After I dialled 999 I waited by the body wondering who could have done such a thing and trying not to look at the blood which dripped steadily on to the green carpet . . .'

She managed to break in. 'You can't say that!'

'Why? Isn't the carpet green?'

'I mean you can't print any of it. It wasn't like that.'

'What colour is the carpet?'

'Brown. Never mind the carpet, the whole thing is rubbish.'

'I'll read you the rest.'

'No. I don't want to hear another word.'

'There's a bit where you say he hadn't been at the paper long enough to make many friends but you hadn't realized he'd made such a desperate enemy.'

She spluttered incoherently. He said: 'I thought that was rather neat. We all know everybody hated him.'

She thought of the Rileys and the Linleys and said he was exaggerating. 'Not a line of that nonsense is to appear under my name.'

He cajoled, without success. She said: 'Anyway, why me? Dick Tavett found him.'

'Oh, come on,' he laughed, 'you know the rules. Our readers don't want to hear about balding neurotics. They'd much rather read about pretty blondes.'

She argued and he made placatory noises before ringing off. Then she left the receiver off the cradle and with mounting unease went out to buy newspapers. The most imaginative obituarists in Fleet Street had struggled vainly to eulogize a heartily disliked man, but once she had smiled over that, Rain found the papers as mischievous as she feared. In spite of Wickham's reservations, there were many inches of speculation that the killing was political. The blood dripping onto or soaking into the green carpet featured in two; the carving knife (or variously a hunting knife) jutted from MacQuillan's body in all except the paper which had found it lying in a pool of blood at his feet. Several remarks she remembered being made by her colleagues in the pub re-emerged from her mouth. One paper mentioned the knife in the pond, saying it was being construed as a threat against Linley. And so it had been, by everyone who saw it taken from the water, although none of them had been melodramatic enough to put that into words. It was interesting, if unreliable, to read that the police thought so too.

* * *

On Saturday morning the newspaper office was dead, its noise and vitality cut off as sharply as the murderer had ended Hal MacQuillan's life. In the typists' room close to where he died, Wickham and Sergeant Marshall were discussing the pathologist's report.

'A lucky strike then, sir, to kill him with just one blow.'

Wickham remarked drily that a stab in the back was not the most reliable way of killing anyone. 'According to this . . .' He tapped Dr Midwinter's report. '. . . it was a very determined thrust while MacQuillan was bending forward and it sank the blade in far enough to reach the heart. If it had been a less effective blow MacQuillan might have cried out and been heard in the circulation department across the landing, or might have tried to telephone for help. There could have been signs of a struggle before he collapsed and died. Whoever attacked him chose a weapon with a suitable blade and wounded him in the right place. It was either luck, as you say, Jim, or he knew precisely how to go about it.'

Dr Midwinter had found little bleeding because the weapon had not been withdrawn before death which had been quick. It was not possible to fix the time of death any more accurately than the circumstantial evidence had already done. But Dr Midwinter could add that MacQuillan had eaten a light lunch, although there was nothing suspicious about the partly digested contents of the stomach. The knife wound alone was responsible for his death. The hands had been minutely examined yet there was no defensive injury which a victim might sustain when grappling with an attacker carrying a weapon.

Wickham was sitting on one of the typists' chairs, shirt sleeves rolled up, tie loose. There was no natural light in the room, no hope of air apart from what the defective air conditioning system provided. He pivoted to face Marshall who rested his weight on the edge of a desk. Already the sergeant's shirt was stained with sweat and his baby face glowed damply. Wickham asked: 'How were the Linleys this morning?' He had sent Marshall to collect the knife found in the pond and it had been sent for examination.

'I think Linley had done a good job of reassuring his wife, but he was a bit perturbed himself. While she was present he was laughing the incident off as a practical joke, but once she'd left the room his attitude changed. He wanted to know whether I thought the knife was a threat.'

Wickham raised an eyebrow. His impression of the deputy editor was that he was the type who would refuse to admit being worried about anything. Worry seemed altogether too active a state for Linley. The man's manner, from his drawled speech to his casual movements, suggested a cultivated laziness. Wickham had expected Linley to regard the business of the knife with disdain. 'Did he suggest any reason why he might be threatened?'

'No, he said the office had been teeming with madmen yesterday and it was possible to believe anything.'

'And prove nothing!' They had ample choice of suspects with motive or opportunity but a paucity of evidence. Scotland Yard's anti-terrorist branch had offered nothing to support the idea of political assassination. Wickham said: 'Jim, if the attack was carried out on the spur of the moment — say someone heard something he didn't like, grabbed a knife from the canteen and lunged at MacQuillan — there would have been evidence scattered everywhere, with luck prints on the weapon. But my feeling is this murder was planned with care. All we have found is a piece of thread and a snippet of paper, which might both be unconnected with the crime. There isn't a trace of anything on the knife.'

'They all think criminals wear gloves these days, sir.'

'In this weather I'd regard a man with gloves in the office as a vital clue.'

Marshall gave a tentative laugh. He was not always sure when the superintendent meant to be amusingly flippant. He said, to counter the laugh: 'No gloves have been found on the premises, sir. And the knife didn't come from the canteen kitchen.'

Another troubling aspect of the case was that the two people first on the scene gave conflicting reports. Marshall did not challenge Wickham's preference for Rain Morgan's version, but Garside, the fingerprints man, had told him with a leer that Wickham had once been rather keen on her. Marshall scoffed and Garside had said: 'The trouble with you, young Jim, is that you never believe anybody.' Marshall had retorted: 'That's what coppers are for.' And he had observed Wickham with renewed interest.

Wickham paced through into Mona's room and back, saying he hoped Tavett would make more sense that morning than he had done so far. He accepted Marshall's suggestion that Tavett had been covering something up, and Marshall was encouraged to expand. He broke off at the sound of the lift humming up to the second floor. Neither of them stirred until Tavett, wearing the same sort of casual clothes he wore on working days, appeared in Mona's office.

Tavett wiped his forehead with a handkerchief and said he was a bit early because traffic on the drive from Greenwich had been lighter than he anticipated. He accepted the cup of coffee which Wickham offered and Marshall fetched.

While it was on its way Wickham asked Tavett to clarify some points from their first interview when he had been confused and contradictory. This time Tavett was eagerly talkative. If he was hiding anything he had worked out how best to do it.

He did not falter until Wickham wanted to know whether he had made an appointment to see MacQuillan. Tavett squirmed before answering: 'No, I just came up. I was going to ask Mona to tell him I wanted to see him, but she wasn't here. I knocked on his door and went straight in . . .'

'You thought you heard a response to your knock?'

'I . . . No, it was as I said. I knocked and turned the handle.'

Wickham pushed on. 'What did you expect to see? Miss Washbrooke taking dictation? Or Mr MacQuillan having a nap at his desk? Or what?'

Tavett shook his head. 'I don't know. I just went in.' He cast a glance at Marshall taking notes.

Wickham let him suffer a few moments before saying: 'I understand you'd been warned by the editor that Mr MacQuillan had plans for your department which would effectively cost you your job.' Unhappily, Tavett agreed. Wickham followed with: 'So when you came up here you were rather angry, to put it at its mildest, and as Miss Washbrooke wasn't there to prevent it, you burst into Mr MacQuillan's office.'

Tavett said in a small voice that yes, that was how it had been. Once the admission was made, he relaxed a shade. Wickham believed it possible he had given up what he had been hiding. But when he pressed Tavett for details about his trip to and from the second floor there was more of the obfuscation which had earlier made him a difficult witness.

Tavett excused himself. 'You see, things became a bit blurred after I barged in and found him. I'm almost sure I didn't get a step inside the door before I guessed he was . . . In fact, I might not even have gone in. I think I kept hold of the handle . . . But I can't really be certain . . .'

The lapse of a day had apparently made events on the landings less blurred. Tavett was, for the first time, sure about the lifts. He said he had definitely taken one from the first floor and it was still at the second floor after he found the body. He got into it, on his way to tell Luke Eliot what had happened, but changed his mind when he saw Rain Morgan on the landing. Until then he had seen no one since leaving the newsroom. He had never noticed the position of the other lift.

An hour dragged by and Tavett clung to his version of events. If he had been suggestible on Friday he was unmovable on Saturday.

'He's wrong, sir,' said Marshall after Tavett had set off home. 'If Rain Morgan's telling the truth, then Dick Tavett can't be.'

Wickham took his jacket off Mona's hanger and walked through to MacQuillan's room, holding the garment over his shoulder by its loop. He stood in the doorway, hand on knob and looked up the room. 'It's not possible he stayed here, or even a step inside, and wasn't seen by Rain when she came in pursuit of him.'

'She said MacQuillan's door was closed, sir.'

'Jim, go back to the typists' room. Look up when you hear this door open and tell me what you see.'

Wickham dropped his jacket on a chair, gave Marshall time to enter the typists' room and then shot out of the landing and across the corner of Mona's office and on to the landing.

Marshall reported: 'I saw what she said she saw, sir. I'd only just got here so I had to turn my head when I heard the door. You were nothing more than a flicker of movement. It's these, sir . . .' He slapped a hand on a bank of filing cabinets topped with plants. 'They cut off what view I might have had, and the angle from MacQuillan's door to the landing did the rest.'

Wickham asked what he had heard and Marshall replied: 'After the door, nothing until you got to the landing. Once you were off the carpet and on to the marble I heard your steps.'

Wickham picked up his jacket again. 'Tavett made no sound when he came across the landing this morning. He was wearing the same green shoes he wore yesterday.'

A telephone rang in the typists' room. Marshall answered while Wickham reflected that all they had learned that morning was that Rain Morgan's story was credible, not that Tavett was hiding anything more serious than his degree of panic when he found the body. Wickham suspected he had accepted Rain's story all along, not because it made more sense but because he knew her. From the outset the MacQuillan case was one where the professional and the personal were intertwined.

The telephone call was from the forensic science laboratory reporting on the cotton thread and the triangular piece of paper which had been found in the cupboard in MacQuillan's office and sent to them for examination. The paper had proved to be newsprint identical to that on which the *Post* was printed. It was old and friable and had been cut, not torn. But the cream-coloured thread was a manmade polymer fibre and not cotton after all. Comparison with reference sets of fibres kept at the laboratory had established that it was used for a fabric called Trilyn. Under the microscope the thread bore signs of fraying: it had been neither cut cleanly nor snapped sharply. Trilyn was used for clothing but was not one of man's most successful efforts to replace cotton or linen because it discoloured with repeated washing and in the lightweight versions did not stand up to heavy wear.

Wickham said: 'What on earth do they use it for? Have you ever had any clothes made of it, Jim?'

Marshall admitted he had never heard of it. He asked whether MacQuillan had not worn a cream-coloured shirt. Wickham said yes, but there was nothing frayed about the MacQuillan wardrobe. The brown linen suit was new, the shirt expensive cotton. He pictured MacQuillan as he had first seen him, slumped on the desk, his dark hair spilling forward and the knife protruding from the smooth jacket. Wickham had already learned that MacQuillan had dyed his hair to cover encroaching greyness. He had been careful about his appearance in other ways, too: his hands were manicured and clean. At the post mortem the routine of scraping beneath the nails had been carried out but the subsequent tests revealed nothing significant.

Wickham led the way to the landing. They had an appointment to keep. He said that if someone had lain in wait in the cupboard for MacQuillan to return from lunch there would have been the risk of MacQuillan going to the cupboard to hang up his jacket. He could still have been stabbed in the back but not in the same way. Back wounds were frequently caused by assailants coming at people from the front and tangling with them so that the weapon-bearing arms wrapped around the victims' bodies. Dr Midwinter had been clear that the angle of the knife in MacQuillan's body and the force with which it had been driven in indicated a downward blow while the man was leaning forward in his chair.

'How could anyone have been sure MacQuillan wouldn't open the cupboard and find him?' Wickham wondered. 'If he'd been discovered it would have been noisy and messy. Whoever did this was intelligent enough to realize that.' They got into the lift.

Marshall said that if the man had an accomplice he could have arranged a telephone call so that MacQuillan got himself into an appropriate position for the killer to strike. Wickham rejected that. 'No one knew whether he was going to lunch, or when he was coming back, and the telephones in his room and Miss Washbrooke's were switched off.' He pressed the button for the ground floor, thinking that the answer to this was going to be very simple and he would feel foolish that it had not occurred to him.

CHAPTER 7

Maureen MacQuillan had left a trail of bad marriages in the way other people leave bad debts. At twenty-nine she was a woman with a chilling determination and no obvious admirers. She was the result of her father's early runaway marriage and when she imitated his folly and secretly married very young, Hal forgave her, bought off her husband and sent her to college. Her later marriages were made with Hal's grudging blessing but any son-in-law who dreamed he would be allowed a hand in the MacQuillan till was disappointed. Maureen herself meant to run the empire after Hal's time.

She had shown no interest in milk cartons but her enthusiasm was fanned once he moved into newspapers. The editor of his first paper was powerless to stop her joining his reporting staff. In London Luke Eliot thought he had kept her out, until the day he discovered her working for the gossip column and Simon Linley admitted to bowing to her father's pressure.

Detective Superintendent Paul Wickham knew that much about Maureen MacQuillan before he rang the bell at her London flat the morning after her father's murder. The information had not prepared him for Miss MacQuillan in person. She looked vulnerable, her obligatory black dress giving her the appearance of a young girl wearing clothes too old for her.

There was an Irish look to her face, something about the eyes and the mouth, and she had her father's short, light build. Her hair hung long and free and was without doubt her natural light brown shade. Wickham caught her idea instantly: she presented herself in a way that declared there was no artifice. He did not, for an instant, believe it.

She invited Wickham and Marshall into an acreage of sitting room with three sofas grouped about a table bearing an elaborate flower arrangement and beyond it a view of a park through full-length windows. An old-fashioned pull hung beside a marble fireplace and she rang for coffee.

They sat down, taking a sofa apiece which was overdoing things as far as comfort went but allowed them all to watch each other. After the preliminaries Wickham asked about her movements the previous day. He was prepared for her to thrust forward the theory that her father was the victim of a political assassination, because she had been lavishly quoted in the papers saying such things. But she appeared content to answer his questions.

'Mayfair,' she said in a quiet firm voice. 'I was here all afternoon but in the morning I went to see a dress designer.' She mentioned a fashionable name.

'What time did you leave him?' Wickham asked.

'About noon. I telephoned Daddy from the salon and asked him to meet me for lunch, but he didn't turn up. I'd been waiting at the restaurant half an hour when there was a message to say he couldn't come. I ate and came home, thinking trouble at the paper had kept him and he'd tell me all about it later. We lived here together, you know.'

She put a hand to her face and Wickham gave her a moment before asking whether the call from the salon was the last time she had spoken to her father. She said it was. He asked whether she could remember how the conversation went.

She leaned forward, elbows on knees, thin hands cupping her face. 'Mona — that's his secretary — put me through. I said something like: "Are you busy, Daddy? I'd really like to have lunch, if you can make it."' She flicked a look at Marshall writing it down. 'And he said: "Darling, I'd love to but we have a problem here and I think maybe I ought to stay around." He didn't give in until I said there were things I wanted to tell him and they were better discussed away from the office. I didn't expect to see him that evening because I was going to the theatre.'

Wickham asked what she wanted to talk to her father about but she dodged the question and went on to say her father chose a restaurant and said he would book a table for 12.45. At 1.15, she said, she got the message to say he wasn't coming.

'Can you remember the message?' Wickham asked.

'The owner came and said: "Madam, I regret to say that Mr MacQuillan is unable to join you. There has been a telephone call." I think those were his words.'

'Was there any indication whether your father himself had telephoned?'

'No, but I guessed Mona had rung for him.'

'There was no explanation for his change of plan?'

She swung back her hair. 'No, but he'd already said there was a problem and the paper wasn't produced last night because the printers walked out. That's never happened to him before. When he knew things were so bad he must have decided he couldn't leave the office after all.'

Wickham felt Marshall's eyes on him, waiting to see what he would do. Wickham told her. 'Miss MacQuillan, we know your father *did* leave the building yesterday. He went out a few minutes before 1.30 and returned to his office at 2.15.'

Her eyes widened. She walked to the window, a hand to her face again, her back to Wickham. After a moment she asked: 'Where did he go?'

'We don't know yet.'

She wrapped her arms around herself as though the room had grown suddenly cold. Then she walked away, as far as the fireplace so that Wickham had to twist round. He saw she had reached a decision about what she would tell him.

'Daddy was a remarkable man,' she said. 'His family were poor Irish Americans, the type who survived when they got over there but never did any more than that. He did it all. He made every bit of the American Dream come true. When he invented that milk carton he had the patents drawn up so tight they squeaked. He was very fond of reminding people that the whole world had been waiting for a drinks carton that really popped open when you wanted it to, and that Hal MacQuillan was the only man able to create one.'

Marshall cleared his throat. Wickham wished he had not. He did not want to appear impatient with trite family history because the key to the whole affair might just as easily lie there as anywhere.

Maureen said: 'Newspapers were the big adventure. He plunged in where other men wouldn't dare and his ideas worked. His American paper is strong and rich now, he gave it a leadership it had never had before. And over here, with the *Daily Post*, he was doing the same thing. In just a few weeks he made a real impression on Fleet Street . . .'

Marshall scratched the side of his nose with his pen. Wickham wished he would not do that, either. Maureen said: 'What I'm leading up to is that people don't achieve Daddy's sort of success without making enemies. I'm not talking about the grousers amongst his employees — you'll find plenty of those wherever he forced improvements. He made bigger enemies than that, businessmen in the States and politicians here.'

She stopped, inviting a prompting question from Wickham. He played according to her rules. 'Who were his enemies here?'

She crossed the carpet again, coming to rest on the arm of a sofa opposite Wickham. 'I really didn't expect to have to spell this out for you. Daddy made the *Post* the only national paper in Britain to campaign for the British to get out of Northern Ireland. His enemies include all of the present government. It's obvious he was killed to stop the campaign.'

'Are you suggesting he was killed by someone acting for the British government?' Wickham kept the scorn out of his voice. The press was trying to get him to say that the kitchen knife between the shoulder blades was a likely method for a terrorist to use, and now the dead man's daughter was proposing it for government agents.

She backed off. 'It's not for me to say who killed him. That's supposed to be your job.'

He asked whether MacQuillan's life had ever been threatened, and she gave a harsh laugh as she said: 'It went with the job.' From a desk drawer she took a file. 'I kept them, every single one since I found out it was happening. He used to throw them away before that, but I made him hand them over.'

Wickham was looking at an extraordinary document, a file with clear plastic pages into which letters and envelopes had been slipped. Each letter was a threat to kill, injure or otherwise take revenge. Some were signed and bore addresses, some were written in the marked handwriting of the mentally unstable, some were pasted together from words snipped from newspapers, some were digressive diatribes and some were Anglo-Saxon and to the point. The date when each entry was received had been added by Maureen.

Wickham concentrated on the most recent arrivals. 'Only two since your father took over the *Post*?'

'*Only* two! Do you think he liked getting those things?'

Wickham was annoyed with himself for being clumsy. Marshall asked: 'Why did you keep them, Miss MacQuillan?'

She stared at him as though it was an idiotic question. 'Because if anything ever happened to Daddy the people who hounded him in this way could be responsible.'

Wickham asked whether she had any idea who might have sent the two most recent letters, both unsigned and posted in London. She said not. He closed the folder and put it down beside the flowers. When he said he would like to take it away with him, she hesitated only momentarily before agreeing. Then he asked her again what she had intended to tell her father at the restaurant.

She gave an impatient glance at her watch. 'It was confidential, a business matter. Now if you'll excuse me, I'm expecting a caller.'

All she would add was that if they really wanted to know they could ask Stuart Pascoe. Then she was ruthless about showing them out. They sat in Wickham's car down the street and Marshall opened a bag of peppermints. The plastic inside the car was burning hot and the air hung heavy.

'Paranoid,' said Marshall, sucking on a sweet. 'That's the word for her. Collecting death threats and spotting enemies everywhere . . .'

'That's not a very helpful observation, Jim.' He helped himself to a sweet. 'I want you to see Pascoe and find out what she was getting at. It sounded like a hint at fraud.'

'Should I tell Pascoe . . . ?'

Urgently Wickham interrupted. 'Jim, do you see who that is?'

Marshall looked up startled. 'Yes, it's that MP.'

They watched as Cecil Hunter-Blair hurried into the block of flats they had just left.

CHAPTER 8

The Sunday papers were as bad as anything Rain could have imagined. Reporters she had not spoken to attributed lurid statements to her. The ones who had interviewed her preferred their phrases to hers. Her former colleague had clung to almost every word she had forbidden him to print, correcting only the colour of MacQuillan's carpet from green to brown.

She fumed while Oliver, reading out the worst of the excesses, found it hilarious. 'Some of these quotes aren't even grammatical,' he laughed.

'Is that supposed to make me feel better?'

He read out another inaccuracy. She interrupted, when he was halfway through the part about 'lovely, lively blonde gossip columnist found her boss butchered', and said she was going out to hide.

'We did that yesterday and it didn't make any difference,' he pointed out.

The telephone rang. He looked at her over the top of a paper. 'It'll be another reporter for you.'

'Then you can say I'm not here.'

Unhurriedly he answered the telephone. She sat still, as though movement could give her presence away. Oliver said: 'It's a journalist, for you.'

She heard Alex Harbury, apologizing for walking in on her on Friday evening and then passing on the information that Maureen MacQuillan had hired a private detective to find her father's killer. 'He's called Brian Berg and my police contacts tell me he's already nosing around. No doubt he'll be calling on you.'

Rain told Oliver: 'That settles it. I'm not staying here to answer questions from Maureen's detective.' They went out.

It was Rain's Sunday off and Holly was editing the column, but by mid-afternoon they had gravitated to the office. It was a fairly quiet news day, the main excitement being the breakout from a maximum security prison. Several readers rang to ask whether MacQuillan's murderer had been caught and Ruby Dobby, a well-known psychic and self-publicist, rang to offer her help. Riley put her on to the police.

There were messages stuffed into Rain's typewriter. Four people wanted to talk to her. In three cases she could guess why. One would deny a paragraph she had published about his involvement in a stock exchange swindle. One would be maligning a former lover in retaliation for revelations published in another paper. One would be cajoling her into mentioning a dress shop she was opening. The fourth was a mystery. She telephoned the fourth.

The warm American voice of Crystal Daly, a voice Rain had not heard in years, came on the line. 'Rain? Could you come by? I have something for you.'

Rain needed more than that. Crystal said: 'It's about MacQuillan.' She gave a chuckle, the chuckle Rain remembered her giving before things went sour between them. They fixed a time, 5.30 p.m. at Crystal's art gallery.

Maureen was in the office that afternoon, clearing her desk. Holly was dialling a telephone number but without luck. Maureen told her to keep trying. Holly murmured that of course she would and escaped to the library. She had been trying to reach Donaldson, a businessman about whom MacQuillan, through Maureen, had demanded the column publish a flattering item. Having failed to persuade Rain, Maureen had won with Holly.

But there was a long way to go before the item got into the paper and Rain could kill it at any stage without a public confrontation with Maureen or Holly. She determined to do so.

Maureen produced a box, packed into it as much as it would hold and asked Oliver to carry it up to the second floor for her. She took a few things herself.

Holly came back having spent her time in the library deciding to air the Donaldson question. 'Rain, I know you don't like the Donaldson story because it was offered by the MacQuillans, but Maureen insists . . .'

'She has no right to insist.'

Holly said calmly: 'It's a good story wherever it came from.'

Rain doubted this. She believed Holly was influenced by the story originating with people who were promising to promote her. Controlling the content of a newspaper was seldom a matter of issuing instructions.

Holly defended her viewpoint, concluding that if Rain held it up any longer the story would be picked up by another paper. Rain said the fact it had not appeared elsewhere only confirmed her suspicions.

Neither of them wanted a conflict. Until Maureen joined the column their relationship had been good. Only Oliver had ever suggested Holly was committed to wresting Rain's job from her, and Rain had vigorously rejected the idea. Now it was more difficult to do that.

In the challenging silence that followed their last remarks, Oliver returned with the empty box and the news that Maureen was delayed by an argument with Wickham about the need for her to move into her father's office. When she reappeared she was tense with anger, and snapped at Oliver that he was to refill the box and carry the next load upstairs.

And then Wainfleet rang to ask Rain's opinion of a story he had been given by Hunter-Blair. 'He's told me a yarn about an incident on Friday at the demonstration outside the army camp, and says he was there. But you know what he's like, always trying to take credit for things which are nothing to do with him.'

Hunter-Blair was not the worst politician in this respect, but he was known to be bad. Wainfleet was troubled because he believed Hunter-Blair delivered his Irish column to the *Post* on Friday afternoons.

Rain told him one of Tavett's current woes was that Hunter-Blair had not delivered his copy and, now that MacQuillan was dead and Eliot could be expected to make a renewed effort at editing, Tavett did not know whether to chase the missing column or not.

'Well that's good enough for me,' said Wainfleet. 'If Hunter-Blair wasn't in Fleet Street he could well have been at the army camp.'

Guardedly Rain agreed. Wainfleet picked up her caution and she admitted to misgivings because Hunter-Blair had given her the impression he had been to the office.

'Oh, maybe he did that before the demonstration. It didn't start until lunchtime.' Wainfleet was eager to be satisfied and rang off.

Rain sat at her desk, listening to Holly interviewing Donaldson and remembering what Hunter-Blair had said to her at Linley's party. It occurred to her he could be using Wainfleet to give himself an alibi for Friday afternoon, because it was not possible for him to have been at the demonstration and then in London before MacQuillan was killed. But he would only fabricate an alibi if he was certain he had not been seen in the newspaper office. And if he had been there why had he not delivered his copy?

* * *

'Have you heard, sir?' said Marshall coming into the typists' office. 'There's been a breakout from Gorstone. Sniffy

Wilson's over the wall and half a dozen others, mostly members of the Clarke gang.'

Wickham rolled his eyes. 'It took us long enough to get them behind bars, you'd think other people would take the trouble to keep them there.'

'Sniffy was one of yours, wasn't he, sir?'

'Burridge was in charge of the case. But, yes, Sniffy took up nearly a year of my life. We got him for armed robbery in the end, the legal advice was that we didn't have firm enough evidence for a murder charge but I've personally never doubted his guilt. When I arrested him and he heard the charge there was a look of relief on his face that was all the confirmation anyone needed.'

Marshall could not see what difference it made, Wilson had been sent to prison for ten years and a life sentence might not have been more. Wickham said: 'If we'd proved in court that he was sent by Clarke to kill two members of the Goad gang, he would never have got out of prison alive. The Goads would have arranged a fatal accident for him. If they'd already had the proof they would have taken their revenge before we got him into the dock.'

Garside put his head into the room to ask whether Wickham had heard about Wilson. Garside said: 'I can't see why they bother escaping. They seem to be inside for no time at all these days, what with remission.'

Wickham pointed out that Sniffy had never qualified for remission for good behaviour and during his current sentence had earned another year for his part in a prison riot.

Garside shrugged. 'Donovan's out. And Wytcherly. They came out last spring, and no doubt they're back at work with Goad. I suppose we shall be arresting them for something else before long.'

Marshall suggested that perhaps they would like to own up to the MacQuillan murder so that he could go home and take the leave that was overdue.

'This killing doesn't bear the mark of Goad,' said Wickham. 'The mind behind it is altogether more subtle and intelligent.'

It had been so careful that the assailant had left them hardly anything to go on. Inside the room Garside had found only fingerprints belonging to MacQuillan or Mona Washbrooke and on the door frame Mona's and Tavett's. However skimpily the contract cleaners dealt with the rest of the offices, Hal MacQuillan's had been dusted, polished and vacuumed. Wickham needed to know how long those fragments of paper and yarn might have been in the cupboard.

According to the cleaning company the work was done thoroughly every day. Their Mrs Smith who was responsible for it had gone to a family wedding and could not be reached on Friday. It was Sunday before she went to see the police.

She was a short vigorous woman who clearly expected to be accused of neglecting her duty. 'I was very particular,' she said as Marshall introduced her to Wickham. He invited her to sit down but she gave the typist's chair a doubtful look and remained standing. 'I'm the head of the team, sir, so I always see to the top man's office myself. Then I can be sure it's done properly.'

Wickham asked what time of day she cleaned MacQuillan's room and she explained that it was done each morning at around 8 a.m. 'Some offices we do in the evenings but, of course, with a newspaper things have to be different. People work here quite late and it suits us better to come in the mornings. We don't have to be early, either. My team starts at 6.30 and we do an office near the Law Courts before we get over here,' she said.

She had never, she said, seen MacQuillan and rarely encountered anybody else, except for one or other of the night security men who let the cleaning women in and out of the building. A man called Stan was usually on duty but occasionally he was replaced by one called Ed.

Wickham asked her to show him what she did when she arrived at MacQuillan's room. She warmed to the idea of a demonstration. 'Shall I get my things, sir? My vacuum and polish and dusters are kept in a cupboard on the ground floor. The key will be at reception — I usually get it from Stan when I come in and hand it back when we go.'

But Wickham said all that was unnecessary. Mrs Smith looked a shade disappointed but went about her mime with a will, being very careful not actually to touch anything. 'It's always very tidy, sir,' she said, and showed how she dusted everything first, then polished the desk and chair with an aerosol polish and buffed the brass fittings to a high shine. Her final job was to vacuum.

'I plug the cleaner in over there—' she pointed to a wall socket '—and then I can reach all round the room. The lead is quite long enough, not like some machines where you're always looking for the next socket before you can get on with the job.' She stopped, hands on hips. 'Well, that's it, sir.' And yet she knew she had failed him.

Wickham said: 'Do you ever clean inside the cupboard, Mrs Smith?'

She flung up her hands as the recollection hit her. 'Oh yes, every day. Thinking about it made me forget. If you'd let me have my duster and cleaner I'd have done it automatically.' She had to be restrained from rushing to open the cupboard to demonstrate how she ran the vacuum cleaner over the carpet and whisked her duster along the coat rail and over the hat shelf. 'You have to do it,' she said. 'Clothes cupboards are nasty dusty things, a day or two missed and it would show.'

She was quite adamant that she had done the cupboard as thoroughly as the rest of the room on the day MacQuillan died. Before she left Wickham had a final question. 'What do you wear when you're cleaning, Mrs Smith?'

'Overalls. Last week it was the blue and red. Do you want to see it?'

'Yes, please. And what about your hands?'

'Gloves,' she said and held up a blotchily pink hand. 'The cleaning things we use bring my hands out in rashes so I always wear gloves. They go on the minute I get here and they don't come off again until I leave. I'll bring those for you as well, shall I?'

'Thank you very much, Mrs Smith. You're being most helpful.'

'Oh, it's no trouble. I'll be back in two minutes.'

When he looked puzzled she laughed and told him: 'I won't have to go home, I keep them in the cupboard with the cleaning stuff.'

She bustled away to fetch them. Wickham gave Marshall a jaundiced look. 'I thought you said no gloves had been found on the premises.'

Marshall did not take this personally, he had only reported on the search, not made himself responsible for every bit of checking. And he could see why Wickham was irritated: there was little enough to go on, the press were insistent that he should be seeking a political assassin and his men were overlooking whole cupboards full of potential evidence.

Wickham stared out of the window into Fleet Street. The place was never entirely deserted on Sundays like some parts of central London. In morning paper offices journalists were creating Monday's pages and each of those papers would want to tell its readers something new about the MacQuillan case. He had given a quote to an agency reporter and insisted he was not to be disturbed by any others. The officer handling press enquiries would take care of the rest, going through the motions of a press conference on the days when the insistence of the reporters succeeded. Only when Wickham wanted to make a public appeal for specific information would he hold the conference himself. He had decided early in his career that it was a mistake to be too willingly interrupted. Empty, determined words looked foolish when the newspaper cuttings yellowed on unsolved crimes. Besides, reporters who seldom heard him were more eager in their response when he wanted their help.

Mrs Smith trotted back, unfurled a flowered overall and held it against her like a woman at a dress shop mirror. 'My blue and red, you see. My green is in the cupboard at the office near the Law Courts and my spare is at home. That's yellow. I can usually make them go a fortnight unless there's a spill and they get splashed. Of course, it's different with the girls who wash the floors. They have to change more often.'

She twisted away from Wickham to show the other police officers who were also taking such interest in the overall. Wickham drew her attention again. 'Have you brought the gloves, Mrs Smith?'

'D'ye know, they weren't there. I must have thrown them away. They were only those thin polythene ones but they do get sticky inside as your hands get hot. I remember thinking I ought to chuck them out and start with a fresh pair on Monday.'

'Can you remember whether you discarded them or not?' Wickham waited while she thought about it, but the answer was unchanged: she *must have* thrown them out, not she *had* done.

Marshall said to him: 'Nobody found them when the waste bins were emptied, sir.'

'I might have taken them home to throw away,' Mrs Smith said. 'I'm sorry I can't be definite.' She had been praised for her helpfulness and was patently sorry to be so useless now.

'Never mind,' said Wickham. 'If you remember anything about it there'll be somebody here you can tell.' He took the offered overall and Marshall showed her out.

'There's no hurry about the overall,' she called as she went. 'I can wear my yellow next week.'

When she was out of sight it was folded, put into a bag and labelled. It wasn't all blue and red flowers. The background was a creamy colour and it was possible the thread found in the cupboard had come from it. 'The seams are frayed,' said the man who folded it. The package was sent to the laboratory.

'She says she's going to ask her Arnold about the gloves, sir,' said Marshall coming back. 'That's apparently her husband. He's unemployed, at home all day and certain to know whether she took her gloves home on Friday.' He made a wry face. 'It's not a lot to go on, is it? A pair of disposable gloves that might have been disposed of, and a thread that might have come from her overall.'

'No, it's not much, Jim. But people have been hanged on less,' said Wickham.

Apart from the tiresome business of Maureen MacQuillan moving her belongings upstairs, Mrs Smith was the highlight of the day. The other hours were spent in checking and counter-checking, comparing one person's statement with another's and sifting for discrepancies. It was the painstaking work which was the framework of every investigation and not the stuff of which press conferences are made.

Wickham stayed late, mildly guilty that Marshall felt obliged to stay, too, when he could just as well have gone home to his wife. Eventually he accepted it was improbable any more would be learned that evening, said as much to Marshall, and they left. In the entrance hall Marshall pointed out the cleaners' cupboard. A short passage linked the foyer with the printers' composing room and the cupboard was in that passage. It was locked and the security man was not at his desk but after Mrs Smith's visit her equipment had been examined and the contents of her vacuum cleaner bag sorted through. There had been no more threads like the one found in MacQuillan's room.

Marshall and Wickham parted in the car park, the sergeant accelerating away before Wickham had turned the ignition of his own car. He had not the same enthusiasm for getting home. Marshall's Sheila would be sitting in front of the television, waiting to feed him. There would not be even the sounds of television as Wickham opened his door. The flat would be very quiet, very empty.

Other policemen's wives broke away because of the constant demands of the job. They wearied of cancelled social engagements, trying to fit family life around the edges of an erratic working week, being shut out of a world their partner found utterly absorbing. The Wickhams had been different. Vanessa's own work was no less engrossing, her pursuit of it no less excluding. She had not even liked him to see her work in progress, her studio was a private place and she had sometimes slept there so that the thread of her concentration would be unbroken.

Wickham was held up by traffic lights in Trafalgar Square. Tourists milled about, scampered in fountains and lounged on lions. St James's Park was peppered with barely dressed people. London looked like a seaside resort. He switched on the car radio and heard a weather forecaster say there was no sign of a change. He half expected the crowds outside Buckingham Palace to raise a cheer.

His last case had been a child murder. A little girl had been snatched and choked by a man who let her help him feed the ducks in a North London park. It had happened on a sunny afternoon within a hundred yards of the child's mother who was sitting on the grass talking to a friend and breast-feeding her new baby. The killing was the kind of frightening, frightful crime that made every parent feel vulnerable. The victim could have been any child, the killer had said so when he made his confession. Any child would have satisfied his urge to touch young flesh — and if it struggled and screamed, to silence it. The police inquiry had been efficient and the conclusion speedy, yet it was the type of case which illuminated defeat. Society was no more able to understand and deal with the man's condition than he was. Wickham was relieved to be immersed quickly in another major investigation.

But the MacQuillan case was not just another case. Meeting Rain Morgan again had stirred secrets. There was a tug of emotion he did not care to name. The wounds of his failed marriage were tender and since his call to the *Daily Post* on Friday his memory had been constantly nudged about the events of that cataclysmic year when he had met Rain, arrested Sniffy Wilson and married Vanessa.

* * *

Rain rapped with fingernails on the glass door of the Daly Gallery in Portal Street. Distantly she could see Crystal bending over a desk with a mess of papers on it. Against the desk and walls stood paintings she had not yet hung. Others fringed the room or lay haphazardly on the carpet.

Crystal ran to the door, thick black hair bobbing, long red cotton dress flapping. 'Hi!' She swung an arm around

Rain and kissed her cheek, as though they were the dearest of friends, not acquaintances who had backed sharply away from each other. Rain did not trust that kiss. Although her smile never faltered, her heart sank. She feared she had been fooled, that Crystal wanted only to manoeuvre some publicity for her new exhibition. She did not blame Crystal for trying, she'd had a tough time since Simon Daly had left her and withdrawn his money from the business. Rain prepared to keep smiling and defend herself.

But Crystal, whisking open a fridge and taking out a half-full bottle of too-cold white wine, said: 'MacQuillan had a mistress, right here in London. And . . .' She stepped delicately over a painting as she held high the long-stemmed glasses she had overfilled. 'And . . .'

She offered a glass. Rain utterly failed not to look avid for more of Crystal's gossip. 'And?' she prompted.

'And he was killed because certain people in this country did not care for his attitude to British involvement in Ireland.'

Rain was disappointed, she felt she had heard that bit before, and Wickham had scorned it so why shouldn't she? She should not because Crystal Daly, gallery owner, gossip and attention-seeker, was telling her that a man called Georgie had mentioned it to her with some authority. 'He was quite convincing, he said he got it from Joey and Joey got it from . . .'

Rain burst out laughing. 'These sound like budgies!'

'Oh, you'd be surprised how Georgie was singing.'

Rain declined to mention that it was traditionally canaries who sang. She asked, more tactfully, how Crystal — or Joey or Georgie — had come by this information. Crystal said she thought Georgie was 'something to do with British Intelligence, one of your MI numbers'.

Rain swallowed most of her wine and very little of the story, while Crystal chattered on. Then Rain fixed her with a gimlet eye and demanded: 'How did you do it?'

'Uh?'

'You don't look like the KGB or the CIA or any of our MI numbers, so how did you get Georgie to . . . er . . . sing?'

Crystal advanced with the wine bottle. 'Like this? Would you believe that?'

'No,' said Rain firmly. She let her glass be refilled.

Crystal wore a slight but unmistakable blush. 'Do *I* enquire into *your* sex life?'

Rain could recall the time, but denied it with another firm: 'No.'

Crystal shrugged and set the bottle down on the desk. 'It's over,' she said, expecting Rain to follow her thoughts back to Georgie. 'Quite finished. Except that *I* haven't quite finished.' She giggled, as nearly as a woman of forty-seven is allowed.

Rain asked whether she was expected to believe that after the stabbing Georgie rushed round to the gallery to tell Crystal who had done it and why. Crystal said: 'No, Georgie told me, way back, that Joey thought it should be done.'

There was more but none of it either plausible or publishable, although Rain's impression was that Crystal wanted to use a newspaper to embarrass Georgie. She wondered whether anyone but Crystal referred to the men as Georgie and Joey, and hoped Crystal's habit did not extend to calling her Rainy.

Some time later, after telephone calls and no more than the usual amount of bribery, Rain had confirmed Crystal's story that a rich American woman living in Mayfair had been MacQuillan's mistress. She put on her most sympathetic attitude and rang the doorbell. A Filipino maid was beguiled into admitting her. Rain heard distant grumbling and then brisk footsteps along the tiled hall. A somewhat overdressed middle-aged woman arrived, her irritation with her careless maid ill-concealed behind an enquiring smile.

Rain suggested to her that Hal MacQuillan had been a friend of the James family and for some while Mrs James expressed her sorrow at his death, her admiration for his business achievements and the strength of his character. And she remembered, fairly often, to say 'we' instead of 'I' so that it should be clear she was speaking for the entire James family. Eventually she gave it up, suspecting how much Rain already knew. They talked on, the word mistress was bandied, and by the time Rain left Mrs James had unburdened the whole humdrum story. The relationship went back years and had been revived once MacQuillan had bought the *Post* and followed the James family to London. But in the week he died, Mrs James had not seen him because she had accompanied her husband on a business trip to Paris.

CHAPTER 9

The scream rang through the newsroom. Rosie, the gossip column secretary, stood rigid, fingers splayed against whitening cheeks. At her feet was a knife, which had landed on its point and stuck into the carpet.

Her scream brought people from all corners. Holly, who was nearest, reached for the knife but Rain caught her arm. 'Don't touch it. The police will want to know about this.'

It was late morning on Monday and Rosie had been opening the mail. She was wearing the outfit she had bought on Saturday and if anyone had been told she was modelling for the fashion page they would have believed it. Until that scream.

Holly comforted Rosie while Rain rang Wickham. He came with Marshall and another officer who carefully lifted the knife and the packet it had come in and took them away. The package was addressed to Rain.

She followed the police to the second floor and going through Mona's room noticed some of Maureen's belongings. 'Is Maureen going to work there instead of in her father's office?'

Wickham said: 'She was persuaded — eventually.'

'Mona will hate that.'

'She won't be there. Luke Eliot has claimed her back.'

She smiled. Maureen had lost a round or two. Wickham said: 'Rosie thinks she touched the knife so once we've fingerprinted her we might be able to discover who else handled it.'

Rain noticed a stress on 'might'. He was not expecting much. She said: 'This must be somebody's idea of a joke.' And was unhappy that he could not agree.

He asked who she could think of who would play such a trick but she was at a loss, unless it was the Patriotic Ten or the free speech folk. Friday's fury spent, both groups had sent members to the office that day to continue working on their draft statements. Wickham said: 'The murder weapon is a very common type of knife and the papers have described it. It doesn't follow that both knives were in the possession of the same person. The one sent to you might be connected with the MacQuillan case, but on the other hand it might have come from any reader of the tabloids who enjoyed your descriptions of the murder scene and decided to give you another frisson.'

She started to deny making those remarks, but then realized he was being mischievous. 'You loved seeing me misquoted!'

He admitted as much. 'That was one of the lighter aspects of my weekend, imagining how you felt finding yourself on the other side of the fence for once.'

'Don't be too unsympathetic, Paul, or I shall withhold the information that Maureen has hired a private eye.'

'Mr Berg? Well, you can't trade that for anything. I trust my police contacts to be at least as good as young Harbury's.' Alex Harbury's keenness was becoming as much of a joke with Wickham's men as it was with his friends among the journalists.

She gave in, said she had nothing to offer in exchange but was desperately curious to know how the inquiry was going. He told her, a story which was basically one of lack of progress. Then he said: 'What would you say if I told you I saw Hunter-Blair going into the block of flats where Maureen lives?'

'I'd say I'm surprised, because I wouldn't expect him to be on visiting terms with her or with the other occupants, either.' She told him who the others were.

Before she left him Marshall arrived with the news that there were only Rosie's fingerprints on the knife. 'It's the same as the murder weapon and the knife in the pond, sir. There's no sign of a useful print on any of them.'

Marshall's flat comment made Rain nervous. Wickham had undermined her confidence that the Linley knife and the one sent to her were jokes. She meant to go on treating them lightly, rather than appear jittery, but her real feelings had changed.

Downstairs Rain discovered Tavett, much alarmed. Holly was trying to soothe him but with difficulty as she had an arm around Rosie who was crying. Rosie was not the tearful type but a month of the unhappy atmosphere engendered by MacQuillan, capped with the suspicion that someone in the office was a killer, had jangled many people's nerves.

'Come and look at this, Rain,' Tavett urged in a whisper and took her to his desk. She caught her breath. On it lay another knife, identical to the one she had received. Tavett said: 'They must be threats. It said in the papers the one in the pond was a threat against Linley's life. We found the body and we're being warned off.'

She tried to laugh. 'Off *what?* We aren't doing anything.'

Tavett said he had not told the police because he wanted her to see it first, which she thought silly until she remembered her own failure to summon a doctor. She lifted the telephone on his desk. Again Wickham, Marshall and the man with the delicate way of collecting suspicious items came.

'I didn't touch it,' Tavett volunteered in a whisper as they drew near. 'It slid out as I opened the package.'

Like the knife sent to Rain it had come in a padded bag. The bags were new and bore plain labels on which names and addresses had been typed. They had not been through the post. The knives were loose inside the bags with no other wrapping and nothing to identify their source, not even a manufacturer's name stamped on a blade.

'I wonder how many more of these will turn up,' mused Marshall, and sent a shiver down the spines of listeners.

Wickham gave him a disapproving look but his apology was drowned by an eruption of noise from Eliot's office. Maureen MacQuillan rushed into the newsroom, collided with a secretary carrying a tray of beakers and sent iced water splashing down the woman's dress. Without faltering Maureen rounded the corner to the landing and the lifts.

Behind her came a cadaverous young man in an expensive lightweight suit. People looked away as, with a more measured pace, he went out the way Maureen had gone.

'I'm always nervous when Ron Barron puts in an appearance,' Tavett muttered to Rain.

Wickham overheard. 'So that's Mr Barron? Jim, tell him I'd like a word with him before he leaves the building.' Marshall sped after Barron.

While Wickham was still discussing the knife with Tavett, Rain went to the cloakroom to fetch water for her pot plant and met Mona. She was holding her wrists under a cold tap to cool herself. Mona looked happier than she had done for weeks, and her relief that MacQuillan had gone freed a torrent of criticism of him. Rain hoped Mona's relief was not premature because Maureen was still there.

Mona said: 'Whatever happens she won't get me to work for her. I only left Eliot because MacQuillan told me he was leaving. I understood that if I didn't move upstairs I would work for Linley, and he's rather difficult.'

Rain seized the chance to learn the truth behind a rumour. 'Is it true MacQuillan sacked Eliot?'

'Well . . .' Mona looked around in case anyone had crept into the room. 'Just between ourselves, of course . . .'

'Of course.'

She said the day MacQuillan moved in he told Eliot to go but Eliot's contract protected him. MacQuillan had been trying to force his resignation, and had been annoyed that Linley was not more active in helping oust Eliot. 'Obviously,' she said, 'Linley wanted to take over from Eliot without making himself totally unpopular with the staff, but MacQuillan didn't appreciate that as his own methods were so crude.'

And then Mona revealed that Maureen and Barron had that morning renewed the demand for Eliot's resignation and Eliot's calm refusal had enraged Maureen. Mona dried herself on a paper towel and changed the subject with: 'What's the news this morning? Have those prisoners been rounded up yet?'

They had not and it seemed to Riley that every member of the law and order lobby was on his newsdesk telephone pleading to be quoted on the laxity of the governor and the undermanning of the prison service. It was Rain who got the call from Sniffy Wilson.

'Got something for you,' he said without preamble.

Like Mona and Crystal Daly, he had given her good stories in the past. Her fingers reached for a pen. 'About the Great Escape?'

'No, about MacQuillan.'

She heard the characteristic sniff that earned him his soubriquet as she asked: 'Do you know who killed him?'

'Well, not exactly, but I know what he was up to. He didn't get anything he hadn't earned. I'd have told you before but I wasn't on the telephone then.'

'No. Well . . . What have you got?'

But something had happened to change his mind and he rang off. She hoped he would try again once the danger had passed but he did not.

* * *

Late in the morning Maureen cornered Sergeant Marshall and demanded to know how much longer it would be before the police would leave. Marshall curbed the inclination to say it could not be soon enough for him because the building with its crippled air supply was one of the least comfortable he had ever been inside. Instead he replied formally that it was normal for an incident room to be established at the scene of a serious crime and that inquiries were continuing.

Maureen was scathing. 'Your inquiries are leading you nowhere. You ought to be rounding up Unionist extremists. Those are the people who killed my father.'

Marshall had never come across any such group operating in London, but was saved from saying so because Maureen added: 'Ron Barron won't be seeing your superintendent. He's got an important appointment.' She strode away.

Had she stayed he would have told her the restaurant manager believed MacQuillan himself had telephoned her to cancel their lunch. At least, the caller had an American accent and gave that name. But as she was being so unpleasant Marshall did not call her back.

Marshall found Wickham in MacQuillan's office, looking through an open window into Fleet Street. Marshall relayed the message about Barron.

Wickham said: 'Miss MacQuillan has gone with him. They've just run across the road together and now they're getting into a taxi.' He doubted Barron's reluctance to spare time for an interview was other than bad manners. No one had suggested Barron had been near the building on Friday.

Wickham pulled the window shut to kill the street noise. On the boardroom table were piles of papers several inches deep and to one side single sheets spread out. There were five of these, each the statement of someone whose whereabouts were uncorroborated during the time the murder took place. These people could not, in the phrase Shildon objected to, be eliminated.

He took up the nearest. Stuart Pascoe said he telephoned to make an appointment with MacQuillan on Friday but failed to get through. He had begun trying at 12.30 p.m. but given it up to go to lunch half an hour later. When he returned at 2.00 p.m. there was still no answer so he went to Mona's office and left a note asking her to telephone him about fixing an appointment. She did not.

Wickham asked: 'Do we know why Pascoe wanted to see MacQuillan?'

'The officer who took the statement says it was something to do with the finances of the paper but Pascoe didn't want to give him any details.'

'All the same, we'll have them.'

Marshall made a note that Pascoe was to be questioned again. Wickham continued: 'And I want the precise wording of the note. If he really left it, it could be significant that someone bothered to take it.' In her statement Mona Washbrooke denied finding such a note when she returned from her shopping and hairdressing jaunt just after 4 p.m.

Wickham set Pascoe's statement aside. He put Tavett's with it: there was still no confirmation of his movements in the minutes before he told Rain that MacQuillan was dead. Wickham took up the statement made by Zak Smythe. The Patriotic Ten was a group on whom the police had a file without finding cause for alarm as they looked and talked more fiercely than they acted. And there had only ever been nine of them, the name being chosen because they preferred the ring of it and because it was an indication of anarchy to declare yourselves Ten when you were but Nine.

On Friday, it was generally agreed, when the patriots ended their meeting with the editor, Smythe had asked a reporter where the toilets were and been directed to the door next to the wire room. Smythe insisted he had been in there the whole time he was absent, but other men had gone in and out and not seen him. They included one of the gang, Tony.

Wickham said: 'If he picked the wrong door he would have been on the back stairs and could have gone up, entered MacQuillan's office, stabbed him and returned to the newsroom.'

Marshall added that Smythe could have used the cloakroom at the top of the back stairs which would explain why he was never seen in the other one. But he was not surprised when Wickham said: 'The flaw, Jim, is that it would have been harder for Smythe to kill MacQuillan than for any of the others. Smythe wouldn't have known the stairs were there and he wouldn't have known they led to MacQuillan's office. He could only have got to MacQuillan by a series of chances.'

Marshall's pen slid from his sweaty fingers. He stooped for it and, straightening, said: 'He'd got the motive, he hated MacQuillan.'

'But Smythe carries a flick knife — or did until we took it from him on Friday. He'd have used that, not bought a kitchen knife which doesn't fold and slip into a pocket.'

Marshall wiped his hands on his shirt front, remarking that nobody had seen anybody carrying a knife or anything which might have contained one. Wickham pointed out it only meant they had not been on the lookout. He turned to Shildon's statement.

'That all adds up now, sir.'

'When anybody has changed a statement I like to be sure I understand why.' In the first version Shildon claimed not to have left the building at all, and to have been in the newsroom all along except when he fetched a sandwich from the basement canteen. He could not say what time he went there.

Early on Monday morning Shildon had been questioned again because his colleagues said he had not spent so much time at his desk. His second attempt was more detailed: he had been to the library to look at back numbers and search for a file of cuttings which he carried to his desk; he suggested his visit to the canteen took place around 1 p.m.; and he remembered two other occasions when he went out of the newsroom — during the printers' meeting he had stood in the rear yard for a short time and he had subsequently been to the composing room. A handful of printers confirmed he had been in the yard.

'He's vague about times,' Wickham observed, 'but that's probably sheer honesty. Anyway, I want to talk to him.'

Marshall jotted Shildon's name on his list. Wickham began to read Linley's statement, then laughed, startling the sergeant. 'I can almost hear his drawl coming out of the page.'

After being so irritatingly hazy when Wickham had seen him, the deputy editor had decided to own up. He admitted being away from the office most of Friday because his publisher had arranged a couple of interviews to publicize his book on Etruscan pots. One of them took place over a lengthy lunch in an Italian restaurant.

When his taxi brought him back to Fleet Street, the *Post* was besieged by free speech campaigners and rather than run the gauntlet Linley asked the driver to drop him off at a coffee bar. A while later he slipped down one of the narrow alleys which spill into Fleet Street and entered the paper by the back door. The printers were not there and he went up the back stairs without meeting anyone. Hearing a commotion on the first floor, he opened the door a chink and grasped that there was a considerable disturbance of which he had no wish to become part. He ensconced himself in the head printer's empty office near the rear entrance and wrote some short book reviews he ought to have delivered to the literary editor a week before. When he had done that it was almost four and, as he was tired and it was clear the paper was not coming out that night, he went home.

'If it wasn't equally clear he had no reason to do away with MacQuillan he would have provided himself with a better alibi,' suggested Marshall. 'He can't name the coffee bar, so there's nothing that can be checked after he left his publisher and interviewer outside the restaurant.'

'Put him on the list all the same, Jim.'

Marshall nodded. 'If he was where he says he was, he should be able to say who came in and out of the back entrance, and whether Shildon really was in the composing room.'

Wickham ran a hand over his head, a gesture which reminded him so forcibly of Tavett that he stopped halfway through. He said, in the tone he reserved for understatement, that it was a shame neither Linley nor Shildon had much idea of timings on Friday afternoon.

Marshall dropped his pen once more. 'What order would you like them in, sir?'

'I don't think I can cope with any more of Tavett yet, we'll leave him until last. Start with Pascoe. At least he admits having been to the second floor before the corpse was found.' He looked at the clock on MacQuillan's wall. 'I'd like him at 1.30, if you can organize that.' It was nearing 1 p.m.

Marshall fixed the interviews and then Wickham suggested; 'Why don't you go for lunch now and get some of what passes for air in central London in a heatwave?'

'Can I bring you anything back, sir?' He worried slightly that Wickham could be careless about lunch. Superintendents who did not bother with food could forget their sergeants wanted some.

But Wickham said he was going to take a closer look at the canteen before the Pascoe interview. Marshall did not waste time asking what drew Wickham to that steamy underworld. He was merely thankful not to have been asked to join him, and left before the thought might occur to Wickham.

Marshall crossed the rear yard and took a sequence of lanes until he cut through to New Fetter Lane. He had known the area well in the past when Sheila, who became his wife, had been a secretary in a solicitor's office near Lincoln's Inn. This was a sentimental journey, leading to Leather Lane where he and Sheila had often jostled together through the street market.

A modern building had risen at the Holborn end of the lane since those days, and he ate a pie in a pub in one corner of the new block before plunging into the throng. He enjoyed the vivacity of the market, the exaggerated claims of the stallholders, and he was even prepared to forget about the crime wave and believe in the bargains.

A busker with no voice but much cheek sang 'You Are My Sunshine' (although the crowd had more sunshine than they wanted) and attempted to tap dance. He was old and drunk and pathetic, but the war medals clanked on his chest and people tossed him money.

Marshall checked his watch. He ought to turn back because it would not do to keep Wickham waiting, but he persuaded himself there was time to go a little further and buy a small gift for Sheila to remind her, too, of their early days.

A stallholder was doing graceful things with silk scarves, making them fly and flutter in the humid air, their vibrant colours reflected against his skin. Marshall bought a blue one and turned to go. But then the crowd at the next stall roared and swayed with laughter and he thought he recognized the murmur of a familiar word. Two women near the back of the group conferred: 'What did he say, Pat?'

Pat had not heard either but a shy young man told them: 'He says it's like the one that stabbed MacQuillan.'

Then Marshall was worming his way through until he had a good view of the stallholder, a man with shaggy, dyed-yellow hair and an impish grin. In his hand he flashed a knife, demonstrating the efficiency of its blade, making sawing and carving actions in the air and then chopping a carrot on a board. The actions were accompanied by repetitive banter which ended with his new joke, that the knife was ideal for stabbing. Until he had the crowd clamouring, money in fists and begging to be served, he did not attempt to make a sale.

Marshall got out his three pounds and held them high. He never saw the man's eyes alight on him but when it was time for the selling to start the man said: 'Let's serve the policeman first, he must have believed what I said about MacQuillan.'

The crowd giggled and Marshall, embarrassed, got his knife.

CHAPTER 10

The canteen had a smell of elderly rissoles and older cabbage. It was utilitarian, adequate and uninviting — rather like the food. Few people used it during the day and those who were there when Wickham entered appeared not to notice him. He opted for a salad with leathery hard-boiled eggs under a neon dressing, and picked a table which gave a clear view of the room from the entrance to the service area.

Unfortunately, there was a distracting painting which had something of Vanessa's style about it and sent his thoughts scurrying back to her. She was not destined to be a great painter but she had the confidence and luck to be a successful one. When she was not steeped in work she was warm and gregarious, almost as though she was ensuring a queue of admirers to buy up her next batch of paintings. Had it been a ploy it would have been a rewarding one, but Vanessa was not given to ploys. She balanced periods of intense isolation with others of frantic social activity, because that was what her nature demanded. Wickham had identified the pattern early on and learned to live with it.

But one winter she got flu, her work was sapped and for the first time the critics were unkind. She ran off to friends in Crete for sunshine and consolation, and returned with renewed vigour. Her zeal was repaid as painting after painting achieved the intensity that marked her best work. Wickham had been proud of her, and was devastated when she said they should separate. Their rows centred on his failure to be available when she needed his support rather than her ability to be physically present but absent in every other way.

But there was not much time for rows because he was conducting the Halpern case which eventually sent three youths to prison for the torture and murder of a crippled old woman. He asked Vanessa to wait until it was over, but having waited her opinion was unchanged. Even then, he believed there was hope and persuaded her that they should take a holiday together. Again she went alone, because the Goad case came along and he had to hunt down a gangland killer. During the case Vanessa moved out.

He forced himself to ignore the painting and pulled his mind back to the MacQuillan case. Mrs Smith's Arnold had confirmed she took her gloves home on Friday and threw them in the dustbin and . . . Then Rain came into the canteen. She carried her sandwich over to join him, saying: '*My* excuse for being down here is that I haven't a moment to spare. *You* must be snooping.' She had three reasons for haste: she was trying to track down Crystal Daly's ex-lover, Georgie; the diary desk was unmanned as Holly had gone to interview Donaldson and Rosie had a lunch date; and Eliot wanted to talk to Rain.

'Investigating,' Wickham corrected. 'And I'd do it more effectively if you didn't block my view of the door.'

She shuffled her chair to the right. 'Better?'

'Excellent.' He kept a tantalizing silence until she prodded him to say what he was looking for. Then he disappointed her by saying he was checking whether it was possible for someone to go in and out unobserved, and how crowded it would be at that time of day.

She explained that it was never busy until evening when the printers took their meal breaks, although it was open from mid-morning. 'In cold weather some people come here rather than leave the building but there's not much enticement when it's dry and sunny outside.'

'There'd be more enticement if they improved the food.' He rejected the second half of his egg.

'It's been tried,' she said, hoping she did not sound as though she had the temerity to defend the canteen. 'Once we had a catering manager who introduced health foods but the printers made a dreadful fuss. The management had a choice of throwing out the canteen manager or bringing out the paper. They chose to bring out the paper.' She had noticed when his attention shifted and she resisted looking round. 'Who's come in?' she added softly.

'Miss Washbrooke.'

Her face told him Mona was not a regular canteen user. The woman spoke to one of the counter staff and then went hurriedly out. Rain watched her for the last few yards, noting how the morning's cheerfulness had been replaced by anxiety. Mona was not seen again that day.

'She left me a note,' Eliot told Rain when she reached his office. 'It says she isn't well and has to get home. It's rather sudden, she was in good form earlier.' He fingered his tie, a particularly vivid one that day, and went straight on to the purpose of their meeting, which was to ask her to help Frank Shildon who was investigating aspects of the MacQuillan empire. Shildon had made remarkable progress in a short time but needed help as he was trying to do his normal work for the business section at the same time. 'He asked for you, he thinks you would work well together.'

The suggestion was puzzling. She and Shildon had never had occasion to work together so what made him think of her? Eliot said: 'He believes it would be sensible to use somebody who is not a business journalist. People would not be alerted by questions from you. He's probably right.'

Rain agreed to do it, but Eliot held up a hand. 'Before you commit yourself you ought to consider the implications. Shildon is in charge of this inquiry but it could become impossible for either of you to continue working here.'

She could not help grinning. 'Luke, it's been intolerable for weeks. I'm not clear what you hope to find, but if Shildon digs up anything to embarrass the MacQuillans I'm prepared to share the credit.'

Eliot said he was not entirely sure what he hoped for, but Shildon would explain the rest. His telephone rang. Before he answered it she slipped in a question about the length of time Shildon had been working on the assignment. 'About three weeks,' he said. 'I wish it had been done months ago but Stuart Pascoe felt it was unnecessary. Everything that's happened since MacQuillan came has convinced me I was right.' He lifted the receiver.

She was eager to talk to Shildon and impatient for him to return from lunch. By then the office would be busy and they would have to contrive a meeting where they would be unobserved. She recapped what she knew of him, as if he were someone she was about to interview. A few years older than her. Divorced. Had worked in the United States for a while and returned to England minus his American wife. One of the office loners, discouraging friendships. A solid reliable reporter who could be safely ignored. All in all, extremely uninspiring company.

She looked around the nearly deserted room. A secretary on the newsdesk was typing, the wire room machines chattered unattended, a few people sat with heads bent over telephones or newspapers. Then a messenger brought more mail and criss-crossed the room leaving a pile for the features editor, some for reporters, and a handful of things for Rosie. There were letters and a padded bag.

Rain felt her stomach tighten. She opened the letters but the bag was a test of nerve. Even when she had turned it over and seen the franked stamps she was childishly afraid. The bag had been re-used, the original sender's label was there but a small plain one had been stuck on top of it.

It was nerve-racking to remember Rosie's shattering scream as the knife sprang from the bag and hit the floor, but the memory of her distress forced Rain to tug at the staples that secured the bag. If she left it unopened Rosie would face it when she got back from lunch and Rain could not be that heartless. As she grappled with the staples she could feel inside the bag the firm shape of a book. Women's Word had sent her their latest offering: someone's reminiscences of running a lingerie mail order catalogue. She tossed it aside and renewed her efforts to contact Georgie and perhaps learn more about the murder.

Meeting Donaldson for lunch had reinforced Holly's belief in the value of the story about him. She wrote a few paragraphs and got up, the typed sheet in her hand. Rain interrupted her telephone conversation to ask to see it. To her annoyance Holly pushed the carbon copy on to Rain's desk and went away with the other. The caller was still on the line, Rain had to give him her attention.

Shildon telephoned next, from a callbox, to say he had heard from Eliot that Rain was willing to work with him. 'We'd do best to meet away from the office,' he said. 'How would you like to come somewhere cool and tranquil?'

'I didn't realize there *was* anywhere like that.'

'I'll be at St Paul's about 6 p.m.' he said and was cut off as his money ran out.

She read the Donaldson story. There was nothing wrong with it except that she doubted it was true and was certain Holly was showing it to Maureen for approval. At Holly's request Rosie had added it to the list of diary items Rain would offer at the afternoon conference. This was normal and not provocative but Rain was provoked. She satisfied herself by pausing on the way to the conference to score it out. The Donaldson matter was petty and tiresome but much of office life was made up of the petty and tiresome. She supposed she ought to be thankful that she and Holly had spent several contented years together before things had become prickly.

After the conference Sniffy Wilson rang again. 'Rain?'

She recognized his voice and automatically lowered hers conspiratorially. 'I've been wondering what happened to you.'

'It got a bit difficult. Look, I haven't got long. What I want to say is I picked up some information in Gorstone about MacQuillan funding a terrorist group in Northern Ireland. I've got some names and I want to use them to do a deal.'

'With the police?'

'With Wickham. He's on the MacQuillan case, isn't he?'

'Well yes, but . . .'

'Just tell him, Rain.'

'Very well, but how does he contact you if you're on the run?'

'Through you. I'll ring you again.' He put the receiver down before she could ask more.

Wickham heard the story with amusement. 'A deal? Is he hoping we'll agree not to look for him very hard?'

'Heaven knows. Perhaps he wants it as credit to set against his future crimes.' They both laughed. She said: 'You will talk to him next time he telephones, won't you?'

'If I'm here. In fact, the novelty of being offered information by Sniffy wouldn't let me miss it. He's never been known to give away anything.'

Because of the meeting with Shildon, Rain left the office early. Alex Harbury was coming into the building after covering the formal opening of the MacQuillan inquest. His face brightened as he saw her. 'Just the person I want to talk to.'

She said she had no time but gave way at his offer of an iced orange juice. For the second time that day she went to the canteen. They sat in the corner and he pumped her for any information she might have gleaned from Wickham. She said she was drinking his orange juice under false pretences because she had none.

'Nothing about the Pascoe business?' As she looked blank he went on: 'Wickham had Pascoe in for questioning this afternoon. Riley says Pascoe wasn't at all happy when Sergeant Marshall told him he was wanted.' Harbury's green eyes were alert for her slightest response.

'Nobody enjoys that kind of thing.'

'No, but he was more upset when Wickham had finished with him. Riley said he was white and blotchy, quite ill. And he said he was going to telephone his solicitor. Riley says he looked very, very guilty.'

'*Pascoe*! Why should Pascoe kill MacQuillan?'

Harbury surmised that he had more reason than anybody: he had been severely demoted, he had been given a rough time and he was partly responsible for Martin Ayling selling to MacQuillan. 'He must have cracked.'

'Oh no, I don't believe that. He went to Linley's party on Friday evening. Would he have done that if . . .'

'Yes,' said Harbury. 'He'd have to carry on as usual or else it would look suspicious.'

They stopped, suddenly awkward at calculating Pascoe's guilt. It was second nature to weigh up a situation and draw conclusions but this was not just another news story, this was different. Neither had previously assessed whether a colleague was a murderer. Rain swilled ice round in her glass. 'If I hear anything about Pascoe I'll pass it on.'

Harbury had no intention of letting her off so easily. 'You can do more than that, with your contacts.' Inevitably his challenge succeeded. Before she swallowed the last of the drink she had promised to ask Wickham for the facts.

St Paul's is only a short walk from Fleet Street but it is uphill and after her diversion to the canteen Rain was short of time and forced to hurry. The heat was overpowering. Shildon had been rash to promise tranquillity: hundreds of tourists sat on the steps of the cathedral, hundreds more flowed in and out of the doors.

Rain pushed through, her pace slackening as she regretted not fixing an exact meeting place. She stood out of the way of a party of scantily clad Scandinavian women who were leaving, then waited while her eyesight adjusted to the contrasting darkness. A finger jabbed her between the shoulder blades. 'You're late,' Shildon accused as she twisted round.

'And you lied about tranquillity.'

‘Not at all. This is perfect. We’ll sit over there and no one will follow a word. Most of the people in here don’t speak English, anyway.’

When they were seated he relayed Eliot’s suspicions about the funding and spending of the MacQuillan empire. He unfolded a sheet of paper from his pocket. There were names on it linked with lines zig-zagging the page. ‘These are all companies within the empire and the lines indicate the way the money is moved around them. It’s done to confuse.’

Rain was impressed by the amount of information he had gathered in a short time. He said simply that he had known where to go for it, and moved on to explain that when Hal MacQuillan made a bid for the paper it was supposed to be his personal fortune that was financing it. The way money had been shuffled around his business suggested otherwise.

One company especially interested him: HM Supplies. ‘It receives money from the others but it’s not apparent what else it does. There’s nothing to link it with the drinks cartons or newspaper publishing. It’s a bit of a mystery.’

He produced another sheet of paper on which he had typed some notes. There were three people he wanted her to talk to: Martin Ayling, Stuart Pascoe and Cecil Hunter-Blair. She gave him a look which asked: ‘Is this all?’ If it were, she would rather concentrate on finding Georgie and checking Crystal Daly’s unlikely but colourful story.

Aloud she said: ‘You know these people too. Why do you need me to approach them?’

‘I thought Eliot had explained. If I ask questions they’ll wonder what I’m up to but you can wheedle information out of them in general conversation.’

‘But I don’t have general conversation with them.’

He said: ‘You see Hunter-Blair at parties or he rings you up when he wants his name in your column.’

‘Yes, I know but . . .’

‘And you still have some contact with Ayling since he left. Aren’t you going to a charity ball at his house soon?’

'On Thursday but . . .'

He said: 'So those two are easy, aren't they? As for Pascoe . . .'

'As for Pascoe, he's a financial man. That's *your* sphere. Surely you'd be more effective?'

'Not necessarily. He's not responsible for anything now, but my hunch is he knows what's going on. All you've got to do is chat to him about Tuscany and then twist the conversation around so you can slide in a few of my questions.'

His face was only inches from hers but she could not be certain whether he was sarcastic. She said nothing and he spoke again. 'Rain, people will chat to you. That's what you're for.' She was still not sure about the sarcasm. The only thing she understood was that having told Eliot she would help Shildon, it was impossible for her to back out.

CHAPTER 11

The two death threats sent to Hal MacQuillan in London appeared dissimilar. The first was handwritten, with certain nouns and verbs leaping into capital letters in the eighteenth-century manner. There were flurries of underlining too. Predictably, there was no signature. The burden of the message was that good men were dying in Belfast for lesser sins than MacQuillan was committing and unless he changed the *Post's* tune he would be shot. It was scrawled on blue lined writing paper.

The second, received eight days later, was typed and brief. 'You are a destroyer, MacQuillan, but the time is approaching when you will be destroyed.' No over-use of capitals, no underlining. Just a neatly typed sentence in the middle of a sheet of A5-size paper.

This last letter did not chime with the rest. Some of the American crop were typed but their tone matched those handwritten or made up of letters and words snipped from publications. Hatred oozed from them. They were occasionally obscene as well as vitriolic. None of them shared the icy restraint of the last letter. Wickham had said as much when he spoke on the telephone to Ray Darby, the documents expert, telling him the file was on its way to him. On Monday afternoon he went to see Darby.

Darby was a cheerfully relaxed young man who compiled cryptic crosswords for a monthly magazine in his spare time. There was nothing he liked better than a good puzzle. He grinned a greeting as Wickham arrived.

'What have you got, Ray?' Wickham fetched himself a chair.

Darby reached for Maureen's file. Its cover was black and the plastic envelopes inside were rather smaller so that each page was displayed edged with black like a mourning card. He flicked the file open at the last letter. 'It was done on a manual Adler typewriter, a machine about ten years old. The keys were rather dirty and the ribbon wearing out, which is why the letters which ought to be open, like the 'e' and the 'a', aren't giving sharp outlines. You'll see far more clearly on the enlargement.'

The enlarged image, taken from a photograph of the letter, illustrated how ragged the letters were and also how uneven. Darby said the machine had obviously had heavy wear and not been well maintained: the 'd', for example, was slightly twisted and the capitals in 'MacQuillan' did not sit firmly on the line. Poor typing skills might account for the jumping capitals but the shift of the machine could be at fault.

A typewriter was as individual as a fingerprint, or a set of teeth, or a gun barrel scoring a bullet. Darby joked: 'All you've got to do now is round up all the typewriters of the correct make and vintage and I'll tell you which one dunnit.'

'Can you wait until tomorrow?' Wickham responded ironically. Then: 'Did the paper tell you anything?'

Darby beamed. 'That has a highly individual characteristic too. It looks like an average piece of A5 bond at first sight but it isn't actually a standard size at all. I'd guess someone has chopped up offcuts.'

'With a guillotine?'

'Yes, it's a proper job, not a scissors or razor blade effort. And there's no gummed edge so the paper wasn't ripped off a pad. I'd say you're looking for a business where they have a heavy demand for rough paper. What do the journalists type on at the *Post*?' He gave the cheeky smile which always accompanied his guidance about the way other people ought to conduct their investigations.

'I've thought of that, Ray, but the answer's no. They use that magic carbon paper. You know the stuff: there are no separate carbon sheets but several layers of impregnated paper and each one a different colour.'

Darby was momentarily crestfallen before saying: 'I still think it's an office you need to find. The combination of a typewriter that has taken years of heavy battering and a piece of guillotined paper of a non-standard size suggest that rather strongly.'

Merely to deflate Darby's confidence again Wickham commented that anyone could buy a tired secondhand machine and stand a good chance of buying inexpensive packs of paper offcuts. He took up the file and studied the plain white paper envelope the letter had been posted in. The same typewriter had been used to address it, it bore a second class stamp and had been posted in London WC1.

'No,' said Darby, 'there's nothing distinctive about the envelope. It's very ordinary office issue but also available in small packs for domestic use. Both the envelopes and the writing paper have lots of smudged fingerprints, the only identifiable ones belonging to Maureen and her father.' Wickham dropped the file back on the desk.

They walked together down a passage, Wickham on his way out and Darby seeking a colleague. 'Tell me,' said Darby suddenly, 'would "Lady at the forefront of the fleet up against turbulent seas" lead you to "Vanessa"?'

Wickham said he thought it would work very well. The name had jarred him as Darby tossed it innocently into the conversation. Wickham wondered how long that sort of thing would go on. Intellectually he had accepted that the marriage had been a mistake, that it had been largely *his* mistake. He had never seriously blamed Vanessa. In the beginning — and it had felt like the beginning although he was past thirty when they met — she had been an art student falling out of love with a young man on her course. The young man then died an unheroic death, riding his motorcycle underneath a lorry in Hammersmith and Vanessa's emotions fed on the tragedy until she was convinced he had been the love of her life. The emotional flux produced haunting paintings.

With sufficient work completed for her first show, Vanessa had exhausted her theme and recovered her interest in the living. Paul Wickham, whose occasional presence had been a pleasant adjunct to her dogged mournfulness, was discovered to be her new love. He, unsurprisingly, was less precipitate. He was very fond of her but it strained imagination to see how she could fit into a policeman's life. Beside the wives of his colleagues Vanessa was an exotic creature with her flare of red hair and highly individual nature.

When she became engrossed in some new work he made her preoccupation an excuse for drawing away from her. Absence was painful. Sometimes, as he sat at his desk over a dull report, his hand strayed to the telephone and he called her. She sounded vague. He guessed that was how she would always be, blocking out everything for the preferred world of her own creation until an idea was spent. Then one day she rang him with the triumphant news that she had finished. He squeezed time to dash to her studio. There were other people there, he had been demoted to the same rank as her many friends. It was as a mere friend that he went to the private view of Vanessa's second exhibition and met Rain Morgan.

Driving back from seeing Ray Darby, Wickham was stern with himself for having twice in one day fallen into reminiscence about Vanessa. Normally he could go for weeks without being so indulgent; but the MacQuillan case had brought Rain Morgan back into his life and with her some poignant memories. Paradoxically, he had once used Rain in an attempt to take his mind off Vanessa. And he was confused by his enjoyment of Rain's company now when he ought, if he wanted to spare himself those memories, to have avoided it.

Early on Monday evening Wickham tossed the papers he had been scanning on to the desk and stood up. 'You can buy me a pint, Jim.'

Marshall was relieved. He seemed to have sat for hours mulling over people's recollections of events on Friday. A colleague had been dispatched to the market to enquire about the knives and Marshall had taken notes during a series of interviews. Tavett had been shaky but in the end unmoved: he added nothing and changed nothing of what he had said on Saturday. Wickham had let it become obvious that important parts of his story did not coincide with the version supplied by the only other person on the spot but Tavett maintained that what he said was correct.

The deputy editor had tried to be helpful. Linley had called his publisher and asked the name of the restaurant where they had lunched and also the time they had left. He offered these details for the police to confirm but was still unable to remember seeing anyone enter or leave by the rear door of the *Post* building. The restaurant manager told the police Linley had left at 3 p.m. He had no doubt about this because the party were the last people to go and they all went out together.

The other two interviews had been more remarkable. Shildon had excused his initial omissions on the grounds that he had concealed that he was engaged in work which was not for the business section. Wickham had remarked that covert freelance writing for another publication did not justify making a misleading statement during a murder inquiry. And Shildon had explained that he was not freelancing but investigating MacQuillan's finances. Shildon had been polite and apologetic and twice begged that his investigation be kept secret.

Pascoe arrived prepared for more questions about his trip to the second floor and provided the wording of his note to Mona: 'Mona. Urgent I see MacQuillan today. Please telephone me. Pascoe.' He had also written: 'Friday, 2.10 p.m.'. Pascoe staunchly refused to go further than his earlier explanation that he wanted to speak to MacQuillan about finance. He grew cross when Wickham demanded more and extremely so when Wickham pursued Maureen's hint of fraud. Marshall expected Wickham to draw back, let Pascoe's temper subside and then wheedle the truth. The chance did not arise because Pascoe left in a purple-faced fury.

Wickham and Marshall emerged into Fleet Street. 'The Cheshire Cheese is just along there, sir,' suggested Marshall.

Wickham gave a teasing smile. 'Maybe, but we have work to do, Jim. At the Black Friar.'

The Black Friar is one of London's unlikelier pubs, an *art nouveau* collision between the ecclesiastical and the most secular. Even the friar swooping like a ship's figurehead from the prow of the building is no preparation for the interior. At one end of the bar marble columns and curves suggest a memorial chapel with tables for drinkers replacing tombs. It was apparently in there that MacQuillan ate his last meal.

Wickham asked at the bar for two pints and then for Doris Clay. 'You're a bit early, Mr Wickham,' said the barman who had a fine memory for faces from television screens and newspapers. 'She doesn't come on for about ten minutes.'

They carried their drinks through to the 'chapel'. Cool. Private. Only a handful of people were in the pub and they were all at the other end. Wickham took from his pocket a photograph of MacQuillan. One helpful aspect of the case was that there were good up-to-date photographs of the man. Too often he had been forced to work with snapshots several years old, maybe fuzzy enlargements of little faces glimpsed in group poses. Also, MacQuillan's face was well known and it was inevitable that someone had noticed him that lunchtime.

Doris Clay, part-time barmaid, had not been to work on Friday evening nor over the weekend. It had been mid-day Monday before she mentioned, in conversation with one of her regular customers, that MacQuillan had been to the Black Friar. The man she told was a printer at the *Post* and after sharing the news with his colleagues he decided to let the police in on it too.

They drank a few refreshing mouthfuls before a slender blonde with high-heeled shoes and bright-blue eyelids swayed down the room towards them. Marshall's instant thought was that she was waiting to be picked up. She was actually Doris Clay, her tartiness only the variety adopted by certain barmaids who hoped to look just a little more glittering than real life.

Doris gave Wickham a cheerful smile and said in a pleasantly modified Cockney accent that she was positive it was MacQuillan she had seen. Marshall drew up a chair for her. She said: 'He wasn't somebody I'd ever seen in here before, perhaps that's why I took notice. Now don't ask me what time he came in because I can't be exact. What happened was this: a group of people at that table . . .' She pointed to one in the main part of the bar. '. . . well, they got up and left so I thought I'd clear their glasses as soon as I'd finished with the man I was serving. I put their empties on the bar and, of course, I glanced in here to see whether there were any more to clear away. That table . . .' She tapped the one next to where they were sitting. '. . . well, that needed doing. And as I got in here I saw that one of the men sitting just where you are was Hal MacQuillan. There's no doubt. You can tell how close I was and he was facing me.'

Wickham showed the photograph just to be sure. She nodded: 'Yes, that's the man.' He encouraged her to go on with her story. She said: 'The man with him was doing all the talking. Now don't ask me what was said, I wasn't taking that much notice. I grabbed the empties and got back behind the bar. I didn't come in here again until around half past two. We were so rushed there wasn't time. He'd gone by then, they both had and a couple of office girls were sitting there.'

Wickham asked whether MacQuillan appeared to have eaten at the Black Friar and she said yes, because both men had plates of food in front of them. She was certain MacQuillan had not gone to the bar because she had been there all the time until then. Wickham suspected he looked dubious because she hurried on: 'Oh, I know you're thinking

I might not have noticed him at the bar. People always think we ignore them when they're waiting but it isn't really like that. We never miss a face, but we know what order they come in and we try and serve them in turn. I don't remember any unusual faces that lunchtime and I would definitely have spotted a famous one like that.'

Doris smoothed a hand over her rounded knee and waited for the next question. 'The other man,' said Wickham. 'What can you tell us about him?'

She frowned. 'I've been trying to remember, ever since one of your men telephoned to say somebody would be along to talk to me. I'm afraid I can't tell you much. He was sitting like this . . .' She leaned across the table to Wickham as if she were the man facing MacQuillan. 'He was speaking quietly, and MacQuillan was giving him all his attention. Even when I recognized MacQuillan and he might have sensed me looking, he didn't glance up at me. He had his eyes on the man's face the whole time.'

'Hair colour?' asked Wickham, 'Clothes? Anything you can remember about the man?'

She bit her lower lip. 'He was wearing a jacket, I'm sure of that. MacQuillan was too. Not many people are in this weather, are they? MacQuillan's was brown but the other man's . . . It might have been cream. No, I can't really say. And the hair . . . That was just ordinary. Not blond, not dark like MacQuillan's, not red. Just hair.'

'Did you get an impression of age? Or stature?'

'Younger than MacQuillan and slim.'

They talked a while longer but Doris Clay could do no better. 'An appeal for the other man, sir?' asked Marshall as they walked back to Fleet Street. Doris and the barman had agreed to ask customers whether they had noticed MacQuillan and a man in or near the place.

'I don't see why not. The papers might as well be handed that titbit in tomorrow's press statement. It doesn't look as though we shall have anything more sensational for them.'

Marshall said: 'Young Harbury was chasing you again this afternoon. He wanted to know whether you'd solved the case yet.' Marshall knew Wickham would be ruefully amused by that 'yet', carrying as it inevitably did an accusation of tardiness.

CHAPTER 12

On Tuesday morning Stuart Pascoe resigned. He had spent most of his working life on the paper and was not far short of retirement so the move was astonishing. A diplomat of doubtful authenticity was holding a hostage in a Middle Eastern embassy in London, an English tennis player was being tipped to win Wimbledon and the Princess of Wales was rumoured to be pregnant, but at the *Daily Post* the big news of the day was Pascoe.

Holly was bubbling with the story of him arriving at work to find someone else installed in his office and his personal possessions in a heap in the corridor. He had dictated his resignation to the first secretary he encountered.

Rain saw her chances of falling into conversation with him, as Shildon wanted, seriously diminished. She had meant to try, although she had learned where Georgie might be found and was rather more interested in seeing what one of Crystal's lovers looked like. She had an acute mental picture of him. The name George and the tenuous link with 'an MI number' suggested a rather solemn civil service type. She asked where Pascoe was.

'Doing a lap of honour to say his farewells,' said Holly. 'He's been to circulation and advertising and now he's with the editor.'

Rain had no time for anything but the direct approach which promised, under the fresh circumstances, to be the most appropriate. She caught up with Pascoe by the lifts and told him she would like to talk. He surveyed her doubtfully through his pebble glasses. She explained a little more. Pascoe shook his head. 'No, no, I want nothing more to do with it.'

'But . . .'

The lift came and he stepped inside. 'If you want answers you can get them from Ron Barron.'

Rain grabbed the doors and thrust herself into the lift. Pascoe scowled at her. He said: 'I've told you, Rain, I'm having nothing more to do with this paper. It's no good bullying me.'

But she did persevere as the lift skimmed downwards. Pascoe's colour rose and he shocked her by the vehemence of his refusal. When the doors opened he charged across the foyer, scattering people, and disappeared into Fleet Street. Rain recovered herself but not before Shildon, the only person waiting for the lift, had registered the scene. He got in and pressed the button for the first floor. 'Not one of the great interviews of our time?' he suggested drily.

She resented his tone but told him the real news, Pascoe's resignation. Shildon said he would probably change his mind in a day or two and be itching to talk. As they stepped on to the landing he signalled her to go ahead while he hung back so they should not be seen arriving in the newsroom together. Rain doubted this was necessary but did as he wished.

She had only ever had a vague impression of Frank Shildon and was interested in how far that was at variance with what she was discovering. Already she had learned that his quiet inoffensive manner could be accompanied by sarcasm and that the steady reliable way of working could lapse into over-cautiousness.

On her way to her desk she tried to collect a beaker of iced water but the machine was empty and a knot of querulous men were standing around it demanding something be done. Among them were Zak Smythe and one of the free speech people, both bands having once more turned up to perfect their statements. Smythe had dispensed with help and advice and was enjoying the writing, while the free speech folk had decided it was more appropriate for them to publish a cartoon balancing Oliver's offensive one. Much to Oliver's annoyance they turned out to be rather good at it.

Wainfleet rang Rain. 'Hunter-Blair's been on,' he began.

'So?' She wished Wainfleet would find a way of checking his stories without phoning her, it seemed to happen rather frequently.

'He says Stuart Pascoe has been sacked.'

'Actually he resigned. It's not in doubt.'

'Oh. Well, that doesn't matter much. The story I've got is that he was forced out because Ron Barron was threatening to prosecute him for fraud.'

She echoed the word in disbelief. Wainfleet said: 'If there was some cooking of the books when Pascoe was in charge, then the implication is that Ayling was involved, too.'

'John, this can't be right. Pascoe wouldn't . . . and Ayling *certainly* wouldn't . . .'

He chuckled, delighted at having amazed her. 'It looks as though they did.' He had a riveting story, even when his lawyers had toned it down it would be a good one and, of course, the *Post* would not run a line on it. He laughed some more but Rain switched tack to ask why Hunter-Blair had told him.

Wainfleet objected. 'Does it matter, if a good story comes along?'

Her mind flashed to Donaldson. 'Quite often,' she murmured. Then: 'Hunter-Blair's up to something.'

'Yes, he's trying to make himself look useful so the next time he wants his own name in the paper I'll remember and do his bidding. He's an MP, they're all the same.'

But they were not. Hunter-Blair took a lonely stand in British politics and until MacQuillan gave him a platform he was a nonentity. Hunter-Blair owed the paper much, and after MacQuillan's death he was trying to hang on to his position. It made no sense for him to be engineering bad publicity.

Wainfleet breezed on. 'While I'm on the line, what's the latest on Frank Shildon's spot of investigative journalism?'

She pretended not to know what he was referring to but he would not be fooled. Not only did he know of it, he also knew she was involved. Eventually she let him win and asked who told him. 'Shildon,' he said, relishing hearing her surprise a second time.

'Shildon!' She spoke more loudly than she intended and Holly looked up, questioning.

Wainfleet said: 'We have an echo on the line. I'd better go.'

But she kept him until he had explained some more. He insisted he had not mentioned the matter to a living soul but Rain detected an unspoken 'yet'. It could only be a matter of time before Wainfleet was using the information for his own purposes. He said he had bumped into Shildon on Monday evening and urged him into a pub, taking the opportunity to make up the quarrel begun on Friday. After a few drinks Shildon had mentioned the work he was doing for Eliot.

Rain had to be guarded so that people around her did not follow what the call was about. She suggested meeting Wainfleet at lunchtime to hear the rest, confident he would not turn her down. He was always flattered when he had information others wanted.

They got to the pub early. Wainfleet ignored his usual perch and followed her to a shadowed corner. She had to go through the ritual of pleading for information while he pretended reluctance, but then he told her what appeared to be everything. Shildon had given him a somewhat more detailed account of his findings than he had given Rain, which rankled.

'Luke Eliot picked the right man for the job when he asked Shildon,' said Wainfleet gesturing to the barman for refills.

Rain agreed Shildon was thorough but Wainfleet said he had not meant only that. 'He was enjoying it, he loathed

MacQuillan,' he said and reminded her that Shildon and he had worked for MacQuillan when he bought his first paper. 'Frank's been around the course already, he knew what it would be like if MacQuillan got the *Post*.'

Shildon, he explained, had been dismissed from the Detroit paper towards the end of a long and exhaustive investigation which, if the results had been published, could have had serious repercussions for MacQuillan's political associates. Instead, MacQuillan had been alerted and sacked the editor and reporter. 'Naturally, it was never admitted they'd been thrown out because of the investigation. There was some trumped up nonsense about false expenses claims, but everyone knew the real reason.' Wainfleet paid for the drinks.

Rain asked whether they had not been able to get the story published elsewhere. Wainfleet gulped his whisky. 'MacQuillan was smart. A very watered-down version which drew different conclusions appeared in his paper, and that very effectively killed it.'

Wainfleet refused to tell her any more as he wanted to pump her about Hunter-Blair. She laughed him off, saying he was becoming obsessed with that MP and it had already been noticed that his column carried far too many stories about him. Wainfleet's eyes flicked over her shoulder at each new arrival and he did not delay her when she was ready to leave. He followed her up to the bar and she heard him noisily latching on to Riley who, she was positive, would not buy him a drink.

Back in the office Holly had received a curt memo from Maureen asking why the Donaldson story had not been published. Rain assumed Holly would put it in Friday's column while she was at Ayling's ball. The atmosphere was distinctly unfriendly.

She was frustrated, too, that Hunter-Blair was being so elusive. The telephone answering machine at his London house said he was not there, his secretary at the House of Commons had no idea of his whereabouts, there was no reply when Rain rang his country house and his car telephone service failed to contact him. Rain confessed as much when Shildon checked up on her progress. Pascoe had rejected her, Hunter-Blair was in hiding and she would not see Ayling until Thursday. But she had been told where she could find Georgie early that evening.

Just before she left to go there, Eliot called her into his office to say he had Shildon on the telephone from a callbox. He held out the receiver to her. Shildon said: 'Are you free for a meeting this evening?'

'Yes.'

'Can you suggest somewhere private?'

She offered her flat.

* * *

An accountant responded to the appeal, published in the *Standard* on Tuesday, for information about the man who lunched with MacQuillan at the Black Friar. He did not know the man's name but was certain he had seen him before and believed he knew where he worked. 'The accountant's here now,' Marshall told Wickham. 'He said he came because he couldn't discuss it on the telephone, but whether he really wanted to see inside the *Post* I can't say.' He cleared his throat before admitting a failure. 'He also insists on talking to you.'

'Show him in, then.' Wickham recognized the type: willing enough to help but he must be allowed to go back to his friends with the news that his information was so valuable he had been allowed to talk to the man heading the inquiry, and if he could throw in a description of a place as exciting as a newspaper office so much to his credit. But the man did not look like one of those. He was about thirty-five with an athletic figure and an attractive open face. His voice was firm and his demeanour self-confident. He stuck out his hand for a handshake. Wickham was left in no doubt who was supposed to be in control of the interview.

'Richard Beales,' he said. 'I work for a firm of accountants in Shoe Lane. Thank you for seeing me, Mr Wickham.

I could have given my information to any of your officers but I prefer to tell you because I must be guaranteed that the source of the information is kept secret. I should be in some embarrassment if my name were to appear in the newspapers, for instance.'

Wickham grasped the position and Beales confirmed it, saying: 'I had lunch at the Black Friar with a woman friend. My wife also works at the accountants in Shoe Lane and she believes I was elsewhere, with a client.'

Wickham assured him there was no reason why his name should be mentioned to the press or anyone else. Beales said: 'I was sure you would say that, but I've taken the precaution of declining to give it to your men. I don't suggest it would have been deliberately divulged but Fleet Street is not the easiest place to keep a secret.'

Especially not, Wickham thought, the *Post* office. Marshall had taken to calling it the rumour factory because a disproportionate amount of time seemed to be wasted on chatter. He did not give much for Beales's chances of getting in and out of the building unremarked.

Beales's story was that he met his friend in the pub just after 1 p.m. He knew the time because they had arranged to meet on the hour but he was a few minutes late and she was waiting. They had sat in the area Wickham thought of as the chapel. Beales had not taken any notice of other customers until a man he recognized as MacQuillan came to the next table.

MacQuillan was out of breath, as though he had been hurrying. Another man had been at the table for some time but Beales only looked at him at this point, curious to know who MacQuillan was with. He did not know the man's name but the face was familiar.

'I don't know what he does but I've seen him around this area. Several times I've spotted him going into a building further up Fleet Street. He speaks with an American accent.' He pushed across Wickham's desk a scrap of paper on which he had jotted the number of the building the man went into.

'I walked up the street and checked this before I came here,' he said. 'Now, you'll want his description.'

Once he had gone away Wickham gave instructions for someone to go to the address in Fleet Street. The American accent was the only distinguishing feature of MacQuillan's companion, the rest rather dispiriting: ordinary, mousy hair, average height, not heavily built. So on.

Wickham turned his attention to the typewriter which had been used for the death threat. The newest machines were used by the administration and advertising staff, the oldest by the journalists. Those that matched Darby's description had been borrowed from the newsroom and the wording of the death threat typed on them.

Any queries about the machines being taken away had been answered with the half-truth that the police needed them for their own use. Four samples of typing had subsequently been brought to Wickham, each identified by the registration number of the machine and the name of the person whose desk it normally stood on.

To Wickham there was very little difference between the notes. A ribbon was fainter on this one, or stronger on that. However, he could not discern the blocked out 'a' or 'e'. He sent the samples to Darby but prepared for disappointment.

The stationery cupboard had not provided paper similar to that used for the note and when Richard Beales left a systematic search was still going on of shelves and desks where some might have been overlooked. 'Meanwhile,' said Marshall, 'if you want a laugh you could read what the staff say they were wearing on Friday. Holly Chase, for example, mentions a *soignée* little number in pink voile.'

Marshall was unable to stop smiling. Wickham thought it extraordinary how the frivolity of the journalists was spreading. He suspected that if he were to walk into the newsroom and make an arrest there would be only a momentary gasp before someone was out with the first of a new crop of jokes.

He did not take the sheaf of notes Marshall tendered but made him recite the relevant ones and in that way learned that three people said they had been wearing clothes which were, at least in part, cream-coloured. They had not been asked about materials because a layman's opinion, or even a manufacturer's label, was not reliable. A female clerk in the advertising department owned up to a cream skirt; Tavett to cream trousers; and Linley to a cream shirt.

'The garments are being collected for examination now, sir,' said Marshall. 'We've done some cross-checking, asking people whether they could say what other people were wearing. The women remembered fairly well but the men weren't good. Some couldn't say what they'd been wearing themselves, but their female colleagues usually gave us some idea.'

Marshall continued, stressing the amount of work which had been done and offsetting, he hoped, the poor impression caused by his light-heartedness. He was not good at knowing when a bit of humour would go down well, but by late afternoon there was some news that cheered them all.

Ray Darby telephoned to say that three of the four typing samples had been ruled out immediately but the fourth had looked promising although not identical with the death threat. The letters of the machine used for it had been brushed clean and the worn ribbon replaced at some time after the letter was typed, but all the other characteristics — including misalignment of the 'd' and the unreliable shift control — had shown up in the enlargement and eventually confirmed that Wickham had found the machine he was seeking.

It was a small success, very far from proving who murdered Hal MacQuillan and not even proving who typed the letter but it was a promising line of inquiry: MacQuillan had been detested, his death had been welcomed and someone, who was probably on his staff, had actually thought of killing him.

Marshall said: 'He's not in the building now, sir. Shall I telephone his home and get him to come back?'

'No, Jim. If he's already gone home tomorrow morning will do just as well.'

Marshall deduced that Wickham wanted to surprise the man, to see how he reacted when confronted with the fact the police knew a death threat had been typed on his office machine. It was probable he did not realize the police had the letter and he might not have guessed the true reason the typewriters had been borrowed. In fact, he had not been in the room when they were taken.

Wickham saw Marshall's sly smile and understood what he was thinking. But his own reasoning was different: there were questions he wanted to ask and things he wanted to consider before it became common knowledge that MacQuillan had received a threat typed on a newsroom machine. His hand went to the telephone but withdrew. He could get some answers in a telephone call but there was a more pleasant way. He dithered. He talked to the man who had completed, with no success, the search for paper like that on which the letter was typed. He wondered aloud why they had not heard from the officer who had gone to check on the man seen with MacQuillan at the Black Friar.

He went back to the telephone, prompted by the recollection of an awkward scene where he had been made to feel unwelcome, a situation created by a man to whom he had taken a dislike. Yet he did not make the call. Instead, he gave the number he might have dialled to a colleague and said he would be there unless at home. It was not necessary, he could have rung once he had arrived, but in this way he committed himself.

* * *

Rain met Georgie on a houseboat at Chelsea. He was staying there since giving up his flat at around the same time he had given up Crystal Daly. One of her contacts had breathed the information down the telephone and she had clambered aboard *Perfidia,* her professional charm switching itself on and eager to deal with any obstacles between her curiosity and The Truth.

A fairly young man in Italian leisure wear from the waist down and nothing but a tan from the waist up appeared from a cabin, ready to repel boarders. Another young man in nothing but a tan lay on the deck watching her through sunglasses. She concentrated on the one with the trousers and said she was looking for George.

'Why?' demanded the one in the glasses.

The interview did not go as the interview with MacQuillan's mistress had gone and Rain was soon climbing ashore, silently cursing Crystal Daly's gullibility. George, the one in the dark glasses, was the least likely member of MI anything that she had ever met, unless she counted the one in the trousers. He was Joe.

They'd had a joke with Crystal, they said, and told her lots of nonsense instead of confessing they were out-of-work actors. Before Rain disappeared over the side of *Perfidia* again they tried very hard to get her to admit they were very talented out-of-work actors to have been so convincing.

CHAPTER 13

Eliot arrived at the flat before Rain. He had brought Harbury with him and they were in the shade of the planes when she drove into the square. 'Where's Oliver?' Harbury asked, remembering the previous time he had visited the flat when Oliver had encouraged him to stay and Rain had encouraged him to go.

'He's at the wine bar.' She led the way upstairs. The flat was sweltering although curtains had been drawn all day to keep the sun out. Rain opened the doors to the garden and fetched cushions so that it was bearable to sit on the scorched chairs. Once they were settled, Shildon came. He looked disgruntled to see Harbury, despite Eliot's explanation that he wanted Harbury to give what further help Shildon needed. Harbury was young and ambitious and went at things with a daunting eagerness. This might not have suited the older, more cautious, Shildon. From what Rain had seen, Shildon meant to keep control of his inquiry. He would prefer an assistant who was prepared to be directed, not one who would dash away under their own steam.

It crossed Rain's mind that Eliot might have planned all along that Harbury should help but that Shildon had proposed her instead. He had picked somebody he thought he could work with smoothly rather than somebody who might try to steal the credit. A further idea came to her: Shildon had preferred to work alone, it was Eliot who had urged him to have assistance. As a result Shildon had given her tasks which ought to have been easy. They might also have been superfluous because he was now saying he had succeeded on his own.

He did not waste time describing his route to the truth. He said: 'The nub of the matter is that MacQuillan never had the money to buy a paper in Fleet Street or do battle with the unions.' He waited until their faces reached a satisfactory degree of indignation then, over the next half hour, his low north-country voice spun out a story which revealed that political interests in the United States had channelled money through MacQuillan's companies to enable him to acquire the *Post* (or any other major British newspaper which came on the market and could be turned into a propaganda tool). All pretence that the paper ever belonged to MacQuillan personally had been given up and the title transferred to a newly formed company within the MacQuillan empire.

Harbury dived in with a question about the legality of such a transfer which, like much of what MacQuillan had done, was contrary to the conditions on which he had been allowed to acquire the paper. Shildon said legality hardly mattered, nothing could have prevented MacQuillan switching the paper from one of his pockets to another. 'He ought to have been stopped from buying the paper in the first place,' he said.

There had been attempts and he knew that. Eliot, who might have defended himself, let Shildon's bitterness go unremarked. He put a question about the precise roles of Ron Barron and Maureen MacQuillan if the paper was a mere facet of the MacQuillan business. Before Shildon got very far with his answer the doorbell rang again. Wickham's voice came over the entryphone. 'Is this a bad time?' he asked, allowing Rain to put him off. She said it was fine, providing he did not mind being one of a crowd.

As he ran upstairs she wondered why she should be so pleased he had come, he would only want to dredge up information to help in the murder case. If he had ever wanted to see her socially he could have done so at any time, but there had been only chance meetings since his marriage. She did not know Vanessa well enough to gauge whether she was one of those wives who deliberately peel their husbands away from former friends.

Wickham bounded up the last flight, shirt-sleeved, jacket in hand. He appeared happy, full of energy and suppressed excitement. Rain was holding the door for him and as he entered he stooped to kiss her forehead as he used to do. He flung his jacket on to her couch and then stopped, looking ahead into the garden. 'You can tell me all about this while you pour me a drink,' he said quietly and they went into the kitchen. She told him Shildon's story.

Wickham had been impressed with Shildon when he had interviewed him after his amended statement. Shildon displayed the confidence of the experienced professional and as Rain relayed the story of Shildon's investigation into MacQuillan's business life, Wickham found the impression reinforced. He wished he could be sure of always working with police officers who brought the same degree of tireless persistence and intelligent analysis to solving a puzzle. More than that, he believed it possible that he, as much as Luke Eliot, would value Shildon's research into the dead man's background.

Dazzled by the evening sun the people in the garden could not see into the sitting room and had no idea who Rain's visitor was until Wickham joined them. The reaction was comical. There was a polite shunting of chairs to make space for an extra one, and Eliot managed a few pleasantries while Shildon looked thoroughly annoyed by the intrusion and Harbury could not contain his delight. Harbury had been failing all day to reach Wickham, which was especially frustrating as Wickham was in the same building and Harbury felt proprietorial about the crime. He hated being fobbed off, as he believed, with press releases from Wickham's subordinates. Even Marshall had brushed aside all suggestions of having a few minutes to spare to give Harbury something exclusive.

Harbury tried to grab the apparent opportunity but Wickham neatly turned the conversation so that Shildon was able to go on where he had left off. This was not simply courteous, Wickham was as attentive as the others. At first Shildon shied away but Eliot urged and the next batch of revelations were made. 'You all know about Stuart Pascoe resigning,' Shildon began. 'There are two stories about him. One is that he led a wretched existence since MacQuillan took over and that he lost his temper when he found his office taken over by someone else. The other story is that last Thursday MacQuillan accused him of fraud and demanded his resignation in return for a promise not to prosecute.'

There were astonished interjections from Harbury who had heard nothing of this before, but Shildon went on to say that the accusation stemmed from the sale of the lease on the top part of the Fleet Street building a few years earlier. According to MacQuillan and Ron Barron the deal was a very poor one for the paper and Pascoe also pocketed some of the proceeds.

Wickham asked whether there was evidence of fraud. Shildon said: 'The deal wasn't favourable, I think that's been recognized by a number of people for a long time. But it was Ayling's decision to go ahead with it, Pascoe's job was to see it through. Neither of them was competent to do that type of business and they made an expensive mistake. Strictly speaking, I suppose it's possible to say Pascoe was negligent.'

'But it would be unfair,' Eliot retorted. 'If anybody was at fault it was Ayling, although the rest of us who were consulted didn't understand the implications either. We assumed they had taken care of the details and Ayling and Pascoe believed everything was all right.'

'What went wrong?' Wickham asked.

Eliot said Ayling believed the sale of the lease would have brought the paper the huge sum of money it needed to refurbish the part of the building it was to retain and to update its rather old-fashioned equipment. It was a Fleet Street joke that there were so few word processors in the *Post's* editorial departments. In the event the money was nothing like enough because the new owners were able to force Ayling to pay for structural work which needed to be carried out to the upper part.

Shildon said that the financial situation had become a mess and that records could be made to prove almost anything, but he did not believe there was a serious intention to prosecute. It was MacQuillan's way of letting Pascoe know he was to leave, he said.

When Wickham asked why Pascoe had not been paid off Shildon adopted his sarcastic tone. 'Oh yes, they could have done that. But it would have been costly because he'd worked at the paper for so long. Making life hell so he resigned, and threatening to expose his negligence to ensure he made the minimum of fuss, was much more acceptable to MacQuillan.'

'I see.' Wickham did not entirely see but this was Shildon's meeting and he was an intruder. He held back his other questions. There would be ample time to sift the fine detail from Shildon next day. As if he read Wickham's mind, Shildon wrapped up the discussion, said he had given them the important stuff and the rest could wait.

Rain showed Shildon out. Eliot was on his feet ready to follow. Harbury had not stirred, seeing a further chance to tackle Wickham. Eliot was unhelpful to him: 'Come on, Alex. I'll give you a lift. I'm going near Fulham.'

'Oh, there's no need.' He saw his chance slipping.

'Yes, of course I will. I dragged you here, after all.'

Despondently Harbury stood up. As Rain showed him and Eliot out, he hung back and whispered to her. 'I'm relying on you. I can't get a word out of him.'

She was laughing as she went back to the garden and Wickham. 'Alex is so . . .'

'. . . earnest?'

'Precisely. There isn't really anything funny about a reporter trying to ask questions, and if he was a bit more ruthless about it . . .'

'. . . or made up the answers, as you found on Sunday?'

'Yes.' She sank into a chair, the last of the sun flaming her pale hair. 'Well, then. *I'd* better answer *your* questions in case you're tempted to make up the answers.'

He assumed an expression of profound gravity before saying the most pressing question was where he should take her for supper.

They went to a restaurant in a cool cave-like cellar. Rain had never heard of it but Wickham and the rotund Italian who owned it were familiar. Because it was early in the week only a few tables were taken and they were led to one where they would be least disturbed by the comings and goings from the kitchen and the noise of the other diners. The menu was full of good, simple things. After they ordered, Wickham toyed with a table knife and told her that he knew where the ones which had been sent to her and Tavett had come from.

'Who sent them?' She leaned forward eagerly.

He reminded her he had said 'where', not 'who'. She flopped back, exaggerating her disappointment, then let him tell her how Marshall had discovered identical knives on sale in Leather Lane. 'They're imported from Korea. The first shipment arrived a few days ago and the stallholder got his stock on Friday evening. He says he did a deal with a man in a pub, a man whose name he can't remember and he'd never met before.'

'In other words he was sure they were stolen, and so are you.'

'Supplies haven't gone into the shops yet so the person who sent the knives to you and Tavett almost certainly bought them from the market, unless it was from another man in another pub.'

Leather Lane is a weekday market so they could not have been bought there before Monday, and the bags must have been dropped into the letterbox later that morning. Suddenly Rain laughed: 'Paul, I hope you don't mean to swap this inconclusive stuff about knives for any worthwhile information I might have. After all, anybody who read the description of the murder weapon in the Saturday papers could have sent the knives. You told me so yourself.'

'I know I did, but that was before I knew the labels were typed on Dick Tavett's typewriter and that the bags matched those in the *Post's* stationery stockroom.'

She felt her stomach tighten but kept her tone teasing as she asked: 'Anything you wish to add to that statement, superintendent?'

'Only that the same typewriter was used to send MacQuillan a death threat.'

CHAPTER 14

'Paul, before you arrest Dick Tavett . . .' She lowered her voice to a whisper, '. . . you should know that everyone has access to every typewriter in the newsroom. None of us lay claim to any particular machine, we're just happy if there's one to hand when we want one.'

Wickham said this tallied with what he had already been told, but it was undisputed that the old Adler currently on Tavett's desk was usually there. She could not recall a specific time when it had been moved. Wickham refilled her glass, telling her to cheer up because he had nothing like enough evidence to lock up Tavett. 'Besides, it would be extraordinarily inept to use one's own typewriter for such messages, wouldn't it? Unless, of course, one was indulging in a complicated bluff.'

'You'd have to be fairly arrogant to do that. Tavett isn't and wouldn't.'

He nodded agreement. 'Who can you think of who could be and might?'

The answer was no one. He fed her names to see whether she thought any of them capable of sending the knives or the death threat, either as unpleasant practical jokes or to intimidate. She found each one inconceivable.

Before they had left her flat he had telephoned colleagues to say where he would be if he were needed. Rain hoped it would not happen and they reached the coffee before it did. Then Wickham was invited through to a back room and a telephone. There were developments in the MacQuillan case. His apologies to Rain were hasty and then he was gone, leaving her with her coffee and the Italian with instructions about calling her a cab.

The man murmured his commiserations and she joked with him. But at heart she felt let down. The conversation had seldom strayed from the case and Wickham's bouncy arrival at the flat and invitation to supper had encouraged her to expect something more. Not a taking up of the old ways, but she had anticipated that for at least part of the evening they would move from professional matters to personal.

She sat dully in the cab while the driver talked non-stop about foreign tourists who would dominate his trade for a few more months to come. As they turned into the square she saw there were no lights on in her flat. She had wanted Oliver to come home before her and find her note saying where she had gone. But he had not been in and the note was as she had left it. She crumpled it, threw it away and went to bed.

* * *

Rain woke very early, stirred by the sounds of a London which never sleeps. Her window had been wide all night and as she got out of bed she looked down on the dusty heads of trees where sparrows were fussing.

She thought she might find Oliver sleeping on the couch which he sometimes did if he came late and did not want to disturb her, but he had not come home. She treated this with equanimity. He would say he had met a friend at the wine bar and gone on somewhere and found it too late to get back. He might say he had tried to telephone her, and this time she might believe him.

Rain set up her coffee machine, thinking as she did so that Oliver had probably not been with Linda Finch although he might encourage her to believe that. As she fetched sugar and milk and her favourite cup and saucer, she made up her mind to break with him. Permanently, she told herself. There should be no more nonsense about one or other of them moving out for a matter of days or weeks only for the unsatisfactory relationship to resume just as unsatisfactorily as before.

Still wearing her fine cotton nightdress, she carried her coffee into the garden and sat, high above the other gardens and in total privacy. Some sparrows invaded that privacy, crossing from parapet rail to chair to flower tub. While she watched them she planned how to deal with Oliver.

She would explain, calmly and directly, that she felt there was nothing in their relationship worth preserving and she would ask him to move out straightaway. Experience had taught her that allowing him time meant, in effect, allowing him to stay. So she would be ruthless about making a clean and immediate break. It would be no use him arguing that he had nowhere to go because he so often found other places to spend nights. As she set down her cup, startling the sparrows, she thought she might even pack his belongings.

While the idea was fresh she began, putting the contents of his drawers into his bag. He owned very little and the packing did not take long. She lugged his bag out into the sitting room and left it, like an object stranded by the tide, halfway between the doors to the flat and the bedroom. The symbolism of this did not strike her at all, as she went back and forth, showering and dressing and rehearsing all the reasons why he was to go. Not least was that his presence diminished her chances of enjoying a happier relationship with someone else. She caught herself wondering whether by someone else she meant Paul Wickham.

All that went completely out of her head when she went to buy the morning papers and read John Wainfleet's assertion of an affair between Maureen MacQuillan and Cecil Hunter-Blair. The account relied more heavily on innuendo than bald statement but the message was clear. There was even a smudgy photograph, apparently taken at a party, which showed them together over the canapés.

Rain stood in the street with the open page in her hand and cursed Wainfleet for not telling her about it. She could have published nothing, but the implications for the *Post* of such a liaison were considerable. People stepped around her as she stood there, debating how much of the tale was true and where Wainfleet had got it.

She pulled herself together and set off across the square. Trees cut her view for part of the way and when she could see the street door leading to her flat she noticed a man dawdling by, looking up and down the pavement and then strolling back the way he had come. He was doing nothing yet appeared purposeful. She slowed her pace, willing him to go away before she drew close. He did not. He crossed to the edge of the grass and craned to look at the top of the building. He had thinning hair and a very lightweight suit in cream and white pinstripes. She thought he imagined he looked smart, but the clothes seemed not to belong to him, as though he were dressing up. She pictured a straw boater and a bicycle and as her smile spread he abruptly faced her.

There were liquid blue eyes and a clipped fair moustache. Oh yes, Rain thought; definitely a boater and a bike. Then she realized he was smiling back, approaching.

'Rain Morgan?' His voice was husky.

'So I am.' Her fingers tightened on the wad of newspapers. There was no one else around. He did not look like anyone she had libelled lately. Perhaps he was going to try to sell her a story for the column? But people reached her at the office and the office had a rule banning employees' home addresses being revealed. She felt herself shrinking from him, preparing to fling the papers in his face and run if she had to.

He was feeling in an inside pocket, an action which prolonged her uncertainty. Then he whisked something out and lunged forward. She stepped back. The papers fell. 'Brian Berg,' she heard him say. 'Private investigator.'

Berg was holding out his credentials, a plastic folder containing a laminated card with his photograph on it. She flicked a glance at it as she gathered her newspapers and remembered. 'Aren't you working for Maureen MacQuillan?'

He had been cunning, arriving so early that she could not pretend to be rushing to work. Although she told him she had nothing to say which might help, he was very persistent. Rather than have him insinuate himself into the building later and perhaps annoy her neighbours, she capitulated and invited him to the flat.

'Going away?' he asked as he noticed the bag on the floor.

She grunted a reply and offered coffee. He said: 'No thank you, I don't drink coffee. But might I trouble you for a cup of hot water?'

She brought hot water and watched as he unwrapped a sachet and dropped it into the cup. A sweet aroma rose. 'Verbascum,' he said. 'I find it very helpful for my sinuses.'

Rain smothered a smile. Of all the detectives she could afford, Maureen had hired this odd little man who looked as though he were play-acting, managed to be obtrusive when he was doing absolutely nothing and carried around a herbal cure for his blocked nose. But perhaps she was wrong to mock him: he had found her, got into her flat and persuaded her to answer his questions.

The questions were what she expected. She was asked about finding the body, about her colleagues, about the Patriotic Ten and the freedom of speech people. He was especially interested in the patriots. Whether or not he believed Maureen's claim that her father met his death at the hands of political opponents, Brian Berg was dutifully pursuing that line. And when he would not be persuaded that Rain had no more for him, she mentioned Georgie and Joey and wished she could be aboard *Perfidia* when Berg cornered them, as he surely would. Sadly, Crystal would never know that there had been a joke at their expense too.

After a while Rain stood up and took Berg's empty cup, a movement calculated to speed the interview to its end. Berg responded by getting up too, saying he must go but popping in another question as he backed towards the door. Before she could warn him he caught his foot against the bag and fell backwards, twisting to save himself, and ended in a contorted heap. It was a heavy fall and Rain's first thought was for the nervous old woman who lived in the flat below. But then she saw the pain on Berg's face.

He waved her away as she ran to help. Agonizingly slowly he raised himself. 'My back,' he gasped. 'I've got a bad back, you see.' At last he was on his feet but moving with difficulty, sharply drawing in his breath as pain shot through him. 'I'll have to see my osteopath. He'll put me back together in no time.' He tried very hard to smile.

Rain left him supporting himself against a table as she fetched her shoulder bag. She felt entirely responsible for the accident although Berg croaked that it was all his own fault. He asked whether she would mind calling him a cab and she dangled car keys and said she would drive him herself. So they went downstairs, Berg wincing at each step and clinging to the banister rail. The nervous neighbour peeped around her door to ask if everything was all right, which Rain took to be a reprimand about the noise.

Her car was parked a few yards away from the building. She took Berg's arm and helped him towards it. His osteopath had premises near Regent's Park and all the way Berg kept apologizing for all the trouble he was causing and Rain kept assuring him it was none at all. With some relief she deposited him with the receptionist to await emergency treatment. Then she drove into Regent's Park and stopped.

She was far too early to go to the office, it was a waste of time to go home and she could think of nothing to do. The café was shut, she did not want to walk as the grass had withered to an unappealing brown, and she had left her papers at home. Remembering them brought back to mind the Wainfleet item. She found a callbox and rang Shildon, asking whether he wanted her to continue pursuing Hunter-Blair.

When he learned where she was, Shildon suggested she went to his flat, a short drive away.

The Lloyd Baker estate is a few streets of plain Victorian houses reaching up a slope near King's Cross. Shildon's flat was easily identified from his description of a treacherously unsafe portico. There was a look of impermanence about his occupation of the flat, as well as about the portico. Rain had to squeeze past a half-full packing case to get through the passage to the sitting room and then there were stacks of books on the floor.

She had interrupted his breakfast and accepted an invitation to some toast. The kitchen was rather primitive with the wooden things painted red and a red and white gingham curtain hanging, café-style, across the lower half of the window. 'I'm not really living here,' Shildon said. 'The tenant's a friend and she's letting me use this place while she researches a book in Italy.'

'Not *Etruscan Pots Reconsidered Yet Again?*' Rain joked.

He just said: 'Nothing like that.' He picked up a paper open at Wainfleet's column. 'Did you know about Maureen and Hunter-Blair?'

She confessed she had not and sensed criticism of her failure. She said: 'I hope there's nothing in it, it could make the difference between Hunter-Blair's column continuing or being axed.'

Shildon washed down the last of his toast with tea before replying. 'Whatever Maureen thinks, Ron Barron will keep things going in the direction her father pointed them.'

She thought that was supposition until he reminded her that Barron had forced Pascoe out after MacQuillan's death. Then he said: 'It's not just rhetoric, you know. MacQuillan wasn't only talking about getting the British out of Northern Ireland, he was using HM Supplies to channel money to terrorist groups. I don't know whether Hunter-Blair or Maureen know that, but Ron Barron does.'

Rain said if Maureen did it suggested a powerful reason for her certainty that her father had died for political reasons.

Shildon said he believed that, too, and asked how the police inquiry was going. There was little she was free to tell him, but he was very interested in what she said and sorry to be interrupted by his telephone. He took the call in the sitting room and Rain sat on a red-painted kitchen chair and wondered how he came to be living in such circumstances. The friend in Italy was only half an answer. He joined her to say he would not be in the office that morning, a contact in the city had an exclusive story for him and they had arranged a meeting.

The news when Rain reached the office was that Tavett was again being questioned by the police; there were insistent rumours of a row between Maureen and Barron; the freedom of speech people were muttering obscenities because their latest attempt at a cartoon had been rejected; and the Patriotic Ten were casting around for a fresh mind to help them get their statement into publishable form.

'Dick Tavett can't have killed MacQuillan,' said Holly, ready to believe he had.

'Of course not,' said Rain, and bit back information about the typewriter used for the packages and a death threat.

Harbury had heard about Tavett's typewriter from one of his police contacts and did not share Rain's inhibitions about discussing it. 'The evidence is just piling up against him,' he said with glee.

Rosie, opening the mail, a task she no longer enjoyed, said it was impossible for Tavett to be guilty of sending the knives because he had been as upset as she was when one fell on his desk. They were all arguing about this when Oliver appeared, furious with Rain and oblivious of everyone else.

She drew him away to the corner by the iced water machine. The machine was still broken. 'What's going on?' Oliver demanded. And complained that she had refused to let him in when he had returned from the wine bar having forgotten his key. He had slept on a friend's floor and spent a very uncomfortable night.

She said: 'I didn't refuse. I can't have been there.'

'You weren't supposed to be going out. There was a hush-hush meeting with Eliot and I was to keep out of the way. Remember?'

She remembered, but also that Oliver had decided to go to the wine bar before the meeting was fixed. She snapped that she was entitled to come and go as she pleased and said an old friend had offered to buy her supper.

Oliver grew more angry, not less, saying there had been rather more to it than supper, hadn't there? Her denials were useless because he said he had returned to Kington Square early that morning and seen her coming out of the flat arm in arm with a man.

Rain said, unfortunately loudly: '*That was Brian Berg!*'

'I don't care what his name is.'

She tried to remind him who Berg was but he cut across her saying he wanted her key so he could go and move his belongings out. Not trusting him to return it, she would not give it. They each stormed away to their desks, Oliver grumbling to everyone in earshot and Rain in silent rage.

Holly offered her a sympathetic smile which was not acknowledged. Harbury pretended the scene had never taken place. 'Did you get very far with Wickham last night, Rain?' he asked and was confounded by the stunned look she gave him.

She recollected fast and said there had been a development in the case during the evening. Harbury went off to quiz policemen.

CHAPTER 15

Stuart Pascoe lived in a spacious house not far from Canterbury Cathedral with a garden that swung down to a river. He had regretted refusing to talk to Rain and rung Eliot to say so. It was not, he said as he ushered Rain into his richly furnished sitting room on Wednesday afternoon, as though he had done anything with which to reproach himself, the fault lay entirely with the MacQuillan people.

He polished his pebble glasses on a handkerchief, a little diversion before he embarked on the full story. Rain settled into a chintz armchair and listened, not rushing him although much of what he had to say appeared irrelevant.

The drive to Kent had been a difficult, slow journey hampered by the volume of tourists who poured on and off the cross-Channel ferries. From London to Canterbury the traffic was solid and the fumes that built up in the car made her head ache. Canterbury itself came as a disappointment. She mourned the loss of medieval buildings, cleared to provide what planners called a shopping complex, and was shocked by the dullness of the modern architecture.

Somewhere there was a photograph of her as a small child standing outside the cathedral with the aunt who had brought her up and taken her one day to visit it. Her mind drifted back to that occasion while Pascoe was talking and she was recalled sharply when she realized he had put a question. He wanted to know whether she would like him to make her a cup of tea or whether they might wait until his wife returned from a committee meeting. Rain chose to wait and Mrs Pascoe arrived soon after, plump and pink.

Rain had never thought about Pascoe being married, having a life beyond the *Post*. Yet if she had she would have imagined for him someone like Mrs Pascoe, someone who gave an instant impression of being a first-class housekeeper (the house was immaculate, everything well chosen and highly polished) and combined energetic work for her local community with a modest reticence about herself. Mrs Pascoe provided tea and a little nicely judged conversation before leaving Rain and her husband to their talk.

'I'm afraid you'll think I'm rambling rather,' Pascoe apologized.

'Not at all,' Rain said quickly, deducing she had been looking bored.

'But you see it's all quite germane. What happened before MacQuillan came had a considerable effect on what he did later. It's important for you to know the ways in which Martin Ayling tried to save the paper and to protect its future if he had to sell.'

As she did not want to reveal how much Shildon had reported, she had to sit again through the complicated story of the sale of the lease. Naturally, Pascoe did not stress incompetence or negligence, the admission was more delicately made. And then he swept on with an account of the several attempts to buy the paper, culminating in MacQuillan offering more money and more guarantees about the way it would be run.

'The rest of the field couldn't compete, and it didn't occur to us that MacQuillan was utterly cynical and making pledges he meant to disregard,' he said. 'I had to endure watching him dismantle all the safeguards Ayling had created. From the outset it was a battlefield, people were being dismissed and demoted quite contrary to the terms of their contracts. My responsibilities vanished but I think they suspected that if I were sacked there would be a public fuss so they had to proceed by stealth. The same was true of Eliot but he was luckier in one way: he could give a little here and hold out against them there. They got the Hunter-Blair column and they got *Girlie* but he prevented a great many other things. My case was more difficult. I had little to do except wait and see how they would attack me next.'

He had not, he said, expected the weapon they chose. It was Barron who had made a show of looking at the figures but it was MacQuillan who had screamed at Pascoe down the telephone accusing him of fraud. 'He followed up with a memo and I sent one back insisting he withdrew his allegations. Needless to say, he didn't. He sent for me and demanded my resignation, and we had the worst row I've ever had in my business life.'

He took off his glasses and wiped them again, remembering the bitterness and rage to which he and MacQuillan had given vent. 'Nobody won. How can anybody when there is complete loss of control? I knew MacQuillan had engineered the scene because he hoped I would blurt out my resignation. I didn't do that. I challenged him with all the dishonesty he had shown and all the damage he was doing to the paper. And he . . . Well, he enjoyed every moment of it, as though he liked nothing better than a brawl. His enjoyment was the most degrading thing about a wholly degrading episode.'

He shuddered and replaced the glasses, before describing how he had spent a sleepless night worrying what he should do and in the morning had made up his mind to tackle MacQuillan again. 'I was definitely not going to bow to his pressure, you see. He had behaved disgracefully on Thursday and I was going to make him face up to the fact on Friday. I was prepared to be rock solid in my refusal to resign and in my insistence that he withdrew that damning memo.'

He made a little face. 'No doubt word has gone round by now that I couldn't get through to him or to Mona on the telephone. I was so aggravated that I was prepared to believe Brenda on the switchboard was lying on his behalf, pretending there was no reply. That's when I went to Mona's room and left a note.'

Rain feared they had drifted so far into the events of the day of the murder that she would never draw him back to other matters. But he said: 'There was something else I was going to say to MacQuillan. Oh, I can see now that it was unworthy and beside the point but at the time I was so exasperated with the man and his perfidy that any ammunition would have done. There he was, trying to blackmail me to leave the company or face a false charge of fraud, and I knew so much about his underhand behaviour. To be blunt I was ready to let him know I was aware how he was using the *Post* and where the money was going.'

Rain forgot her headache and waited for the rest. Pascoe said: 'I do understand that it would also have been blackmail but in the circumstances I wasn't adopting a very high moral position. I just wanted revenge, what Bacon called a kind of wild justice, I believe. MacQuillan was destined to win the contest, but I was prepared to get a strike or two in first. I'd seen other men in other companies, as innocent as I believed myself to be, hounded out because wrongdoers require a scapegoat where the wrongdoing concerns money. They pick on an accountant because an accountant needs a good name and has been partly in control of the funds anyway. They threaten to "expose" a misdeed, probably a genuine mistake or perhaps complete fiction, but the salvation is that if he goes without a murmur the matter will be hushed up. It never is, though. Once he's gone he's their explanation for the missing money and all they will ever be accused of is leniency in not prosecuting.'

He looked out of the window to watch a rowing boat floundering by with novice crew. 'The records were being altered, a new accounting system was being introduced and key people were moved from positions of authority. MacQuillan was draining the paper of its few assets and sending the money to one of his companies in the United States called HM Supplies.'

Rain asked whether he had told anyone else about this and he said not. 'MacQuillan died. I thought that might improve my life but on Monday Barron demonstrated that was not true, so I left. If my information is helpful to Eliot, who apparently has the energy to carry on the struggle against the new overlords, then he is welcome to it. Otherwise I see no purpose in repeating it now that I have no opportunity to provide the proof.' And that proof, he said, was to be found among the financial records of the newspaper, he had taken nothing away with him.

When it was time for her to leave, he walked out into the sun to open the driveway gates. He was relaxed, a contrast to the tension which had gripped him while he spoke of the MacQuillan calumny. She hoped for his sake the memory of his time working for MacQuillan would quickly fade. He said: 'Don't say you're in too much of a hurry to look into the cathedral before you go.'

She promised she would. 'We go to the services quite regularly,' said Pascoe, holding the gate. 'My wife has a nephew in the choir. It's her home town although it's changed a lot since she was a girl. Apparently it's a much more vigorous place now. She approves of that, says it's a good thing to keep up with the times.' He was waving quite cheerfully when she last saw him.

Rain parked near the cathedral and kept her promise to him. A woman barred her way because a service was ending and there was an aggressive demand for a donation on entrance instead of, in the British tradition, a polite request before leaving. She paid up, thinking of the Pascoes praying visitors should do so and save the precious fabric.

When she was allowed through to the nave she discovered dancers rehearsing a performance and robed guides discouraging visitors from proceeding to the site of St Thomas's shrine because their passage disturbed the troupe. Aggrieved, she refused to obey instructions to sit and watch the dancers and took a side door into the cloisters.

Sitting on a stone wall she listened to tourists who sprawled on grass where they were asked not to encroach. Two youths chased each other around a pile of rucksacks and their girls were shrill in encouragement. Someone on the far side of the cloisters made a joke in Dutch and another gaggle of European youths burst into laughter. Rain gave up and returned to her car. She had remembered somewhere else from long ago, doubted she could find it but dared.

Luck was with her. She stopped close to the entrance to St Martin's and walked up the steep path of a tiny church, ancient before St Thomas was born. The gable wall revealed Roman bricks, the simple interior was soothing. She was alone, enjoying an impenetrable peace.

But before long she was thinking about MacQuillan and Pascoe. Irresistibly she returned to the question of whether Pascoe could be the murderer. If Harbury had heard the story Pascoe had just related, he might have been confirmed in his belief that it was possible. Her own imagination suggested how it could have happened. Perhaps there had been a second confrontation after all and another loss of control. In his fury Pascoe might have grabbed the knife — which could have belonged to MacQuillan and been to hand — and plunged it into him.

Her common sense told her that would not do, her imagination was ignoring the facts. MacQuillan had been stabbed in the back, there were no palm or fingerprints on the weapon. It was much harder to imagine Pascoe taking gloves and a knife with him when he went to MacQuillan's office and creeping up behind him, and there was no evidence of a struggle between the dead man and his attacker which would have been the case if the killer had not approached from behind.

She caught herself wondering whether it mattered if Pascoe had done it, whether it was invariably wrong to kill when a murder meant removing a menace. She started to count how many people, who might not confess it in simple language, were relieved MacQuillan had gone. She lost count. Within her narrow experience that man had made many people undeservedly wretched.

The door opened and a shaft of light fell down the aisle. An elderly woman came in, seated herself in a rear pew and clasped her hands in prayer. Rain looked at the roof, at the timeworn stone and the patina of wood, and she tried very hard to remember her earlier visit to St Martin's. It would not come although it must have been on the same day as the trip to the cathedral and her aunt had undoubtedly been with her. The place itself was clear enough in her mind, there had been no surprises when she walked up the path and entered the small high room.

Memory was mischievously selective at the best of times. Trivia stuck limpet-like and the useful filtered away. Sometimes bad things hung on so it was possible to remember an outing as the day the car broke down rather than the day there was a barbecue on the beach and the party went on until the tide came in. But it was equally likely that truly dreadful things were wiped away, which was why she had no recollection of being lifted from the wreckage of the vehicle in which her parents had died. Might not a murderer, she wondered, erase the memory of the deed? She had hoped for Pascoe's sake that the MacQuillan affair would fade from his mind, but perhaps his memory was already concealing from him the truth about the killing.

The old woman still prayed. Rain tiptoed out. The interior of her car was a furnace and she frittered a few moments wandering in the graveyard after opening the car doors to cool it. It had little effect and she had to force herself into the driving seat and begin the return journey. At around the same time the police were setting out to interview Pascoe again.

CHAPTER 16

A large woman dressed like a dishevelled extra from *Carmen* was by the news editor's desk when Rain got back from Canterbury. 'But don't you understand, I only want to help,' she was saying with bosom-heaving passion.

Riley was doing his best to tell her to go away. 'Why don't you write to us about it?'

'No, no, Mr Riley . . . it's essential that I should be given something, I can't work until I have something.'

Journalists wore the amused smiles of people enjoying a good argument which did not threaten them personally. No one tried to shunt the woman away to let Riley get on with his work. As Rain passed Tavett's desk he cupped his face in his hands and moaned for her benefit, saying: 'Have you ever wondered what it would be like to work in an ordinary office instead of a newspaper where every kind of freak feels entitled to barge in and collar you?'

'Boring,' she said cheerfully. 'That's how it would be. Anyway, who says we should throw Ruby Dobby out? She might hold the solution to the MacQuillan mystery.'

'Your friend Wickham says. He won't allow her near the second floor so she's come to us.'

The room reverberated with the fat woman's cry of 'Rain!' as she abandoned Riley in favour of a friendlier face. Tavett crouched over his desk until he felt the swish of air as the woman passed by, purple and pink cotton skirts flapping. 'My dear!' cried Ruby making a theatrical gesture. 'Now *you'll* understand, I'm sure. If I'm to solve this wretched murder case I must have something that belonged to MacQuillan. Anything would do, but it must have been used by him. Then I can begin my mysterious processes.'

By an equally mysterious process Eliot knew Rain had returned and asked Mona to fetch her. Rain walked up the room after Mona with Ruby running crabwise beside her begging: 'Do think of something, Rain. I feel I could be entirely useful if only I could get something to focus on. A garment, perhaps, but anything would be acceptable.'

'I'm sorry, Ruby, I have nothing at all of his. You'd have to ask his daughter if you want something personal.' The suggestion that Ruby Dobby might descend on Maureen was a comic afterthought but from Ruby's point of view completely logical. Her gait slowed as Rain disappeared into Eliot's office, then she asked Mona where she could find Miss MacQuillan.

Rain and Eliot discussed the substance of her meeting with Pascoe and his assertion that evidence to support his story was to be found in the financial records kept at the *Post.* Eliot said: 'I no longer have his scruples so I would love to steal that evidence. Unfortunately I also lack his talent for figures. How are your sums?'

'Not up to this, Luke. Besides, the information is hidden in a computer.'

'I'm assured the thing is what they call user friendly.'

'The antipathy is all on my side.'

Eliot summoned Mona and asked whether she'd had access to the computer while working for MacQuillan. She had, but only to certain files and could not have dipped into others because access was governed by codes and, in the case of the most confidential files, by numbers too. The codes and numbers could be changed to ensure secrecy was maintained. She said that apart from MacQuillan and Barron she did not know who else had been allowed a complete list.

Mona hesitated, then offered: 'If you seriously need that list I could try to get it for you. MacQuillan's copy was kept in a locked drawer of his desk. Perhaps it's still there.' But when Eliot asked how she would get the keys to the desk, she realized her suggestion had been useless: she had forgotten that Maureen had taken them from her.

The door was pushed open and Zak Smythe, who grew more benign as the days went by, appeared. He grinned at Rain and Mona and happily promised Eliot: 'You're going to love this one, I reckon we've got it right this time.' He thrust towards him the most recent attempt at a letter for publication. Mona and Rain faded away.

Just then Ruby Dobby swept into the newsroom with formidable hauteur. 'Rain!' she said, 'I've met the most appalling and impertinent woman. Your Miss MacQuillan says she questions my motives and emphatically will *not* encourage me to identify her father's killer. The bereaved are normally anxious for a speedy conclusion in these tragic cases. I can't think why she's behaving in such a way.'

Rain could not cite a case where Ruby Dobby had brought a speedy conclusion to a murder case. In one missing person inquiry she had claimed success because the runaway girl had telephoned home, but no one could prove or disprove that Ruby's meditation over a favourite pair of tights had influenced her. Ruby's forte was getting her own photograph in the newspapers as she 'arrived at the police station to advise officers working on the such-and-such case'; she was a popular television chat show guest; and she made a decent living from writing about psychometry. What she was not was the answer to a policeman's prayer.

However, Ruby had a resilient nature and Rain had a plan. Rain spent a few minutes sympathizing with the psychic's frustrations and then suggested that she try Maureen again, but with a specific request for a set of keys. 'Keys?' said Ruby, deflating.

'His desk keys. They might be the only thing she has here which he used personally.'

Ruby was sceptical. 'I've never worked with keys.'

'You said anything would do.'

'I know, but . . .'

Rain coaxed her. 'Go on, have a try. Then you can come and sit near me and find out whether they will be of any use. If they aren't you can send them straight back.'

Ruby closed her eyes. Rain thought she was conjuring up keys, clutched in the fingers of the dead man. Actually, Ruby was considering how well publicized her intervention in the case would be if she were to work from the *Post* newsroom. The last time she had been to the office she had been confined in a poky little interview room near the editor's office, but she hoped to avoid that fate this time. 'Very well, my dear,' she breathed. 'I shall brave that awful creature again.'

'Not just any keys mind,' Rain cautioned, and stressed the value of the desk keys.

Fifteen minutes later, when Rain had forgotten all about her, Ruby swayed into the room once more with a triumphant smile. 'She's bounced back *again*,' whispered Holly who knew nothing about keys. 'Is she planning to move in with us?'

'Yes. She's going to use our spare desk for a spot of psychometry.'

'Oh, of course,' said Holly, as though it made any sense to her.

Fortunately Ruby worked with no more sound than the occasional deep breath expelled in a sigh. She dropped down on the other side of the sweetheart plant from Rain, bowed her head, rested her right hand lightly on the keys, shut her eyes tight and concentrated. True, it had taken her several minutes to decide whether the keys should be bunched or splayed but she had ceased fidgeting with them and settled into an abnormal quietude.

Rain intended to get the keys for herself as soon as Ruby had finished with them. Ruby was unhurried. The deep breathing and sighs continued despite the clamour of typewriters and telephones as the working day reached its crescendo of noise and activity. In the middle of it Sniffy Wilson rang. 'Haven't got long, Rain,' he said. 'Is Wickham there?'

Rain got through to Marshall who said he would take the call. Holly asked Rain whether Sniffy had named names yet and she admitted getting nothing from him. At that moment Ruby gave a growl that set her loose flesh trembling. Rosie jumped and people who had taken no interest in Ruby since she had sat down made excuses to walk by the diary desk and see what she was up to. Her hands brushed the keys, her head began to nod, then her body to tremble. Her lips shaped barely audible words.

'Is she ill?' asked Tavett.

'No, it's her mysterious processes,' Rain explained.

'What's she saying?' asked Harbury.

'She says she can feel keys,' said Holly with a smirk.

'Oh, very clever of her,' said Riley sarcastically.

Ruby raised the level of her voice. 'A man,' she was saying. 'A man's keys.'

'Her processes are too mysterious for me,' said Tavett and moved away.

'I can sense evil,' moaned Ruby.

'That's MacQuillan for you,' said Harbury with a shrug. He walked off.

'These keys are linked with evil.' Ruby's voice was fractionally louder.

'This could take forever,' grumbled Riley and went.

'You look like a coven of witches,' Linley remarked unkindly in passing. He was angry that the next day's *Guardian* was to carry a damning review of *Etruscan Pots Reconsidered*, and more angry that this was common knowledge. He doubled back to tell Holly she had written a nice piece on Donaldson. She accepted the compliment with a smile but it was an awkward moment, underlining that Linley and Maureen had approved the story rather than Rain or Tavett.

Tavett was too preoccupied with his fear that Wickham believed him to be the murderer to form any judgments. He was in the office each day but the tide of work flowed around him. He sat at his desk looking over the same papers and repeatedly having the same conversations but unable to take decisions or achieve anything.

For the second time that afternoon Sniffy Wilson rang Rain. 'I've got to be quick,' he said. 'I want a meeting.'

She misunderstood. 'I'll put you through to Wickham.'

'No, I don't mean that. I want a meeting with you.'

'Well, I'm not sure I ought . . .'

'I've got some papers but I can't take them to the police, can I? If I give them to you, you can do your story first and then pass them on.'

Rain asked whether he could not tell her the story on the telephone. 'Sure,' he said, 'but you'd want the proof. Anybody would.'

'The post?'

'Look, I know what you're thinking, Rain, but I can organize it so it's all right. You won't learn where I'm holed up so you can't give anything away. And what I've got for you is worth every bit of inconvenience.'

He had been reliable in the past, she had to trust him. She agreed to the meeting. He said she was to go to Ludgate Circus, stand on the south corner of Fleet Street at 6.30 p.m. and wait for a cab to pull in and pick her up.

'Will you have to wear a carnation and carry a copy of today's *Post*?' asked Holly with a giggle.

'No, but if I'm not here tomorrow morning you might tell our resident superintendent that I'm probably the victim of a gangland killing.'

Rosie laughed, which Rain thought a trifle unfeeling. Then Ruby Dobby grew dramatic again, growling and shuddering and recapturing attention. 'Don't tell me,' said Holly under her breath. 'She's proved psychometrically that they are *desk* keys.'

To their alarm Ruby flung back her head, opened her eyes wide and very slowly brought her face level with Rain's. 'These keys,' she said, 'have an aura. This tells me they have been connected with wickedness.' Then she looked dispirited. 'I had hoped for more, I must confess, Rain. But as I warned you, I have never worked with keys before.'

Rain patted her shoulder. 'Never mind, perhaps you'll be able to get hold of something else MacQuillan owned.' She reached for the keys. Ruby closed her hand around them, saying: 'I must return them, as I promised.'

Rain called over a messenger, saying there was no need for Ruby to deliver them herself. Rain took the keys and quietly asked the messenger to hand them to Mona. She looked at her watch. It was nearly time for her to take up position at Ludgate Circus, but first she had to get Ruby to leave. Ruby did not want to, she wanted to talk about her technique even though it had let her down. Rosie, who was least capable of resisting, heard several minutes of the tremors in Ruby's fingers and the palpitations of Ruby's heart and the pictures flashing through Ruby's mind before Rain propelled Ruby out of the room.

They went downstairs together, Rain anxious that Ruby might also want a taxi at Ludgate Circus. Ruby, however, meant to walk the opposite way and glided proudly up Fleet Street, purple headscarf bobbing and gold hooped earrings glinting cruelly. She was angry. Her parting exchange with Rain had been less than friendly. Ruby had said she would be at the office again next morning by which time she expected Rain to have found something more profitable for her than keys. But Rain had told her it would not be a good idea for her to reappear, she was not likely to solve the case. Ruby saw her chance of publicity disappearing.

If Ruby Dobby had not been offended matters might have turned out differently.

CHAPTER 17

There was nothing distinctive about the black London taxi except that it swooped to pick Rain up when she had not hailed it. The driver checked her name, jerked his head to tell her to get in, and then shot out into the evening traffic. They talked about the weather, as everybody did in those suffocating days. He asked whether the police had got the man who had done in MacQuillan. Otherwise the journey to Wapping was quiet. He dropped her outside the Prospect of Whitby, stressing that the fare was taken care of. She understood and gave a generous tip. As he pocketed it he said, with studied casualness, that the pub terrace had a good view of the river. Then he switched on his 'For Hire' sign and drove away.

Rain pushed open the door. There was the usual pub smell of stale tobacco but the river Thames laps against the old smugglers inn and its odours mingle with the rest. A long pewter-topped bar runs down the room. A barman was polishing glasses with his back to Rain. An old man sat over a half pint of stout. A microphone and musical instruments were placed ready for a band.

Rain walked past them all, turned left and went through open glass doors to a terrace. A cruiser was going up-river, against the tide and churning water. Gulls drifted lethargically on the swell. The boat was making for Tower Bridge, round the distant bend to Rain's right; the tide was running out towards Limehouse Reach, beyond the long sweep of river to her left.

There was one other person on the terrace, a swarthy man with a blue nylon shirt sticking to the contours of his body. Rain approached him, her eyes on the river. When she was near enough he spoke softly. 'It's a white delivery van. The back doors are unlocked. It's parked about ten yards away from the pub, on the left. You can go out through the door behind you. Make sure you're not seen getting into the van.' The terrace was cluttered with wooden benches, empty beer crates and a fire escape which half hid the narrow door he meant.

She did not altogether like the sound of this. It had been easy to agree to Sniffy's request from the safety of the office but it felt different to be taking the orders of a stranger from Sniffy's brutal underworld. She might have backed off, gone into the pub and telephoned for a cab to fetch her; but Holly knew who she was supposed to be meeting and she would feel foolishly fainthearted next day if she had to confess to being too nervous to see the matter through.

She did not bother to ask herself whether Holly would have done what she was being asked to do, or whether it was sensible to care what Holly thought. She did as the man said, and got into the back of the van.

She could hardly breathe. The van was airless and the metal hot against her skin. Some rags, which had apparently been used to wipe it out, gave off oil fumes. Rain perched on a folded piece of carpet which was presumably to be her seat. She hoped the journey would start soon and not take long.

The driver's door opened and the man from the pub got in. 'I hope you're a good traveller, love,' he said and the van rattled away down Wapping High Street. She had a view through the windscreen but no one could have seen her in the back. A few familiar miles rolled by before she was in territory she did not recognize. Traffic was heavy and drivers bad tempered so the white van was forced to jockey for position, the swarthy man stamping on brake or accelerator and his passenger bouncing off her precarious seat.

Gradually the houses thinned to countryside. Trees dominated her rectangular view. It did her morale no good to realize she was in Epping Forest, graveyard of many gangland victims. Ruefully she recalled her quip to Holly. Then the van was leaping over rough ground, getting out of sight of the road. Shade darkened the interior. The driver dragged on the handbrake. 'Stay there,' he said and got out to stand close to the vehicle. A few moments later he said: 'All clear. I'll let you out.' And did.

She stumbled on to the parched grass, taking in her surroundings. The van was beneath a big tree, no different from any of the other big trees. 'That way,' the man said and pointed. She asked whether he would be there when she got back and he said: 'Yes. They said it wouldn't take long.' Then he added with threatening humour: 'But don't get lost.'

Rain set off. Her hands were grubby, her dress marked and her sandals scuffed. The smell of oil clung to her as strongly as it did to the rags in the van. Once she looked round and saw the driver standing, his back to her, leaning against the van.

There was no clear path, she was just winding through trees and keeping as close as she could to the direction he had shown. All of a sudden a voice called her name. Her heart lurched. Sniffy Wilson was crouching a few yards away.

He was neither pallid nor flabby, prison had not marked him in the ways she expected. There was a bit less hair on his scalp but he looked as fit as he had done at their previous brief meetings. She dropped down beside him, saying casually: 'This had better be good. I've endured a terrible journey in the back of a van for you.'

'It's good all right, Rain. Look at this.' He pushed into her hand a folded paper. On it were names, dates, personal details. She asked what it was, who the people were. Sniffy said they were inmates of Gorstone prison, the document a print-out from the prison computer. Some of the dates were release dates but they were not all genuine because one of the prisoners had been able to interfere with the computer and 'reduce' the sentences.

He told her how. She wanted to know who as well, but he refused her and she knew it would become part of his bargain with the police when and if he were caught. The sheet was folded small and put in her pocket. After that she asked him about MacQuillan.

'I told Wickham on the telephone,' he said. 'I was sharing a cell with an Irishman and he reckoned he'd heard from another man in there that there was a plan to kill MacQuillan. It was political, you see. They'd found out MacQuillan was buying guns for terrorists, so they decided he was to be stopped.'

He elaborated but there was nothing he had not already told Wickham. The conversation broke off sharply when he became edgy and scrambled for cover, telling her to go away. Rain took a couple of steps before thinking of asking him to telephone again. But he had vanished. The forest was very still, the only sound the distant grind of traffic. She hurried towards the white van.

The trees all looked the same, the return journey seemed longer. Then she noticed faint tyre impressions on the dusty ground and suspicion crept into her mind. A minute more and she was certain she had walked further than the distance from the van to where Sniffy had called to her from the undergrowth.

She cast about, looking downwards as though she had dropped something. She was right. There were two sets of tyre tracks. To be absolutely sure she followed one of them and came to the place where they curved round in front of a tree and retreated. The swarthy man had taken his van away and abandoned her.

Bemoaning her stupidity at letting him escape she trudged towards the sound of traffic. She blamed herself for trusting him to wait, for not refusing to go to Sniffy without the van keys in her possession.

Harsh grass scratched between the straps of her sandals and made walking uncomfortable. Traffic grew closer and trees sparser until she entered a glade which ran down to the road. The place was obviously an informal car park, the grass worn away and dust stirring beneath her feet as she walked.

There was one vehicle there, a car with two figures sitting in the front seats and apparently looking at the road ahead of them. But as she drew near, the doors flew open and two casually dressed young men got out and closed in on her. 'Police, Miss Morgan,' said one of them.

'How did you know . . . ?'

'Information received, miss,' said the other one.

* * *

She got home to Kington Square at last, still grubby, very hungry, quite dispirited and having had to hand over to the police the document which had cost her an unreasonable amount of suffering. She did not confirm for them that she had been meeting an escaped prisoner and she did not explain the significance of the print-out, but they clearly knew the first and it would be only a short time before they worked out the second. At least, she thought savagely as she climbed the stairs to the top floor, she would get the story about the release dates into the paper. They could not prevent that.

When she went inside she was surprised to find the bag on the floor. The matter of evicting Oliver came back to mind, along with the Brian Berg fiasco. She went straight to the bathroom, stripped off her dirty clothes and stepped into the shower. A second later the doorbell rang. She snatched up a towel and went to the entryphone. Oliver. Sounding rather crisp. She unlocked the door and got back in the shower.

He joined her in the bathroom, drawing back the shower curtain and shouting above the sound of rushing water: 'I've got something to tell you.'

'Yes. I know. You're moving out.' She drew the curtain forward.

He tugged it back. 'It's a message. From Mona.'

'It'll keep.' The curtain whisked across again.

He stood outside it and yelled. 'She says they are not MacQuillan's keys.'

Rain switched off the water. Very slowly the curtain opened. 'Say that again.'

He shrugged. 'That's all she said. You were supposed to understand.'

She took up the already damp towel and swathed herself in it. 'Did she say who owns them?'

'I've given you the total message.' He followed her into the sitting room, and noticed for the first time his packed bag. He averted his eyes from it and went into the kitchen, asking whether she would like an iced drink. She said yes and went to dress, stepping around the bag without commenting on it. It was like having a third person, an onlooker, in the room.

Oliver poured orange juice, drank half of it in the kitchen while looking very thoughtful and then carried Rain's to the bedroom. Before he could speak she said: 'I'm famished. Is there anything to eat?'

'Not much. We could get a salad at the wine bar.' He picked up her sandals, looking at the scuffed leather. 'What on earth have you been doing to these?'

'I took them for a ride in a van and a walk through Epping Forest.' She drew a comb through her wet hair. In the mirror she saw him slide open one of his drawers, checking that his suspicion was correct, that the contents of the drawers had become the contents of the packed bag. The position was clear enough but she thought she ought to enlarge. She began: 'Oliver . . .'

'Thank you for doing the packing,' he said.

They walked to the wine bar, the bag unmoved on the sitting room floor and their attention on Rain's story about Sniffy Wilson. He asked whether there had been other policemen in the forest. She said there had but she did not know how close to where she was picked up. The men who stopped her had done a lot of talking on their radio before taking her to their police station.

Oliver insisted she had been followed from Fleet Street and that it was likely the police had tapped her office telephone. By the police he meant Wickham. When she demurred he said the other possibility was that Holly had tipped them off. 'She's always been after your job. She thought it was within her grasp and then MacQuillan died and Maureen left the department and Holly got desperate and tried to have you locked up.' Even to his ears it sounded wild.

Rain clung to the belief that although her relationship with Holly had deteriorated, Holly was far too loyal to the paper to dream of ruining a story. Oliver said: 'It's Wickham, then.' And at that stage they reached the wine bar and changed the subject.

Harbury was there, so was Linda Finch. Rain waved on her way to a table but Oliver went to speak to Linda. After a while Harbury and Linda detached themselves from a group and carried their drinks over to join Rain. Clearly it was done at Oliver's invitation and Rain would normally have welcomed company; but in her glum mood she expected Oliver would flirt with Linda, and Linda would be amused at Rain's expense, and it would be quite impossible to spoil their fun by mentioning that Oliver was leaving Kington Square. She did not have long to brood because Harbury began talking to her about the MacQuillan case.

Towards the end of the evening she paid the bill and made other obvious signs that she was ready to leave. Oliver was not and the packed bag loomed large in her mind. She wondered whether it were conceivable he had forgotten about it. In the end she left without finding out. 'You can leave the door open,' he said. 'I won't be long.' She could not tell whether he also meant he would not be at the flat long, only long enough to collect his bag and take a taxi to whichever friend's spare room he had negotiated to borrow.

The streets were dusty, the shop lights garish. Nothing looked fresh or interesting. She craved clean air and peace, but there were not many hours to pass before she could point her car westwards and join Ayling in the country. Once she was there it would require a tremendous effort of will to get her back to London — except that she could not leave Holly in charge for more than a day; and except that she was avid for information about the murder inquiry; and except that there were any number of good stories she wanted to pursue for the column and any amount of private gossip she wanted to hear.

As she opened her door the telephone was ringing. Wickham asking whether he could call in on his way home. 'I'd like your help again,' he said when she let him in, 'assuming I'm forgiven for abandoning you so brusquely yesterday evening.' His eyes fell on the bag. 'Are you off somewhere?'

'No, Oliver is. Paul, before you get any help you can tell me whether you arranged to have me followed this afternoon.' Her tone was colder than he would have chosen.

'Yes, of course. I passed on the information which came my way. But my own role is to investigate the MacQuillan murder.' He was speaking with sham formality again.

She persisted. 'Did you get my telephone tapped or did you simply pass on the suggestion that it should be done?'

He dismissed the idea of a telephone tap. 'It wasn't necessary. Sniffy Wilson wasn't going to tell you where he was. He had told me what he had to say about the murder and was free to call me again any time. *Too* free, of course.' She did not smile. He said: 'You'd already said his calls were being made from callboxes, a tap would have been unlikely to trace him unless he repeatedly used the same box and he's too bright for that. What *was* useful was to know that you were being taken to him.'

Her heart sank. It probably had been Holly. 'I assume you won't name the informant because it's confidential.'

He agreed. There were other things he would not tell her either, such as the reason he had been called away from the restaurant. After some confusion, the sergeant who had gone to the Fleet Street address offered by Richard Beales, the philandering accountant, had tracked his man. The building provided London bases for a number of international businesses including MacQuillan's. The man who had been seen at the Black Friar with MacQuillan was Ron Barron.

Questioned, Barron had refused to talk to anyone junior to Wickham and even when Wickham went to his hotel he had little to say except that he had met MacQuillan on private business, that it had nothing to do with the murder and was of no interest to the police. He had hinted, as Maureen had done, that Pascoe was guilty of fraud but did not implicate him in the murder, and invited Wickham to accept that it was a political killing.

Wickham said to Rain: 'Could we talk about MacQuillan now? We interviewed Pascoe again today and he mentioned you had been to see him. I'd like you to tell me whether . . .'

As she answered his questions she could see how the evidence against Pascoe was accumulating. Pascoe had now told the police what he had told her, about a fierce row with MacQuillan on Thursday and an attempt to confront him on Friday. She had initially found it impossible to believe that a respected, churchgoing man could have been pushed beyond the limit of his endurance and have killed. At St Martin's she had imagined him crossing that limit but his mind refusing to accept the memory of it. Wickham's view was harsher. He believed human beings to be conscious of their cunning. A mind could not be read any more reliably than keys could give up the name of a killer. But murder was Wickham's trade. If he suspected Pascoe, Rain had to concede the probability that he was right.

Wickham did not stay long. When he was going he glanced again at Oliver's bag. 'When is he coming back?'

'He isn't.'

He looked at her for what felt a long time, seemed about to say something more, but in the end let the moment pass.

CHAPTER 18

In the morning Oliver, who had come late and slept on the couch, started a conversation which suggested he was wavering about leaving the flat. Rain pretended not to understand his drift. She was determined he should go, a feeling reinforced by that odd unresolved little conversation with Wickham. Another time, with Oliver gone, the appropriate things might be said.

Meanwhile the pretence was maintained that Oliver was eager to pick up his bag and walk out, that it was he who was putting an end to things. He did not, however, show any signs of picking up the bag. He had a great many things to do before he was free to go. He needed to water the plants in the garden tubs. He noticed a loose cupboard door catch which needed screwing tight. There were telephone calls to make and a letter to write. He offered to go to the shop and fetch the papers. None of these were things that had been known to occupy him on other mornings.

While he was buying the papers Rain packed her own bag. She intended to drive to Gloucestershire straight from the office and before she went to work she wanted Oliver and his property out of her flat. There were to be no excuses for him returning.

They settled into an amicable silence as they breakfasted and turned the pages. Suddenly the silence was broken as Rain said: 'Look at this!' She twisted the John Wainfleet page round so they could look at it together.

'Ruby Tells All.' Oliver read out the headline. Beneath it were a photograph of a beaming Ruby Dobby and a few hundred words about her having a psychic revelation that Sniffy Wilson was near London and trying to make contact with a friend. Ruby had 'seen' a blonde woman stepping into a taxi near Fleet Street.

According to Wainfleet Ruby had asked him for a photograph of the escaped prisoner from the newspaper's files, passed her hands over it and discovered that Sniffy was in Epping Forest. Wainfleet added that although the police had closed in on the area they had missed Sniffy.

Oliver found this extraordinarily funny. Reluctantly Rain conceded. She said: 'Ruby seemed to be deep in a trance when Sniffy rang me. I never dreamed she was listening.' She was thankful that Holly was not to be blamed after all. Oliver was grudging about accepting Wickham's innocence. He returned to the letter he had begun typing earlier.

It was a suspiciously long letter for someone who seldom wrote any, and when Rain was waiting to set off for the office he was still tapping away at it. 'You go on,' he said when she interrupted him, 'I must finish this.'

'How much more are you going to do?'

He shrugged. 'I don't know. I'm feeling quite inspired.'

Rain avoided remarking that she was inspired to believe the letter a delaying tactic. She picked up his bag, saying she would put it in her car. He said: 'Don't you bother, that's far too heavy for you to carry downstairs. I'll bring it when I'm ready.'

Testily she said: 'The car's going in five minutes.' She dumped the bag on the floor. He did not look up. The letter proceeded, tap by hesitant tap. Time was slipping by. She carried her own bag to the car and drove away.

Tavett had the Wainfleet page in his hand when she walked into the newsroom. 'We had that crazy woman in here for hours but Wainfleet gets the story!' he grumbled.

Rain told him she had a better one and he went with her to listen as she talked to Riley and the lawyer, Wilmot, about the prison release dates. Tavett grew annoyed when he realized she had already discussed it with the other two the previous evening as soon as she had been allowed to leave the police station.

They were slightly embarrassed that he had been left out, but had agreed at the time that there was no sense in phoning him at home because he would have nothing useful to say. Everyday matters seemed too much for him since the murder, they knew he could not cope with the bigger issues.

Harbury joined them, keen to hear what they were saying but with the excitement of someone nurturing a good story of his own. Eventually it was his turn. 'The police have caught all the others except Sniffy Wilson,' he reported.

'In Epping Forest?' asked Riley.

'No, in Yorkshire. An isolated farmhouse had been rented for them . . .'

'Just like the Great Train Robbers,' said Tavett without much relevance.

'. . . and they were going to stay there for a few weeks until their faces were off the front pages and they could tiptoe away. Unfortunately for them the person who rented the place didn't know that the stables across the yard are let separately as a holiday cottage.'

'I see,' said Wilmot. 'The holidaymakers noticed pale faces behind twitching curtains, did they?'

'Oh no,' Harbury said. 'The holidaymakers were having a party and one of the prisoners went and asked them to keep the noise down. They recognized him.'

They were all laughing at such ineptitude when Wainfleet telephoned. 'You owe me a favour,' he said to Rain. 'I kept quiet about you hobnobbing with Sniffy in the greenwood, didn't I?'

She groaned. 'Do you want to hear the truth about Ruby Dobby?'

'Certainly not. She's far too valuable just as she is, even if her sixth sense didn't mention Epping Forest until after our crime reporter did. What would have been my lead story this morning if she hadn't wafted in?'

'Oh, you'd have found something, another piece about Hunter-Blair, perhaps.'

He said Hunter-Blair was the real reason he was ringing. He was convinced the man had not been at the army camp demonstration on the day MacQuillan died. 'Several people who were present say he wasn't, and a cabby says he delivered him to the *Post* on Friday afternoon. He remembered the time because it was the last fare he carried before taking a tea-break. I do hope he isn't the murderer, I don't want them to lock up one of my best contacts, but if you ever hear where he really was, I'd love to know.'

As they rang off Mona arrived by Rain's desk to discuss the keys Ruby had found evil. Mona still had them but was about to return them to Maureen. Zak Smythe, breezing back from Eliot's room with his rejected copy, joined in. 'You could ask Maureen whose they are, you're all supposed to be good at interviewing people.'

He ran down the room, jinking around the desks. The previous day the free speech people had drawn an acceptable cartoon which Eliot had agreed to publish and so they had given up going to the office. Zak Smythe showed no signs of ever doing so.

Mona frowned after him. 'I wonder whether the Patriotic Ten will ever leave? They seem happier here than some of the staff. I must convince Eliot it's time to approve what they write, but he's enjoying teaching them. The only problem with their copy now is that it's far too long.' Bringing her mind back to the keys she suggested having a photograph taken so that there would be a record of them if it was ever needed. Rain did not think this necessary but dispatched Rosie on the errand.

Across the room Oliver's desk was unoccupied. She knew it was too much to hope he would arrive in the office with all his worldly possessions, but longed for proof that he had moved out. Presently Rosie scuttled back. Maureen had met her returning from the photographers' room, discovered the keys and taken them. There had been no mention of their true ownership.

But even if they had been MacQuillan's they would have been no use. The desk drawers, as Wickham assured Rain later that morning, had been unlocked when the police went to his room on Friday and had remained unlocked. A number of documents had been in the drawers but not a list of computer codes. He called Marshall and asked him to send Maureen to see him immediately.

Maureen's attempt to move into her father's office and her subsequent compromise of commandeering a desk in the room outside it had been gestures of little practical effect. She was seldom on the premises. Whether this was, as the newsroom quipped, because it had dawned on her she had nothing to do there or whether it was, as the police believed, because she had lost her argument with Wickham, nobody could be certain. Either way, she was not around when Marshall went to look. He was told she was at home.

Wickham reached for his jacket. It was far too hot to wear one but an interview demanded the formality, although why his authority as a questioner should depend on the smallest degree on what he was wearing he could not say. This was not a problem which afflicted journalists who were the most carelessly dressed tribe of professionals he had come across.

Maureen looked annoyed as she opened her door. 'You should have telephoned, superintendent.' Then she tried to soften the reprimand by adding: 'I might not have been here.'

'As you are, perhaps we could come in.' He made a forward movement which obliged her to make way. Had he not assumed the initiative it was feasible she would have given a reason to keep them out.

Wickham went through to the sitting room with its view of the park. A man was on one of the settees, a blond man with his back to Wickham and a glass in his hand. He heard movement and turned. Cecil Hunter-Blair. The MP's mouth sagged. He set the glass on the table before rising. By then he was composed if not actually welcoming, but he was too late. Wickham had seen the initial reaction and was not to forget it.

Throughout the interview Maureen adopted her look of vulnerability. She had chosen to have Hunter-Blair stay, saying she had no objection to his presence if Wickham did not. The remark was tinged with the suggestion that she would like a witness, apart from Marshall whom she could reasonably assume to be biased in Wickham's favour.

Wickham asked her about two aspects: the whereabouts of her father's list of computer codes and the ownership of the keys which had been loaned to Ruby Dobby. They parried before she admitted her father's list had been missing since the day before his death, and he had believed Mona Washbrooke had stolen it and was also guilty of going through his papers.

No evidence was advanced of Mona's guilt, except that she resented the changes at the office and was on friendly terms with Pascoe. The desk, Maureen said, was always kept locked and her father carried the only keys. For this reason she had doubted his claim that anyone had touched his papers but once the list disappeared she did not know what to believe. After his death Mona had found the keys on the floor in the secretary's room and given them to Maureen.

Maureen said: 'I didn't think about them again until that psychic woman asked for them, but it was only after I had given them to her I realized they weren't his at all. His were brass and these were steel. I hadn't noticed before, I was too upset for details like that.'

Mona too, Wickham thought, remembering her palpable shock at MacQuillan's death. Maureen said she had got the keys back and intended to try them in the desk, to see whether they were a duplicate set and her father's complaints could have been justified. Why, asked Wickham, had she not told the police? But she had no satisfactory answer to that.

Hunter-Blair sat with unusual reticence throughout much of the questioning, involving himself only when Maureen floundered. He helped her out when her father's meeting at the Black Friar was raised. 'Ron Barron is a law until himself, superintendent. Maureen wouldn't necessarily understand his moves.'

She flicked back her long loose hair. 'Oh, I have the measure of Ron Barron,' she contradicted. 'He wanted to consolidate his position within the company by being appointed head of the UK operation. His argument was that it would free my father to return to the States, but Ron is never so simple.'

Over the next few minutes Wickham learned that MacQuillan had not wanted to leave Barron in control anywhere, that Maureen and Barron had been and still were jockeying for position and that Maureen had enlisted Hunter-Blair's support. 'I'm afraid,' she said, 'you'll find intrigue everywhere you look, but it's what business thrives on.'

A mite sharply Wickham replied: 'Your father didn't thrive, Miss MacQuillan. Someone murdered him.' He reminded her of her concern when she had heard her father had gone out to lunch the day he died, and he put it to her that she had guessed whom he had met. Cautiously she admitted it but said in the same breath that it was of no consequence because her father had died for political reasons.

Wickham said: 'Miss MacQuillan, there's no evidence so far to support that. The death threats he received in London don't point to it, but if you have any other reason for believing that theory I must ask you to reveal it so that it can be properly investigated.'

She shied off, but it seemed unarguable that she was convinced the killing was political: she had hired Brian Berg to follow that line. Wickham wished he knew the truth about the story Sniffy Wilson had brought out of Gorstone, but that would take time, if not prove impossible, to check; and anyway, a plot plotted was very far from a murder carried out.

He believed Maureen would have mentioned such a story if she had heard one and he took the view that she had no proof whatsoever. When he looked questioningly at Hunter-Blair the man shook his head to show he had nothing to contribute.

Wickham revived the Black Friar meeting, suggesting Maureen knew what Barron wanted to talk to her father about and asking why it had been important to them to meet in a pub instead of one of the two Fleet Street offices at their disposal. She repeated the stuff about Barron urging MacQuillan to leave UK affairs to him, but they all knew she was lying.

'I don't think Hunter-Blair knew the truth, sir,' said Marshall as they walked back to their car. 'He looked as keen to hear her answer as we were.'

But it was Hunter-Blair's earlier air of guilt which had impressed Wickham. On the drive back he considered whether the man were guilty of something more heinous than drinking champagne with a rich young woman on an afternoon when his constituents might reasonably expect him to be in the House of Commons.

Part of the answer came as soon as he reached the *Post*. The deputy editor came to see him. 'Actually,' Linley drawled, 'I'm a bit shamefaced about this. I told you a lie. It was rather a small one and it didn't appear to matter at the time.'

'I'm sure you're not alone in that, Mr Linley. But you're the first to confess.'

Linley offered him a sheet of paper covered with double-spaced typing. 'I found this today and it's revived a memory.'

The style of writing would have identified the text even if the page had not been marked as one of Cecil Hunter-Blair's columns for the paper. Wickham saw the point but waited for Linley's explanation. Linley said: 'That is the copy Hunter-Blair delivered on Friday. I discovered it today in the pocket of a jacket I hadn't worn since then. The second I saw it I remembered what happened. It's not true that I saw no one while I was writing my book reviews in the printer's office. I saw Hunter-Blair. He gave me this and asked me to deliver it to Dick Tavett. I'm rather afraid I forgot.'

Wickham made a swift calculation. Linley had left the restaurant at 3 p.m. and taken a taxi to Fleet Street, a journey of no more than ten minutes even on a busy Friday afternoon. He had made a detour to a café where he stayed for an unspecified time before walking to the *Post* and entering by the back door, discovering the mayhem in the newsroom and retreating to the printer's office. It was improbable that he had accomplished all this before 3.30 p.m. but, between then and the 4 p.m. discovery of the body, Hunter-Blair had talked to him.

Wickham asked: 'How did he know you were there?'

'He saw me by chance. It must have been, I was only there by chance.'

'Did you see him come in through the back door?'

'No, I didn't see him until he was standing beside me. That's where the lie comes in, you see. I told you everything I did that afternoon but I didn't bother to mention I fell asleep. There were four short reviews to do and I dropped off between three and four. When Hunter-Blair had gone I finished the fourth one and went home.'

Wickham wanted to know whether Hunter-Blair had explained why he chose not to deliver the copy himself. Linley said: 'No, but that's not of any significance. He doesn't have to discuss it, just hand it in. He might have been in a rush, with a car badly parked or a taxi ticking. The thing that's teasing my mind is that I'm fairly sure he asked me not to tell anyone he'd been there.'

The 'fairly' was troubling but Wickham had to accept he would get nothing firmer. He had the picture accurately now. Linley had drunk too much at his celebration on a very hot day. The coffee at the café had perked him up long enough to tackle the reviews but then heat and alcohol had won and he had nodded off.

The Linley confession was not the only one that morning. Mona Washbrooke, questioned about finding the keys on the floor and confirming what Maureen had said about them, felt foolish not to have spotted immediately that they were the wrong colour. Then she reported another bit of foolishness: she had concealed and taken home a knife which had been sent to Eliot.

Wickham tried not to look as outraged as he felt. 'When was this?'

'Monday, the same time Rain and Tavett received knives.'

'Then why on earth didn't you say so at the time?'

Mona assumed a quiet dignity before saying she had not wanted Eliot upset. 'It was partly panic, superintendent. Knowing what had happened to Mr MacQuillan, it was horrible to open a package and find a knife. My impulse was to hide it. I couldn't see that telling Luke Eliot or the police was helpful. You already knew there was a hoaxer because of the knife in Simon Linley's pond and the two to the office. A fourth didn't seem necessary.'

Wickham could not conceal that he did not share her view. She said: 'Perhaps not, but Luke Eliot is embattled on many fronts. You've been here long enough now to have formed your own impressions of what goes on. There's the constant struggle with Linley, there was dreadful trouble with MacQuillan and now there's Ron Barron and Maureen MacQuillan, all meddling and dabbling in the editing of the paper.'

He stopped her with an impatient gesture. 'You were being the protective secretary, just looking after the boss.'

It was no compliment. She reddened, said: 'I knew you would think I had taken too much responsibility on myself.'

Wearily he said: 'Miss Washbrooke, you have taken the responsibility of deciding that those knives were sent by a hoaxer and not a murderer. That is rather more responsibility than I am prepared to take.'

She looked aghast, tried to defend her view and then grew apologetic saying that newspaper offices weren't like others, the most extraordinary things turned up in the post all the time and it was reflex to laugh them off and throw them away.

Wickham took pity on her, remembering her anxiety on Monday. He said: 'But you couldn't laugh it off, could you? Isn't that why you went home?'

She admitted it. 'I felt quite sickened.'

An officer went with her to recover the knife from her flat although, like the others, it bore no clues to its sender. 'One more knife and we'll have a set,' murmured Marshall when the news came.

'Not a well-matched one, Jim. The one that killed MacQuillan is like none of the others, neither is the one from the pond. Only the three sent to the office match.' He wondered whether there had been others, also tucked out of sight, and he tried again to see a connection between the recipients he knew of. Had the hoaxer or murderer shown him a pattern which he ought to study to find the sender's intention and ultimately his identity? Or were the knives sent to a random group of people to confuse the hunt for either the killer or the hoaxer?

Another fundamental question resurfaced: was the MacQuillan killing a personal matter or linked entirely to the man's business or political activities? The anti-terrorist branch were looking hard at MacQuillan's political life, but Wickham knew someone who would certainly be able to tell him about the dead man's business life. He arranged to meet Frank Shildon.

Before they met, Marshall announced the absurd news that enquiries in the rag trade had revealed that Trilyn, notorious for its inability to stand up to heavy wear, was most frequently used for trouser pockets.

CHAPTER 19

To Alex Harbury's chagrin Riley would not let him work on the prison release dates story and sent him to interview a *Girlie* winner. Harbury rebelled and went to a Women's Word press reception instead. The publishers had hired a room in a large hotel. The room was twice the size of their back-street Holland Park offices but for a couple of hours all comers were invited to believe that Women's Word was on the same financial footing as its big competitors.

'It's not without influence, though,' Rain said to Harbury whom she had found hanging around near the bar.

It was the third time she had failed to agree with his criticism and offered a compensating compliment. She wondered why he was so morose, he wondered why she was so cheerful. He said: 'Marilyn Duxbody's account of running a naughty knickers mail order catalogue won't have much influence.'

'I'd say it already has,' said Rain. 'Look at the extraordinary cross-section of Fleet Street which has turned up for the launch.'

'It gets odder by the minute,' said Harbury. 'Here's Shildon.'

Shildon joined them and they had a comic argument over the relative merits of writing about the event for the business section, the gossip column or the news pages. Shildon said mail order lingerie was an area the business section had too long ignored, Rain insisted that knickers were gossip column fodder and Harbury remarked that it could probably be shown there had been offences under the Post Office Act.

'I wonder how it compares with sending people knives?' Harbury added.

'Three knives to the office equals one dirty catalogue or two sets of underwear? I expect there are guidelines somewhere,' said Shildon.

Conversation trickled away as the Women's Word public relations officer, a bouncy young woman in a tight bodice, said a few welcoming phrases and introduced Linda Finch. Linda was not only Ms Duxbody's editor, she was also one of the founders of Women's Word and her short talk was consequently a mixture of congratulatory remarks about *Revelations* and a progress report on the company.

Once she got away from lingerie interest flagged and Rain found herself puzzling over something which had been said before the speeches began. Before she had solved it she was distracted by a general movement in the room. Guests who were not already close enough to the bar to reach for fresh glasses of wine edged nearer. It was as though a breeze was sweeping the room and carrying everyone to one side. Linda seemed oblivious, even when the whispered conversations threatened to reach the level of her own voice.

Embarrassed for her, Harbury breathed: 'For heaven's sake introduce Duxbody and sit down!'

'I don't think she can,' Rain murmured in reply.

Eventually Linda gave it up and admitted that Marilyn Duxbody was not present but added, with overtones of hysteria, that she expected her any minute. Linda buried herself in the crowd, exchanging words with this one and that and heading for the bar. Harbury snatched up a glass of wine and took it to her.

Converging on Linda at the same instant with Oliver. Rain saw only that he got there first and Harbury was left holding out the wine glass. Then she turned away and came face to face with Emelda Linley.

'Are these events always like this?' Emelda asked. Rain said not quite, and enquired how Emelda's book on the subjection of Italian women was going. The evasive answers told her progress had been minimal, it was going to be some time before Emelda faced a press launch.

Wainfleet interrupted with loud jokes about the disappearing Duxbody. Shildon closed in on them and mentioned he had arrived late because Wickham had wanted to question him. 'Do you know what line he's taking, Rain?' he asked.

Wainfleet got in first. 'Baffled, that's what he is. The police haven't got a clue who killed MacQuillan. I mean *literally*. It was a smart piece of work. Nothing left at the scene, nothing for Wickham to go on. It'll go down as one of the famous unsolved crimes of history.'

'And one of the least mourned victims,' said Shildon. But he still wanted to hear what Rain had to say. She told him about the puzzle of the second set of keys, then Harbury wandered back and began to say what he knew of the case.

Wainfleet could not resist gloating to Rain over his story of a romance between Hunter-Blair and Maureen. 'That's only the beginning,' he said, 'there'll be much more of that one. Mrs Hunter-Blair telephoned when it appeared. She was furious, denied everything and said her husband would be taking the matter up with my editor. Well, I said the usual pompous things but I had a good laugh when she rang off. Guess where I got the story?'

'He *didn't*!'

'Oh yes he did. Hunter-Blair sent me the photograph himself. I don't pretend to understand the man's mind half the time but he's never short of a story.'

She said: 'Aren't you forgetting that they aren't always true? Like the one about the army camp demonstration?'

Wainfleet pulled a face. 'There's bound to be one rotten apple in every barrel.' He drained his glass and went to fetch another.

The room was emptying. A huddle of photographers gathered up their gear and sloped off. Across the room Linda was repeating her apologies, Oliver hovering in the background. The woman in the tight bodice was wearing a rigid smile and promising to arrange interviews with Ms Duxbody later. Word had reached her that the author was not delayed but quite unable to come.

Rain asked her to say goodbye to Linda for her and was about to go. She wanted to avoid Oliver, although she was desperate to know that he had moved out of the flat. Escape was not so easy. A series of people waylaid her to chat before she was out of the room, and then Emelda came, rather excitable. 'Rain, please take Oliver away. He doesn't seem to realize . . .' Her sentence hung as she looked back down the room to where Oliver and Linda were standing alone.

He was doing nothing more dreadful than lingering, making light-hearted conversation and monopolizing Linda's attention. But Linda had lost her author, she had spent too much effort and money on an event which had become a disaster. The affair was both a personal and a professional humiliation and she looked as though she could cry. With a surge of joy Rain knew that Oliver's insensitivity was no longer her responsibility, that she could walk out of the door and not worry that he had upset people who might, by association, be cross with her.

'*Please*, Rain,' Emelda begged.

Rain's joy vied with sympathy for Linda. If she did as Emelda wanted she could free Linda but would be snared herself. Emelda said: '*I've* tried. I offered him a lift and he said he wasn't in a hurry.' Rain sighed and saved Linda.

Out in the street Oliver looked about and said: 'Where's your car?'

'I lied. It isn't here.' She waved down a taxi.

Puzzled, he got in. He had gone to the launch at Linda's invitation. He had not expected Rain to be there and definitely expected her to leave before he did. In fact, he had hung on waiting for her to go, avoiding her. And then suddenly she had swooped and practically ordered him into her car which, it transpired, she did not have. He found women very confusing.

Rain said: 'Did anyone say what happened to Marilyn Duxbody?' She thought that would be a safe subject for conjecture until they reached the office and went to their separate corners.

'The police raided her house and took her, along with piles of her catalogue, down to the police station. They say she'll be there some time.'

'Oh, poor Linda,' Rain said. 'No wonder she's fed up.'

'Fed up? Did you think so? I thought she'd get rather a lot of cheap publicity.'

Rain objected that if that were the case publishers would be getting authors involved in sordid court cases the whole time. And besides, Women's Word had worked very hard to establish themselves as serious publishers. They believed the Duxbody book had considerable sociological interest.

Oliver snorted. 'These little publishers always say that when they bring out a book everyone else rejected as uncommercial. It's a dustbin operation, publishing what nobody else wants.'

Rain had an awful suspicion. 'You didn't say that to Linda, did you?'

'Shouldn't I have done?'

The car swung into Fleet Street. Oliver cleared his throat in a subject-changing way and said: 'Look, Rain, about Brian Berg . . .'

She said quickly that there was no need to apologize, knowing well that he was not doing so. He tried again: 'I've been thinking . . .'

She guessed what he had been thinking and jumped in with a diverting remark. When they got out of the cab she could not shake him off. He waited while she paid and then walked beside her into the entrance hall. A lift was coming and they waited for it. Oliver had one more shot. 'Rain, about the flat . . .'

The doors of the lift opened. As they were about to ride up someone hurried across the hall. Oliver pressed the button for the first floor but Rain held the door open and allowed Wickham to join them. The brief journey felt interminable. There were pleasantries which meant nothing. The lift was small and Rain was trying to distance herself from Oliver without pressing up against Wickham. Her situation, in every respect, was impossible.

Some while later Harbury appeared by her desk looking buoyant. She could not help saying: 'You've perked up. What happened? Was the *Girlie* winner a rich beauty with a weakness for crime reporters?'

He hushed her and flicked a nervous glance towards Riley and the newsdesk. 'I haven't been to see her yet. I've managed to see Wickham.'

Rain narrowly avoided laughing at him. He said: 'He had to see me this time because I had a clue for him.' He looked at Rosie and Holly, drawing them in and lowering his voice for effect. 'I had to go to the pub to meet one of my contacts. While I was there Sean told me the knife he used to slice the lemons with was stolen last Friday!'

Harbury studied their suitably impressed faces. 'Gosh!' said Holly, to oblige.

* * *

With unfaltering confidence the barman identified the knife from Linley's pond as his lemon-cutting knife. He had not deliberately marked it but to his eyes the pattern of tiny scratches on the handle was as good as a signature. 'I knew it couldn't be the murder weapon,' he gravely told Wickham, 'because I was using it on Friday evening, hours after MacQuillan was found dead.'

At Wickham's prompting he painstakingly recalled everything that had happened in the pub that evening up to the time he missed the knife, and recited a list of names of customers who had been there. Had they been discussing any other evening he would not have been nearly so competent but the murder pinpointed the day.

At one stage Marshall opened his mouth to interject but Wickham stopped him. Afterwards, when they were alone, Marshall said: 'If that was an accurate account, one person had ample opportunity to take the knife off the bar and we already know he was at Linley's party.' He picked up the telephone.

'He's the least likely murderer, though, Jim,' said Wickham as they waited for the man to join them. 'All we can hope from this meeting is that he admits being the hoaxer. Then perhaps we can forget all about those knives and concentrate on finding the killer.'

But John Wainfleet would only confess to taking Sean's knife and putting it in the pond as a joke. He adamantly denied sending the other knives.

'All right, I'm sorry about the knife in the pond,' he said, raising his hands in submission. 'It was just one of those things which seemed a good idea at the time. If you'd ever been to a party at the Linleys you'd understand. They're not the liveliest occasions.'

But Wickham's expression was steely. Wainfleet carried on: 'I've apologized — I'll even apologize to Linley if it'll make any difference — but what more can I do?'

'You can do nothing to make up for the time that's been wasted checking for a link between that incident and the murder of Hal MacQuillan.'

Wainfleet protested that he could not fairly be accused of wasting police time with his practical joke because he had not anticipated the police being informed. Wickham thought that a weak defence and said: 'The Linleys were rather disturbed by the incident . . .'

'It would have failed as a joke if they hadn't been, wouldn't it?'

Wickham suggested that once he'd had his fun with the Linleys he could have owned up and put their minds at rest. Wainfleet said: 'I told you, it seemed a good idea *at the time*. Afterwards it didn't, so I kept quiet.'

With more petulance then penitence he described how he had noticed Sean's knife as the barman was called away to serve a customer. He suddenly thought of using it to play a joke on some of his friends at the *Post*, concealed it in his newspaper and left the pub. He had no clear idea what he was going to do but expected a good gathering at Linley's house and thought an opportunity would occur. When he arrived there were disappointingly few people and he felt rather obvious holding on to a rolled-up newspaper. But just when he thought he would have to drop the paper and the knife in the dustbin and abandon the joke, he spotted the pond.

Other people were near the table with the drinks and nobody noticed him slide the knife into the water. Then he threw the paper in the dustbin and planned to stage discovery of the knife later. 'I was going to pretend something had fallen in, reach into the water and come up with the knife,' he said. 'But it was a good thing I wasn't impatient, because the entertainment Linda and Emelda provided was far superior to anything I could have managed.'

His amusement at the scene was rekindled. Wickham quashed it with some hard questions. Wainfleet's answers took them no nearer the truth about the murderer or the sender of the other knives. He appeared irritatingly triumphant that he could not assist, as though that justified his attitude to the knife in the pond. Marshall said, after he had gone, that he doubted Wainfleet could take a serious view of anything.

But while Wainfleet's apology had been specious and he really did not see what all the fuss was about, he was not quite as carefree as he had let them think. He resented being called from his office to be reprimanded. As he walked back up Fleet Street he thought it would be very satisfying to get even with Wickham one day.

CHAPTER 20

Cecil Hunter-Blair's London *pied à terre* was a cramped flat above a pizza restaurant close to Trafalgar Square. It was not a place to which he could take Maureen MacQuillan or any woman, and only partly because he shared it with a fellow MP. His flatmate had a mistress in Hampstead and so was seldom there, but the flat was squalid and the scents of garlic and oregano rose from the kitchens below. When Wickham called no one was in.

He dithered, wondering whether to go to the restaurant for a cup of coffee while hoping Hunter-Blair would return or else to find a telephone and call his office. Uncharacteristically, he decided the telephone call could wait. He was hungry, the smells of food reminded him breakfast had been skipped and lunch forgotten.

Just as he started down the stairs a man ran in from the street and pounded up, head bent and arms cradling a flat box, the tell-tale sign of a take-away pizza. Hunter-Blair looked up, full of surprise. 'Superintendent! You've caught me at a very late lunch. Come in, come in.'

He kicked open the door and rushed to the far end of a large room. There were a kitchen table and two metal chairs, beyond them a worktop with a built-in cooker and nearby china and food cupboards. In the sink were dirty dishes, through a door an unmade single bed. Two other doors were shut.

Hunter-Blair bounced his pizza on to a plate and rattled through a drawer for a knife. He hacked the pizza into pieces and asked Wickham whether he would like some. Ravenous, Wickham declined.

'Oh dear,' said Hunter-Blair, pulling out a chair. 'More questions about MacQuillan, I suppose. Well, you'll have to excuse me. I have to down this and get to the House in half an hour. The Whips will kill me if I'm not there.'

Wickham might have commented that his business took precedence over a vote on the future of the chewing gum industry, but his priorities were not a politician's priorities. He asked instead why Hunter-Blair had not said he was at the *Post* on the day of the murder and why he had troubled to ask Linley to keep his presence secret.

'Oh, that,' said Hunter-Blair, strings of melted cheese linking his mouth to the piece of pizza in his hand. He gulped down the mouthful before saying: 'Well, that's pretty obvious, if I may say so. Nobody asked me if I was there, and it would do my career no good at all to have my name mentioned in a murder case. I've got nothing to hide.'

'Then why hide the fact?'

Hunter-Blair tore off another mouthful of pizza. Then he dropped the rest of the portion back on the plate, went to the fridge, poured the dregs of a bottle of wine into a glass and drank it. 'You see . . .' he said, and, after another false start, 'You've clearly found out I saw MacQuillan. I should have known you would. Well, I mean to say, I've got total admiration for the way you chaps work. I knew you might work it out but I reasoned that if I didn't rush forward to explain all, you might catch the culprit first and never have to trouble me.'

Wickham showed no sympathy. 'We haven't made an arrest and I do have to trouble you.'

'Quite so.' He put the empty glass on the draining board. 'I'd better tell you then, hadn't I?' He looked at his watch. 'I could play games, but I've got to catch that vote so this will have to be quick. MacQuillan was alive when I left him and in fighting form.'

Rapidly he described how he had gone to the paper with two missions that Friday afternoon: to deliver his column to Tavett and to tackle MacQuillan about the increasing anger among the print unions. He had gone in and out by the rear door and back stairs and seen no one but Linley.

Unfortunately he could not offer a time for his visit. He said he had wanted to convince MacQuillan that it was no longer fashionable to manoeuvre unions into illegal acts and invoke the law to take revenge on them. MacQuillan, as a newcomer to the Fleet Street scene and a man who was averse to advice from others, appeared not to have realized this. Hunter-Blair said he warned MacQuillan that it was being whispered around Westminster that the unions had evolved a protective strategy and were looking for an opportunity to test it. The *Post* was thought to be one of the more vulnerable titles.

'How did he take this?' Wickham asked.

'He was livid, as though I had stirred up the printers against him and come to say "I told you so" once they'd walked out.' He said he tried previously to warn MacQuillan of the risks he was running. 'I told him he had to go carefully, he was not in the strong position he liked to imagine. In every other way he was doing wonders but it would all be lost if he fell into a trap and saw the paper closed. That wasn't a truth he wanted to hear so there was quite a heated exchange. After that I forgot about seeing Tavett and didn't remember until I was leaving the building. Then I saw Linley, dozing in the printers' room, and asked him to deliver the copy.'

Wickham asked who else knew about his meeting with MacQuillan and he said he had told only Maureen, adding superfluously that they were close friends. He checked his watch again, saying: 'Look, I've got to get a move on. I've told you everything now, there isn't anything else, I promise. You're welcome to search this place if that's of interest to you, but please, I must beg you not to let the press get a whiff of my name. You know how damaging publicity can be, even to an innocent bystander.'

He rushed out, calling to Wickham to pull the door shut when he went. Wickham gave a jaundiced look at the cooling pizza and followed him down the stairs.

'We're getting warmer, sir,' said Marshall when they met up. 'Now we've got two people who admit going to the second floor that afternoon: Pascoe and Hunter-Blair. I suppose . . .' He screwed up his face. 'I suppose it's just possible Hunter-Blair had a motive as well as an opportunity. If he believed Maureen would run things the way he wanted and her father might blunder into a union trap and have the paper shut down and he would have nowhere to publish his views, then he might have killed MacQuillan?'

Wickham gave him the withering look of a man whose junior reads too many detective stories. Hunter-Blair's deep interest was politics, not newspapers. Warning MacQuillan against his folly was one thing, killing him to save him from it was going too far. All the same, Wickham had been invited to have the flat searched and might sometime do so, although for the moment he saw no justification for it.

Marshall set off in a new direction. 'Ron Barron has left the country, sir. He telephoned his secretary from Heathrow to say he was boarding a flight for New York.'

Shildon had an explanation for Barron's haste. When Wickham met him that evening he told a tale that shook the MacQuillan empire to its core. Wickham's initial feeling was that if it were true the only surprising thing was that Barron had not flown away sooner. Later he reflected that perhaps it was not so surprising because of the conflict Maureen had described between Barron and her father and between Barron and herself.

Wickham was finding Frank Shildon very useful although his thanks embarrassed the man, because Shildon did not fit the stereotype of people anxious to display their knowledge. Many police inquiries brought one or two of those to the fore and mostly their motive was the uncomplicated one of gaining praise and attention. Occasionally they were compulsive attention-seekers who had little to tell and invented where truth fell short.

But Shildon had a tidy card-index mind that produced substantiating evidence for what he said. His replies to Wickham's questions were direct and his information reliable. There was probably no subject, Wickham realized, that at least one person in the newsroom could not discuss with authority but it was a bit of time-saving luck that Shildon had investigated MacQuillan.

'You've been very thorough,' Wickham told him, and regretted that it sounding patronizing. Shildon reminded him that it was not wholly the fruit of his investigation for Eliot, he had a head start because he used to work for MacQuillan in Detroit.

CHAPTER 21

Along with the *Daily Post* Martin Ayling had inherited Hatherley, an estate of hundreds of acres of good Cotswold riding country and a house which would not have disgraced minor royalty. His decision to sacrifice the newspaper to MacQuillan rather than sacrifice the estate to the newspaper had not met with universal approval, but he did not let that trouble him. Indeed it had never occurred to him to sell bits of Hatherley to keep the paper going any more than he had considered using the profits of the paper, in the years when there were some, to pay for the substantial renovation the house had required.

He had the facility for keeping his life, as well as his businesses, in separate compartments. When neighbours who entertained him in Knightsbridge spent a rare weekend at Hatherley they were surprised at the switch from newspaper owner to farmer, a switch so thorough that the paper was not mentioned the whole time they were there. It was not seen, either, and a story was founded that Ayling would not allow it in the house. (The mundane truth was that the delivery boy had forgotten it, but the correction did not circulate as efficiently as the rumour.)

Once a year for several years Ayling had let his town life and his country life mingle. The Hatherley ball to raise money for a hospice charity had become an important event in Gloucestershire because Ayling did what people craved on such occasions: he brought them the rich and famous whom they usually saw only on their television screens or in their newspapers. And in the train of the rich and famous came the journalists.

The rich and famous had not arrived by the time Rain Morgan did, although there were plenty of county folk poised to spot them. She was taken to a comfortable bedroom with stone mullions and changed into clothes appropriate for the occasion. Then she went to find Ayling.

The house was filling up. A squealing young woman called Clarissa was being chased along a passage by a young man called Toby. A band was playing and everyone was talking at increased volume to make themselves heard above it. Rain's arm was gripped by a dowager in green silk, the woman recognizing her from her byline picture in the paper and wanting to know who had killed MacQuillan. Smiling, Rain disappointed her and escaped. There were other similar encounters before she caught Ayling's eye across the room.

An actress cornered her with snippets of information about herself which she hoped Rain would publish. Rain would not; they were far too mundane. And then, devoid of any more self-promoting ideas, the woman told Rain something shocking about another actress. Rain made a mental note to get Holly to follow up the story next day, she could visualize it leading the column on Friday unless anything better turned up.

Better things did. It was remarkable the way people sought her out, often not minding that their conversation was public. There was a particularly promising yarn about a young duke, and Tavett liked a high count of dukes in the column. Rain meant to verify that story herself, the duke himself was less than twenty feet away. She inched towards him, daring him to move before she had shaken off the latest man to accost her. And then she saw Vanessa Kyle.

Vanessa was in the circle of people gathered about Rain's quarry. Patrick pretended to hide when he saw Rain was after him. He grabbed Vanessa, ducked down behind her. The others gleefully pointed him out. Rain felt his antics virtually confirmed her story. She said: 'It's no use, Patrick. I've got you surrounded. You might as well come out.'

He stood up but stayed behind Vanessa, his hands on her upper arms, her red hair brushing his face. 'It's not fair,' he said. 'Someone's been telling tales again.'

His friends demanded to know what tales but Rain and he mocked their curiosity and would not say. Abruptly he stopped fooling and stepped away from Vanessa, saying: 'You two know each other, don't you?'

Together Rain and Vanessa said yes. One of the men said: 'Vanessa, isn't your policeman looking for the man who killed Rain's boss?'

This prompted some quips during which Vanessa's reply was lost. Then Patrick changed the subject and when they were all away on the new tack he took Rain aside. She said: 'It's about the dog track.' He groaned. She said: 'I've got enough but we might as well get it right, mightn't we?'

'Who told you?' She would never tell him, he knew that. He said: 'I'll bet it was Reggie Parminter. It was, wasn't it?' He was right but she gave no hint. He said: 'Well then, *I've* got something to say about *him*, and it's a bit juicier than my nonsense at the dog track. I'm going to have my revenge on young Reggie, but not here. Too many eavesdroppers.' He giggled: 'We ought to creep out singly for an assignation.'

She was fleetingly reminded of Shildon insisting they walked singly into the newsroom so no one should know they had been talking together. She said: 'There's a library. Somewhere over that way, I believe. On the left.'

They fixed a time and he turned back to his friends. Rain glided away, heading for a politician of doubtful integrity.

There *was* a library but Rain and Patrick did not meet there because her recollection was wrong and they blundered into each other in a passage. He told her his version of events at the dog track and then about Parminter. The Parminter tale was utterly scandalous and she would have to persuade

Wilmot to skate around the libel laws if it were to get into print, but she kept these reservations to herself.

Patrick immediately began to justify his breach of a friend's confidence. 'Of course, I'd never have breathed a syllable if he'd kept quiet about the dog track.'

'Of course not.' She wrestled to look solemn.

'I must say, though, I do enjoy getting my own back.'

They moved towards the sounds of the party. Then he asked: 'Rain, you're not going to write anything about Vanessa, are you? She wouldn't be happy.' He looked relieved when she said no one had told her anything.

The evening flowed on. Rain met people who had been avoiding her for months and others she had been dodging. If half the stories she picked up earned space in the column the ball was a success from her rather peculiar point of view. Other people were also having a good time: the level of noise had edged up and up; the charity organizers, women with greedy smiles, were counting piles of money; and Clarissa was still leading Toby a chase.

Eventually it was all over. The band played going-home music; the charity women said profuse thanks to Ayling who had been 'so wonderful'; and the handful of people who were to stay overnight slumped in the smallest of the sitting rooms. Rain had met some of them on previous occasions. Experience convinced her that the man who was drunk would lecture them on the futility of dying, a theme prompted by the first mention of hospices. The others would be pinned there by a courtesy he did not merit.

Rain snatched an early chance to say goodnight and Ayling walked with her to the foot of the stairs, asking after people at the *Post* and showing every wish to go on talking. She failed to smother a yawn and he apologized, saying: 'Go on up, I shouldn't be detaining you. Will you have time to talk in the morning?'

There was something very attractive about delaying her return to the poisonous atmosphere of the office. 'As much as you like.'

'Good. We'll ride for a while. That's the best way to see Hatherley.'

She went upstairs eager for the comfort of her room. When she switched on the light her cosy mental picture was shattered by crude reality. Sprawled on top of her bed were Clarissa and Toby, half-undressed and asleep. They woke in panic and, accompanied by Clarissa's yelps, were thrown out. Rain felt distinctly uncharitable as she straightened the bed and tried to pretend they had never been there.

* * *

When she went down to breakfast there was the background noise of caterers clearing away the vestiges of the ball. Otherwise the house was silent. None of the other guests had stirred, judging by the untouched food in the covered dishes on the sideboard. She filled her plate and sat at a table by a window. Outside was a lawn, clipped trim as a general's moustache, but browning in patches and along the edge as though the general were a heavy smoker. The window was open, the sky unbroken blue.

'I can't think why we didn't hold the ball outside,' said Ayling coming in with newspapers under his arm. 'It would have saved all the cleaning and clearing that's going on today, but I suppose we simply did what we always do. It's remarkable how quickly a tradition establishes itself.'

She took the paper he offered. A slight frown marred her face as she saw the Donaldson item in print, a reminder that the problem of Maureen and Holly was not going to go away on its own. She still did not know what to do about it.

'Is something wrong?' asked Ayling.

Rain showed him the offending paragraphs. 'This. I don't believe it and I tried to kill it.' She told him about Holly and Maureen and the MacQuillan plan for a three-page gossip column. The tale was distressing to Ayling and she knew she ought to have curtailed it but she could not resist going on. At the back of her mind a small demon was saying: 'Why shouldn't he be upset? It's all his fault. If only he hadn't sold to that dreadful man, you wouldn't be having such a miserable time.'

Chastened, Ayling got up to fetch coffee and his own breakfast. He had been up for hours, out on the farm, before eating. 'I trusted MacQuillan,' he said quietly. 'No doubt I was gullible and he was dishonest, but I didn't foresee any of the problems which have arisen.'

'Martin, nobody thinks . . .' she lied.

'Yes, of course I'm to blame. Three generations of Aylings ran a respectable newspaper and I handed it over to someone who sent it plummeting down-market, used it to promote an extreme political view and was a thoroughly bad employer.' There was a lengthy pause before she said he had been allowed no choice. He retorted that the choice had been to close the paper and he wished he had done that because it would have been remembered as a decent publication.

Rain reminded him he would have put hundreds of people out of work. He appeared to ignore her, saying his folly had been to believe one could sell a newspaper with as little responsibility as a man selling apples off a stall. Then he said: 'What are the jobs worth now? I keep hearing of people being sacked or getting out. You must have thought about going.'

She gave a wry smile and said the thought had crossed her mind. 'I want to see what difference it makes now MacQuillan has gone.'

'I'd hoped it would have made an improvement,' he said. 'It looks as though I was wrong about that, too.'

One of the other guests arrived for breakfast and the subject was dropped, only to resurface briefly when the woman discovered in the paper she was reading John Wainfleet's account of Sniffy Wilson's allegations of an Irish plot to kill MacQuillan.

Ayling's final words about MacQuillan echoed in Rain's mind as they went to the stables, especially the tone of them. Bitterness. Anger. Disillusionment. It was virtually impossible to say aloud that one welcomed the death of a fellow human being, but she believed that was how Ayling had felt. Since Friday she had met many people who had every reason to be relieved, but Ayling had come closest to saying he was glad.

They rode out of the stable yard. He had saddled for her a calm, unflustered mare and they hacked peacefully along remarking on the hardness of the ground, the atrophied crops and other manifestations of summer. 'I'll show you something interesting,' he promised. 'We have to be some way above it to see it clearly. We'll go up to the ridge.' They wound up the valley on a broad ride through trees.

She could guess roughly what he was promising but let him keep his secret. He cut into her thoughts with a question about the ball and she repeated her earlier assurance that she'd had a successful evening, adding that in all conscience she ought to have been driving back to London to work on some of the stories.

'London is no place to be in a heatwave,' he said. 'I'm rather pleased to be able to keep away from it.'

She almost asked whether he had not been there the previous Friday but stopped, unsure whether he had forgotten or was deliberately misleading her. Before she could shape a probing question he urged his horse forward and without waiting to be encouraged Rain's mare sped after it. The trees were left behind and the yellowing fields flashed by until Ayling slowed the pace as they crested the ridge. He looked round as she caught him up. His face was glowing with boyish pleasure. 'Over there,' he said.

Rain looked down into the steep cleft of another valley. On the far side rectangular shapes showed beneath the grass. 'Roman?' she wondered aloud.

'Almost certainly. I'm hoping someone will find it worth while having a proper inspection but these things pop up everywhere when the land is so dry. This probably won't rate very highly in archaeological circles but I'm rather pleased about it.'

He said he had first noticed impressions in the earth some years ago when the first of the long hot summers had come. In successive years the outline had grown more pronounced and the current rainless spell exaggerated them yet more. Aerial photographers scanning the country for just such signs had recorded the Hatherley evidence and told him it was virtually certain to be a Roman villa, but that archaeologists would give precedence to the more important sites.

'Until these places are excavated there's no knowing what treasures might be there,' he said. 'It doesn't follow that the bigger sites contain all the best things.' He eased his horse round and they ambled along the ridge until the ground fell steeply away and a great valley stretched below them, a silver river sketched through it. Although it was morning the scene shimmered, a haze hid hills beyond the valley. Nothing was clear, there were only suggestions of villages, churches, farms, woods. Features were obscured and distances confused.

Ayling said he had wasted her time, they could see nothing although this was a famous viewpoint. He led the way back to Hatherley, threading through brittle woods. When they reached the stables a groom took the horses and Rain and Ayling entered the house by a back way. There was a telephone message for her to call Harbury.

'Pascoe's dead,' Harbury said as soon as she got through. In her shocked silence he told her Pascoe had been found dead that morning but no one could get details. 'You know Mrs Pascoe, don't you?'

She said: 'I met her for the first time this week.'

'Well, you know Wickham, anyway.'

A cold apprehension seeped through her. Harbury was saying: 'The Pascoes' telephone isn't being answered. I heard about his death from one of my police contacts but nobody will tell us what happened. The rumour here is that he killed MacQuillan and now he's committed suicide.'

She wished she could tell him that was nonsense but she feared Pascoe's death was confirmation of something she had imagined, not proof of something she had found incredible. She agreed to ring Wickham.

She wanted to get it over fast but Ayling, hearing her put the receiver down, came into the room. He understood from her face that there had been bad news. She prevaricated, wanting the story verified or denied before sharing it with him, but he couldn't be expected to know that. He made her tell him.

Just as her words were out one of the charity women came chattering in through the open doors to the terrace. She had news about the clearing-up operations and enquiries about a necklace lost by someone called Clarissa. Rain abandoned Ayling and telephoned Wickham.

First she got someone she did not know, then she got Marshall and finally she got Wickham. He said he had been informed of Pascoe's death but could make no statement about it. She objected to his formal jargon, although she imagined a glint of amusement accompanying it. Then he said: 'I'm more interested than the rest of you to know whether he killed himself. Until the post mortem's carried out none of us will.'

She wanted details about Pascoe but he offered only that the man had been found dead at home. When she demanded whether there were any suspicious circumstances he refused to be drawn and took over the questioning: 'Why didn't you say Ayling was here on Friday?' He sounded angry; she had been wrong about the amusement.

'You didn't ask,' she said simply.

'I didn't ask Oliver either but he told me Ayling delivered a letter to you. How much do you know about his visit?'

'Nothing at all. The letter was delivered by hand but I don't know whether he brought it himself.'

Wickham said they would know soon enough because he had sent someone to ask Ayling. She guessed he did not know she was calling from Hatherley. She did not enlighten him, rang off and warned Ayling the police were going to question him.

Ayling was unperturbed. 'They'll be wasting their time. I didn't go right into the building. I had an engagement in town that morning so I didn't post the letter. I decided to call round with it and have a word with Eliot if he was there. I walked from Holborn but as I got close I discovered the attraction of setting foot in there again had faded rather badly.'

He said he had planned to use the back door, go through to reception, leave the letter and disappear the same way. When he went through the back door he discovered the printers had gone home and thought at first no one was there. Then he saw Shildon. 'I asked him to hand the letter to you. That's all. I got a taxi as soon as I stepped out of the back door. The police are going to be very disappointed, I'm afraid. I saw nothing suspicious and I know nothing of what happened on the second floor.' He dismissed the matter as a trivial diversion and returned to what concerned him deeply: Pascoe's death.

Rain's mind was only half on what he was saying. She had no reassurance to offer and he was convinced of his own responsibility because the sale to MacQuillan had set in train the events leading to Pascoe's despair.

'Martin,' she said gently, 'it hasn't been confirmed that he killed himself.'

He looked startled. She had not been brutal enough to mention the office rumour and Ayling had not expected his words to be interpreted that way. 'I shouldn't think that at all likely,' he said. 'I believe he was killed by the pressure he was under. We spoke a week ago on the telephone and he told me he was desperate. That was his word, and it struck me at the time that it was extreme language for a man of his temperament. He certainly sounded as though he couldn't stand much more.'

Rain argued that once Pascoe had left the paper he ought to have put it out of his mind. This was an insensitive remark, and Ayling shamed her by suggesting that the things one ought to be able to do were often impossible. He no longer meant Pascoe, he meant himself. Before she could comment he made the point that people did not switch off anger once they had extricated themselves from the risk of further suffering, especially not if they had leisure to reflect on injustice. Bitterness was enduring as well as destructive.

There was an uncomfortable pause while they both thought of Pascoe in his enforced retirement, watching the river flow by his garden and reliving in his mind the wretched end to his career. Then Ayling's housekeeper came to ask how many people there would be for lunch and Rain declined an invitation to stay. She wanted to be gone before the police arrived and Ayling did not press her with convincing enthusiasm. She thought he welcomed some time alone.

Her final sight of Hatherley was from the lane which skirted the park for a short distance. The magnificent Tijou gates of the main entrance were no longer opened and the drive to the house was greening with disuse. A Volvo estate car was parked outside the gates and a middle-aged couple picnicked on the grass verge. The woman bore a disconcerting resemblance to Mrs Pascoe.

Then Rain's car was round the bend and the house vanished. She did not know how many miles or minutes she would have to drive before she left Ayling farmlands behind too. Three villages on she passed a Hatherley Inn with a coat of arms painted on the wall panel above its low front door. And at the junction beyond it she saw a brown car driven by a man whose face was familiar. He was one of the men working on the MacQuillan case.

CHAPTER 22

A spirited argument was going on around the sweetheart plant when Rain got back from Hatherley. People were defending their opinions as to the identity of the murderer and scoffing at others. One of the most pedantic of the sub-editors was saying: 'You're all looking for somebody with what *you* call a reason, but his thinking will be at variance with yours.'

Nobody tangled with that line. Ruby Dobby's earrings became energetic as she insisted that there were more than five senses to be employed in any search for the truth. Rain ousted Zak Smythe from her chair and asked what was going on.

Harbury told her: 'Eliot was also sent a knife on Monday and it looks as though Tavett has been arrested for murder.'

Mona had recovered from whatever embarrassment she had felt at the Eliot knife becoming common knowledge, and said crisply: 'I can't believe that's true about Pascoe, Alex.'

That set them off again, Harbury enthusiastically reciting the string of reasons why the police had questioned Tavett several times; Oliver throwing in that Tavett might have *known* about it but Pascoe must have *done* it; Zak saying it was political assassination and nothing to do with the staff of the paper; Holly reminding him that Scotland Yard's anti-terrorist branch had found nothing to support that; and Rosie hushing the clamour because her telephone was ringing.

In the relative quiet that followed Harbury appealed to Rain for information about Wickham, ignoring that she'd had no success over Pascoe. She wished he would stop talking, because something one of them had said had stirred the memory of a puzzling moment. But she was allowed no space to think about it. Harbury rattled on: 'I know he'd rather make a statement later on and give it simultaneously to everyone. Well, I don't think that's good enough, not when it's *our* murder and our features editor who's been charged.'

'Arrested? Charged? Are either of them true?' she asked. Harbury's loose talk suggested he had few facts.

He said: 'I honestly don't know. Tavett was taken from here by the police yesterday and he hasn't come in today. The police aren't telling us anything — I haven't been able to get as far as Marshall and the others just look mysterious and say they don't know.'

It emerged that Harbury had rung Tavett's home and been told by his wife that he was unwell and had gone to the doctor's surgery. Harbury had chosen not to believe her. He said to Rain: 'I'd expect her to cover up if he was still with the police.'

She said that being a crime reporter was having a bad influence on him, but agreed, for the sake of her own curiosity as much as his, to try Wickham.

Holly said: 'But take care. Today's other rumour is that he's furious with all journalists because of this.' She showed Rain that morning's John Wainfleet column. Alongside the item about Sniffy Wilson and the MacQuillan death plot, Holly had ringed a story about Vanessa taking up with a rich young duke after the break-up of her marriage to Wickham. Wainfleet had not avoided the slur that Wickham was giving more attention to his private life than his professional and this accounted for the lack of progress in apprehending MacQuillan's killer.

Rain thought this unusually malicious for Wainfleet and wondered what could possibly be behind it. Rosie said: 'Ask him, he's always asking you things.'

Harbury intervened: 'But would you mind trying Wickham for me first?'

The line was engaged so she went upstairs, thinking that keeping Harbury happy was becoming a burden. The feeling intensified when she met Marshall who gave a knowing look and said: 'I expect you're working for Mr Harbury.' His fluffy hair was newly washed and standing out like a halo.

'I'm interested on my own account too.'

'Well, it won't do any good. We're rather busy despite what some journalists are saying.'

'John Wainfleet? What have the police done to upset him?'

Marshall smiled contentedly as he said: 'We got him to confess to putting the knife in the pond.'

Wickham appeared on his way from MacQuillan's room to the typists' office. 'Pascoe had a heart attack,' he said. 'That should scotch the suicide gossip.' He had begun to walk on when she asked about Tavett. He repeated the name, waiting for her to expand. She said roughly what Harbury had. Wickham looked at Marshall who said it was the first he had heard of it either.

'No arrest. No charge,' she reported to Harbury. 'They talked to him yesterday afternoon, that was all. Mrs Tavett's honesty is vindicated, even if you harbour doubts about Dick's.'

They forgot about Tavett and moved on to discuss Pascoe and how, when they came to think of it, he had looked very like a man waiting for a major heart attack. While they were saying so, Marshall was contacting Mrs Tavett and learning that her husband had said he was going to the surgery that morning but had not been home since. The doctor's receptionist had not seen him.

'Shall we look for him, sir?' Marshall asked. But Wickham said not. Tavett was free to go where he liked and there were no grounds to hamper him. He looked increasingly more like a confused and inadequate witness than a killer. Even so, Wickham was not ready to shut the door on the possibility.

He had absolutely, however, set his face against accepting help from Ruby Dobby although she had arrived on the second floor that morning full of promises if not promise. She had laid siege to the typists' room for some minutes before Marshall had persuaded her downstairs. In the newsroom, hours later, no one had been able to shift her.

'Oh, what a wretched nuisance that Miss MacQuillan has got the keys back,' she said to Rain. 'I so much want to try again. You see, I was on my astrological cusp on Monday, it wasn't at all propitious for me. But now my powers are fully active.'

Rain murmured that it was a pity the keys had gone and made an effort to get Ruby to go too. Then Rosie burst out with the helpful statement that she had a photograph of the keys and if Ruby's powers were very strong she might manage with that. She gave it to Ruby who crowed with delight while Rain and Holly looked at Rosie with unreadable expressions.

'That creature is a charlatan,' said Rain, sore about Ruby claiming extra-sensory perception of her visit to Epping Forest.

Holly, with unreasonable charity, said: 'She was on Monday but perhaps today will be different. She must be successful sometimes or she wouldn't make her living at it.'

One obvious difference was that Ruby worked more calmly than on Monday. There was little to show for her effort apart from the occasional flexing of her fingers and a long-drawn-out breath. Then she opened her eyes and focused on Rain. 'No good, Ruby?' Rain asked, ready to sympathize and ask her to leave.

'As a matter of fact,' said Ruby confidentially but loud enough to make Rosie and Holly keel over to hear. 'I had a strong sense of . . .'

'Evil?' prompted Holly.

Ruby flashed her a look. 'Yes, evil,' she confirmed coolly. 'Or perhaps not exactly that but . . . *bitterness.*'

'As in lemons?' queried Rosie.

'No, dear,' said Ruby. 'More the sort of bitterness that comes from ruined hope, you know.'

'Hm,' said Rosie who was not certain she did.

All at once Ruby leaped to her feet, flying colours and bobbing earrings. She tossed the photograph on to Rosie's desk. 'I should get rid of this, dear. I feel there's something bad associated with it.'

'But *what?*' wailed Holly, as Ruby floated down the room and out of sight on her way to the street.

Rain put the photograph in her bag. She had no use for it but suspected Rosie had been alarmed. Then they all turned their attention to the real work of the day. There were interruptions: Oliver coming to ask what Ruby Dobby had been up to, and Shildon asking Rain for the latest news about the murder. In each case Rain confessed ignorance and left explanations to Rosie who was in a chatty mood.

But after he had left them Rain wondered whether Shildon might not want to see her about his MacQuillan inquiry, a matter other events had put out of her mind. She dialled his extension. There was a fractional hesitation before he said yes, and suggested meeting after work at a pub off Hatton Garden.

Before then the office came alive with two pieces of news: Sniffy Wilson had been captured and Marilyn Duxbody had been charged under the Obscene Publications Act. Riley said the paper's priority would be Sniffy and the success of the police in snatching all the escaped prisoners. But this was not a wholly popular view as most reporters welcomed the chance to write about naughty knickers for a change and leaven the fare of their working lives. 'Harbury's the crime man,' said a voice, 'what's his opinion?'

'Forget Harbury,' said Riley exasperated. 'From next Monday he's responsible for interviewing the *Girlie* winners and nothing else.'

There were shocked protests but the argument degenerated into a disgruntled murmur as people reflected that to cross Riley might mean ending up as Harbury's assistant on the *Girlie* patrol. Someone went to commiserate with Harbury and Harbury went to lacerate Riley for announcing an appointment he had no intention of accepting.

The room erupted as first Harbury and then Riley stamped into the editor's office. Eliot was taking a day off and they got Linley. 'You're too late, Riley,' said Linley laconically. 'You're wasting your breath telling me what you want done with Harbury. He's just resigned.'

Riley swore and Linley drawled that there was nothing to get upset about, because Harbury had himself cleared the way for the man Riley wanted appointed. Riley pulled an ear and bit a lip and said this was all very well but the trouble was he had learned the other man was unwilling to move to the *Post* after all.

'Oh dear, Riley, we have made a mess of things, haven't we?' said Linley unkindly. 'I wonder why you told everyone Harbury had lost the crime job if you didn't have his successor neatly lined up?'

'Because,' said Riley through gritted teeth, 'I was told to keep up the pressure on him.'

'Ye-es,' said Linley as though he were considering the predicament with sympathy. 'But I'm sure I didn't tell you to do anything silly.'

Riley bridled. 'It's not all that silly — you wanted him to go and now he's gone.'

'But this way you run the risk of a strike. If you'd shuffled him into, say, motoring, no one would have cared. It would have meant the hole was stopped, they couldn't be pushed into it themselves. But this way . . .' He tut-tutted.

Riley snarled and went back to the newsroom. Harbury was doing what Holly would call a lap of honour, circling the room saying goodbyes. Rain trapped him in the corner by the empty water machine. 'You can't leave now,' she said flatly.

'After *that?*'

'Especially after that. It's not up to Riley who comes and goes.'

'But I've told Linley.'

She said that a few cross words with Riley and Linley did not count for much. And when he sagged and said he'd had enough of the place and it was not what he had thought it would be, she said life never was and that if he wanted to stay in Fleet Street he would be foolish to leave without a new job to go to. 'Besides,' she said, 'what you want is a decent story completed, not a good one abandoned.'

He conceded she was right but admitted that the frustration of having the MacQuillan case within feet of his desk and very little more information than reporters miles away had worn down his enthusiasm. Worse, Riley had been chiding him for not providing a string of exclusive MacQuillan stories but the ones he had written were being held over until they were out of date or appeared elsewhere. 'I knew he was doing it because he wanted me out. It's the classic method, isn't it?' he said miserably.

She said yes. There was no other answer which would not have been a lie. It angered her that anyone's work should be treated cavalierly because someone with a little authority regarded a newsroom as a draughts board. She had an idea and asked him to meet her that evening at a time which allowed her to see Shildon first. Then she convinced him he was to say no more about leaving and get back to the story he had been working on when the row blew up.

Holly looked quizzical when she sat down again but she was too busy and too uncertain to explain. An authoritative denial of the Donaldson item came in and Rain passed it to Holly who regretted believing the man or the MacQuillans who had pushed her into writing it.

'I hope Wilmot can handle this,' said Holly anticipating the lawyer's reproach when she explained herself to him. At the editorial conference Rain brushed aside Holly's error of judgement as blithely as if it had been her own.

* * *

Holly was wrong about Wickham's reaction to the gossip column story about his wife. He did not know of it, a thought which after a few minutes occurred to Wainfleet when Wickham encountered him in the pub. Wainfleet had put on his most triumphant expression as Marshall and Wickham strolled in and it was deflating to realize it was wasted.

They could not escape Wainfleet nor his conversation, especially as their arrival at the bar permitted Riley to flee from him. Believing he was rubbing salt in a wound, Wainfleet nudged the conversation towards the matter of Vanessa and the duke, a story he only half trusted but had been content to print. He nudged by mentioning the similar item which had linked Maureen and Hunter-Blair.

'I never understand how you know these things,' said Wickham with candour. His world was not one where people fought to get their names in the papers. Far from it, personal publicity could hinder their work and they were engaged in serious business.

'Oh, you know,' said Wainfleet airily. He decided to be magnanimous, having collected a month's backlog of expenses, and indicated to Sean that he would pay for his companions' drinks. Sean had been bought a replacement knife by Wainfleet and had forgiven him the theft of the first. Wainfleet went on as the drinks arrived: 'All sorts of folk have their reasons for wanting other people's private business, or their own, published. Ours not to reason why.'

He poured a whisky down his throat and pushed the glass across the bar for a refill. Wickham said: 'How did you get your story about Hunter-Blair and Maureen MacQuillan?' He knew better than to expect a detailed answer.

'Oh no, no, no,' said Wainfleet feeling in a pocket for cash. 'Can't reveal my sources.' He laughed as though this were clever comment. He was slightly drunk. Sean passed Wainfleet his change and then Wainfleet dipped a hand into another pocket as he said: 'Shan't whisper a word, not ethical to do so, but, on the other hand . . .' He drew out a sheet of paper, unfolded it on the bar and leaned back as Wickham and Marshall read the note and signature.

It seemed to Wainfleet that there was a peculiar delay in their response. To fill the gap he roared with laughter at his own witty fashion of dealing with ethics. Then he began to refold the paper. Wickham stopped him. 'John, would you mind very much if I took that?'

Wainfleet's eyes were pinpoints of concentration. 'Why? The story's true. Anyway, it's no crime if it's not. This is only the tip, all the facts I could get were in the paper.'

'Even so, I'd like to borrow it. You'll get it back.'

Wainfleet did not want it back, the only reason he was carrying it around was that he had jotted a telephone number on the back. He copied the number into his notebook. 'All yours, superintendent,' he said and skimmed the note along the bar where Wickham caught it.

Wickham asked casually whether the same person often supplied Wainfleet with stories and was told he did. They talked a bit longer until some other people went to the bar and Wickham took the chance to get away. Out in the street Marshall said: 'If that piece of paper is what it looks like we could have found the killer.'

'Or another hoaxer,' said Wickham with justifiable caution.

Ray Darby could not say which but confirmed that the note sent to Wainfleet was on paper identical to that used for the death threat. There was restrained optimism among Wickham's team that this could be the lead they had been waiting for. Wickham told them: 'The note to Wainfleet was written this week but no paper like this was found in the office. Therefore the possibility must be that the sender kept it at home, and that there's more of it there. I think we have good reason to search his flat.'

It was at the flat that Wickham learned about Vanessa and the duke. There were newspapers on a table, the story was on an open page and if Marshall had not closed the paper and pushed it beneath others, Wickham's curiosity would not have been aroused.

He was not upset by the story — Vanessa had freed herself to consort with dukes if she chose — but touched by Marshall's gesture. It never occurred to him that the story was questionable, that Wainfleet had deliberately published something he did not totally believe and that he had done it in retaliation for being humiliated.

The flat was shared and many of the things in it did not belong to the suspect so the search was complicated. But the man raised no objections to a search and had dashed off to keep an appointment, leaving the police to their work. They found paper which appeared to match the death threat to MacQuillan and the note to Wainfleet; and they took away a pair of trousers with worn pockets.

After the items had been sent to the laboratory, Wickham suggested they congratulate themselves with a visit to one of the unprepossessing local pubs. Nothing more could be done on the case that evening and they had cause to hope it was nearing its end.

For a change of subject, they chose Sniffy Wilson, one of them having heard how colleagues had been tailing two armed members of the Goad gang, Donovan and Wytcherly, and at the end of a hair-raising fifteen minutes found they had arrested Sniffy as well. Sniffy was reasonably pleased to see them as the Goad men had been about to wreak vengeance on him for his revelations about the prison release dates being changed.

Wickham had heard all this before and his attention wandered. He was thinking that perhaps he ought to warn Rain where the MacQuillan case was leading. At its mildest, it could be unfortunate if she blundered upon realization of the killer's identity. And if the man were as confident of getting away with MacQuillan's murder as Wickham believed him to be, she could put herself at risk. He borrowed the pub telephone and called her, but got no answer.

He shrugged it off, not convinced that his concern was necessary because she was unlikely to see the man that evening and in the morning there could be an arrest. He was inclined to believe he had been looking for an excuse to ring her, which was foolish because he did not need an excuse.

He decided to telephone her over the weekend, by which time the case could be finished and he would be able to invite her to dinner with reasonable hope that they would be uninterrupted. Now that she and Oliver had separated there were no obvious impediments. The office gossip had been quite useful in reassuring him on that point, and he had been able to view the uncomfortable ride in the lift with them in an encouraging new light.

* * *

Rather later than planned Rain set off for the Old Mitre pub. It is concealed down a narrow alley linking Hatton Garden with Ely Court but patrons have been finding their way to it since the sixteenth century. Much of its period charm persists, along with its claim that no felon may be arrested there. Shildon was not waiting for Rain and the landlord had not seen anyone fitting his description. Rain took a glass of wine into the Cloister, a tiny annexe off one of the oak panelled bars, and waited.

She was late because Crystal Daly telephoned, indignant that Brian Berg had arrived at the gallery and accused her of being MacQuillan's mistress. She had winkled out of him that he got the story from Georgie and she had much trouble persuading him it was a joke. Crystal thought Berg was a newspaper reporter and she assured Rain: 'I didn't spoil your story by telling him MI something killed MacQuillan.' She expected to be thanked for her loyalty. Rain thanked her, not having the heart to tell her about Georgie's other little joke.

After waiting for Shildon for half an hour Rain used the phone in the Cloister and rang the *Post.* A secretary in the business section confirmed he had left long before Rain did. Then she telephoned Eliot at home and after that was about to leave when Shildon came, apologetic and saying he had met somebody who had delayed him.

He sipped the lager she bought him and then he said: 'Tell me what Ruby was up to. Rosie said something about keys but I couldn't make head or tail of it.'

Covering her impatience, she told him that some keys similar to MacQuillan's desk keys had been found and Ruby had been trying to divine from them the identity of their owner. Then she got him to talk about his investigation. He said it had petered out because Eliot did not want him to go any further and did not have a plan to use the information already gathered. Rain felt a surge of annoyance: Shildon could have told her that on the telephone and not wasted part of her evening.

Shildon said: 'If MacQuillan had lived, Eliot could have used the information to persuade people to change their minds about letting him have a free hand with the *Post*. The unions might have seen an opportunity, trustees might have been appointed . . .'

She hurried her drink, anxious to get away and only half listening to what he was saying. But when he mentioned that the MacQuillan business in the United States was in trouble, she automatically asked what sort of trouble.

Shildon said that a superior drinks carton had been invented and the MacQuillans faced the choice of buying the invention or seeing a competitor develop it and steal their market. Trouble flared a few days before MacQuillan's death, when it became apparent the inventor was in effect conducting an auction and the price of buying the securely patented new carton had shot alarmingly high.

The possibility that the MacQuillan empire was facing hard times raised interesting questions about the future of the *Post*, but Rain's glass was empty and Shildon read that as a signal that she was impatient to leave. He finished his drink and they walked down Hatton Garden together.

'Another weekend of parties?' he asked. Even colleagues assumed the gossip column staff spent most of their waking hours at parties. She said she was going to miss one that evening because she had an appointment at a Chelsea wine bar.

Harbury and Linda Finch were together at a table when she got there. 'I've told him to grit his teeth and hang on,' said Linda. Rain reported that Eliot's message was much the same. Harbury gaped to hear she had told the editor. 'Why not?' Rain asked. 'The same rug's under his feet too. The more people who stand firm the harder it is for anyone to whisk it away.'

'Where's Oliver?' asked Linda who had grown as tired of hearing Harbury's troubles as she was of Marilyn Duxbody's.

Rain still did not know the answer to that when she drove to Kington Square another hour on. She parked conveniently beneath the trees and walked towards the flat. But as she mounted the first of the steps to the front door she sensed someone close to her. With a muffled sound she spun round, clinging on to her shoulder bag and ready to fight off an attacker.

Right behind her was Shildon. She recovered herself, grateful that he had either not noticed how jumpy she had been or was willing to pretend he had not. 'There's something else,' he said. 'I thought we might talk, if you've got time.'

In the confusion of the moment she agreed and led the way upstairs, wishing she had dreamed up a reason to turn him away. It was getting late, she was tired and wanted time alone. Also, he had kept her waiting at the Old Mitre and she would have preferred him to say everything then, or telephone now, rather than trail after her.

Then they were in the flat, the first time she had been there since leaving Oliver typing his letter the previous morning. So much had happened since — the Marilyn Duxbody fiasco, the Hatherley trip, Pascoe's death — that it seemed far longer.

Oliver's bag was not on the floor. In spite of everything she felt regret. He had gone, he was not coming back because this time he had taken everything with him. He had done what she had wanted and now she was sorry. Sorry that Oliver had gone, or sorry that she would be alone? She had no time to consider the difference.

Offering coffee, she went straight into the kitchen, her shoulder bag over her arm, and set up the filter machine, talking as she did so about the day's gossip. Once the machine was hissing and the aroma of coffee was spreading through the flat Rain tossed her bag on the couch, kicked off her sandals and opened the doors to the garden.

In as tactful a way as she could contrive she asked Shildon to hurry up with what he wanted to say. He sat on the couch and started a story the burden of which was to illustrate that Hunter-Blair was being paid an exorbitant amount for his weekly outpourings and that he and Maureen were having an affair. Rain frowned as she poured the coffee. None of it was new. As she handed him his cup the telephone rang.

Tavett. Tavett in a callbox and some distress. 'Give me your number, I'll call you back,' she said. When she got through he said he had taken a train on the spur of the moment and was in Bristol. She had panicky thoughts about the Clifton suspension bridge and its alarming suicide rate, but Tavett did not mention Clifton. He wanted to know whether Wickham had arrested anyone for the murder because until then he could not face going to work.

Rain said: 'You don't have to, Dick. You can stay at home. Everyone will understand.'

He assured her they would not, they would think he was guilty, that most of them already thought he was guilty. She knew it would be useless to suggest that running away to Bristol looked more suspicious than pretending a stomach upset and staying at home. She tried to calm him, insisting that no one could believe he was a murderer, and asked whether he had called his wife. He was vague about that.

'I can go where I like,' he kept saying, unconsciously repeating Wickham's sentiments earlier that day. But it was apparent that having gone he did not entirely like it. The problems had travelled with him. Rain asked whether he had money and a hotel room but his answers were not encouraging. She had to talk for as long as he wanted and it was a long time.

And while she was concentrating on Tavett she watched Shildon, reflected in the glass of a painting on the wall in front of her, slide his hand a few inches along the couch, flip open her bag and feel through the contents.

CHAPTER 23

She was suffused with indignation, but it did not appear Shildon had taken anything and the more urgent matter was to get help for Tavett. She put the telephone down on the floor and knelt beside it, facing Shildon and saying Tavett was in trouble and she had to make some calls. She wished he would understand she wanted him to go but Shildon sat there while she dialled and then he went into the garden.

Rain fought back the impulse to grab her bag and check the contents, and then she was through to the *Post.* Wickham and Marshall had gone. She told her story to an officer she did not know and gave him the number of the Bristol call-box. After that she rang Mrs Tavett but the line was engaged.

There was nothing left to do but join Shildon. She followed him into the garden. He was leaning against the parapet rail, gazing down at the brick terrace several floors below. The neighbours who often sat there in the hot evenings laughing and talking had gone out. Voices of unseen people floated up from more distant gardens. Music drifted from open windows and traffic droned down the King's Road. But Rain and Shildon might have been alone, there was no one to see or overhear them.

She had to decide what to do. If she had walked into a room and found him with her bag in his hands, the decision would have been made for her. But to tackle him on the basis of a fleeting reflection was tricky. She digressed, running through in her mind the bag's contents to discover what could have interested him.

He turned from the rail and she anticipated one of the usual compliments visitors paid her garden but instead he asked about Ruby Dobby. She laughed, partly amused at his fascination with the woman and partly relieved at being able to delay her decision. She said: 'You're very interested in her. I'll have to introduce you next time she comes.'

'I'm only interested in what she does and how she does it.' And he went on to ask about Ruby's visit that afternoon. Rain could not understand why, when he had heard from Rosie all there was to know. He asked what had become of the keys Ruby had used.

She opened her mouth to say they were with the police, but abruptly changed her mind. 'I took them from her,' she said instead, fearing mention of police interest would lead on to computer codes and MacQuillan's business methods. She did not want a prolonged discussion, she wanted only that he should go away.

Eventually he did. Then she locked the door, bolted the garden doors and prepared for bed. But before getting into bed she emptied her bag out on it for a final attempt to work out what he had wanted, possibly taken. Everything appeared to be there: purse and cheque book; comb and lipstick; notebook; a diary in which she forgot to write things; a bill she had overlooked; an invitation to a party she had skipped; and a photograph of a set of keys.

She was jolted into realization. He must have been looking for the keys. He had not grasped that Ruby worked that day with a mere photograph and a photograph was all Rain had in her possession. The conversation with Rosie had left him with the impression Rain was carrying the keys, and her own deliberately misleading answer that evening had confirmed it.

She sank down on the bed with the photograph gripped so tightly in her hands that the paper buckled. Her thoughts raced wildly, but each time returned to the idea that Shildon would come back. He had kept on and on about those keys, although she had been deaf to his insistence; he had come several miles to catch her at home and seize a chance to rifle her bag for them; if there had been any purpose to the meeting at the Old Mitre it might have been to get the keys. She imagined him out in the square at that very moment concocting a plan to get into the flat again and make a thorough search.

Before she knew the decision was taken she was struggling into her clothes. The flat that was usually so attractively private had become a trap. If Shildon had waited on the stairs instead of leaving by the street door, he could creep back and force the flat door while she was asleep. The uncertainty was intolerable.

With unsteady hands she opened her door and peered out. The stair light was bright. For as far as she could see there were no secret, unsafe corners. But she could not see all the way, it was feasible that he was on a lower flight and she would come face to face with him. She doubted she would be quick enough to retreat to the top floor if that happened. Clenching her teeth she pulled the door behind her, heard the sharp click of the Yale lock that shut her out.

There were no sounds from the lower flats, no television or music to assure her that people were at hand. She was tempted to tramp noisily down so that if Shildon had lingered he would be scared away, but then she would never know whether he had been there. Softly she slid down the stairs.

Succeeding flights opened up to her view and then she was looking at the lobby. The empty, well-lit lobby. Ashamed of her excess of imagination, she let herself out into the street and covered the few yards to her car under the trees. Just as she reached forward with her car key she saw how the window had been forced and the catch freed to open the door.

Rain did not keep much in the car, because there was always the risk of attracting a thief. But her radio was in place, her maps and street guide and other papers were still present although not exactly as she had left them. Her new torch was where it should have been. All the portable bits and pieces which might have been stolen were there, yet someone had broken into and searched the car. She did not question who it had been or what he was looking for. She started the engine and drove east.

Fleet Street was quiet. The printers' shifts had ended and the delivery vans had screamed away. Stan, the *Post*'s security man, looked surprised as he let Rain in. 'Can't sleep?' he asked. She replied with an equal banality. He went back to his chair and picked up his paper again. Riley had won his argument: the lead story was the recapture of Sniffy Wilson. There was a pile of spare copies on a table in the entrance hall. Rain took one.

'A busy night,' said Stan, and it might have been either a statement or a question. She grunted a reply and checked the lifts. They were both at higher floors so she ran up the stairs instead.

She intended to go straight to the second floor and find a policeman she could tell about the keys, but when she reached the first floor landing she veered into the newsroom instead. Two of the overhead lights were on, one near her desk, another much farther down the room.

There was a shadowy vagueness about the rest with its hulks of desks and clutter of baskets and papers. Waste bins overflowed with paper, in the wire room the overnight news from around the world spewed out, in the typewriters sheaves of messages or half-written copy had been stuffed. It was as though everyone had dashed off on a far bigger, far better story than they had covered in their lives.

For those few moments the atmosphere had changed, was as comfortable as in the Ayling days. It was possible to believe that the sale and all the unpleasantness which had followed it had never taken place. With a sigh she knew that in the morning when the people returned they would bring with them the rivalries and ill-feeling that had spoiled everything.

Then she registered that there was a message stuck on her typewriter too and curiosity propelled her towards it. Rosie had scribbled down the name and telephone number of a caller who had offered a story. Automatically Rain concealed the note. The fewer people who knew where she got her information the better. She pulled open a drawer to drop the note in.

Someone had rummaged through the drawer. She slammed it shut, tried others and each one was in the same state. Edging round the bunched-together desks she checked Holly's and Rosie's and thought they had been tampered with too. Straightening, she saw movement down the room near the exit to the landing. Her eyes strained but it was not repeated.

She set off for the second floor, but there was no police officer there. The doors were shut, the lights off. She went into MacQuillan's room. A street lamp shed light over the front part of it where the boardroom table stood. The rest was darker although she could make out shapes. She withdrew to the secretary's room and was about to close MacQuillan's door when she heard a scraping sound from the adjoining typists' room.

Her hand slid along a wall to a light switch. With the movement of a finger she could find out who was in there. Her hand fell away from the switch and she took a step towards the typists' room, her head cocked. And as the sound recurred she identified it and fled, with a speed which astonished her, through the nearest door.

She was in MacQuillan's room again, her eyes drawn to the desk where he had been found dead. But the door by which she had entered was not the only way out. Diagonally across from where she stood was the door to the back stairs. With minimum sound she moved over the carpet towards it.

Once, her taut nerves convinced her there were footsteps leaving the typists' room and she dropped to her knees at the side of the desk where someone glancing in would not see her. But no one looked. A minute later she scuttled forward, snatched at the door handle and tugged. The door was locked. She had to go back the way she had come.

To begin with she heard nothing to justify her fright, and got as far as the staircase between floors before the lift began to hum. She froze and listened hard. It sounded as though the lift stopped at the first floor but immediately the sounds resumed and it was rising, she thought, to the second floor. She hurried into the newsroom.

A few telephones had direct outside lines when the switchboard closed down at night. Mona's was one. Rain had reached it when she heard a thud from the direction of Linley's room. She pushed back his door.

The room was empty. The sound came again and she understood then that it was from the interview room beyond his wall. Back in the newsroom she approached the interview room with caution. Slivers of light showed around the door. Giving herself the advantage of surprise, she ripped open the door.

Oliver. Oliver who was in the act of lifting a brown leather-covered chair which he dropped with sufficient noise to drown his voluble fright. Angry amazement dwindled into puzzlement of the what-on-earth-are-you-doing-here? variety.

She could see what *he* was doing. He was arranging a row of similar chairs to form a makeshift bed. 'You can't sleep *here*!' she said.

'Why not? There's a shower in the cloakroom, there's a coffee machine twenty feet away . . .'

'This is ridiculous. Suppose somebody finds out?'

He looked sulky. 'You have.'

'I'm not counting me. Suppose the security man finds out?'

'Stan knows. He doesn't care. I'm not going to get thrown out into the street.' He sat down on one of the chairs and stared up at her with an accusing, plaintive face.

She hardened her heart and thought she should swiftly make it clear she had not come in search of him. She told him about Shildon and the keys and her intention to tell the police. Oliver said: 'Wanting the keys doesn't connect him with the murder.'

'Of course not, but the police are interested in those keys too and I want to put a stop to Shildon searching my property.'

Oliver said that could have been easily accomplished by telling Shildon where they really were and if it were Shildon she had heard going through a desk in the typists' room he must already have found out. Oliver had seen only Stan who, for a small fee, had agreed to 'forget' that he was spending the night there.

Stan might truly have forgotten if it had not been for the crash of the falling chair. As it was, the newsroom lights were snapped on and Stan came to investigate. He joined Rain in the doorway of the interview room. 'Well, I don't know what we're going to do about that,' he said and sucked his teeth and shook his grey head and expressed dismay that a leg had been knocked off the chair.

'We'll think of something,' Rain promised. But Stan was oddly unwilling to be appeased.

Oliver understood him better. 'What will it cost to get it fixed?'

Stan rapped out that a fiver should cover it. Oliver felt through his pockets without luck. He glanced towards Rain but she took the lofty view that bribing security men was not her concern. Instead she asked Stan whether Shildon had been in that night. He denied it. She gave him a mistrusting look and altered the question. 'What time did he leave?'

'He said he was only going to be a few minutes. He slipped out again while I was doing my rounds.'

His rounds took him to most parts of the building and Rain was eagerly accepting that it must have been Stan on the second floor making her jumpy when he mentioned that since the murder he did not go into MacQuillan's room or those next to it because the police were usually there. Worse, he told her that naturally he never used the lifts because if one were faulty he could be stuck a long time with no one to free him.

She had other questions but Stan chose not to be side-tracked from the serious business of telling Oliver he could not stay on the premises after all. Turning a blind eye to his presence was one thing, he said, but being party to malicious damage quite another.

Oliver argued but Stan made a grumpy mention of ten minutes and tossed over his shoulder the order that the chairs were to be put back where they belonged. Oliver would have gone on wrangling but Rain said it did not matter, her car was outside. 'You said that once before,' he said suspiciously.

She helped with the chairs — one back to Mona's room, another to Linley's — while Oliver carried the broken one to the library. He took some time because he jacked up the chair on books to make good the missing leg, rather than have an unsuspecting colleague collapse. Then he collected his belongings from the interview room and joined Rain on the landing.

She gestured at the lifts. 'They're both on the second floor now. Stan says he never uses them, we haven't and yet there they are. There definitely is someone else here.' She dashed to the stairs.

Oliver started to ask whether they could not drop it and go home, but it struck him that he was in a precarious position and he kept quiet. On the second floor they found a light in the typists' room and heard the mumble of voices. Rain rushed in.

Shildon was there with a young officer. The speech Rain had prepared for the police about the keys dried. Instead she said something pompous about having information and wishing to speak privately, before backing out to wait her turn.

Outside, she and Oliver whispered about Shildon. 'He's been helping them with background about MacQuillan,' she said.

'He wouldn't have to tell them at this time of night. Anyway, he'd tell Wickham or somebody important, not a junior acting as night-watchman.'

'Well what's he up to?'

They did not have to wait long before Shildon emerged and told them. 'It's Ruby Dobby again, my obsession as you nearly called her, Rain. I think the keys she was playing with were mine and I want them back.'

Rain was going to conceal her knowledge of his searches but Oliver bounced in with: 'Why didn't you ask rather than search Rain's bag and car?'

Shildon recovered fast. 'I'm sorry, I shouldn't have done that. I know it looks rather exaggerated but I wanted them back without a lot of questions.'

Exasperated, she said his behaviour had prompted a great many questions. And with that sarcastic tone she had always disliked he said he was giving her the answers: he had acquired a duplicate set of keys to help in his research for Eliot. When she objected to him sharing the blame with the editor, he brushed her aside and said that without the keys a lot of information would have been kept from him. He showed no surprise when she referred to the list of computer codes.

He had explained all this to the police officer as the man confirmed when Rain and Oliver trooped in to see him. He welcomed the interruptions of what was otherwise a very dull shift. 'Mind you,' he said, 'Mr Shildon didn't say he'd been searching your property or that he ever believed you had his keys. He said he lost them about a week ago and heard today that a set which might have been his had been used by that psychic woman. Apparently he came to the office to get her telephone number and she told him we had them.'

Rain said: 'I think he searched in here for them too.' The man drew open the desk drawers. One stuck and scraped.

He said: 'He took a chance coming in here, I was only away for a few minutes. Stan makes a cup of coffee and I go down and fetch it.' He swung the drawers shut. 'We never use these drawers, if he'd put the light on instead of feeling around in the dark he'd have found that out immediately.'

He laughed at Shildon's stupidity before saying: 'The case is pretty well over, did you know that? Mr Wickham's just about ready to haul someone in.' He pulled a face and said less colloquially: 'I mean, he'll be asking someone to accompany him to the police station.'

CHAPTER 24

On Saturday morning Rain went to the Barbican Centre. A women's magazine was running a feature on what well-known Fleet Street women were wearing and she had been cajoled into taking part. Apparently none of them matched up to the magazine's ideal because far from being allowed to wear what they owned, they were to be fitted out by the fashion editor. And in case they still looked too dull, the photographs were to be taken amidst the bougainvillaea and exotic plants of the conservatory.

On a crisp spring day when the promise was made the warmth of the conservatory sounded a good idea. In a July heatwave, plus camera lights, it was almost suicide. One of the women, a foreign correspondent who knew what it was like to hack her way through real jungle, fainted on to a cactus and was carried out.

The others gamely battled on, discomfort compounded by inquisitive faces pressed against the glass. With some relief they let go the creepers, abandoned the raptured looks of women spotting favourite parakeets and set off for a poolside session.

The Barbican terrace on a dry day which is not even a very warm day has the air of a Continental resort café.

Tables stud the paving, flowers flourish in tubs, people perch on poolside ledges. When the staff of *Metropolitan* and their press gang of models arrived on the terrace the whisper was that bathing suits were to be modelled. But no, fine suede and woollen knits were the preference because the magazine world is a far-sighted one and summer photographs are destined for autumn readers.

Rain dutifully appeared in a high-necked knitted dress and attempted to look as though she were just a fraction chilly. She balanced near the water and hoped that by being biddable the torment would soon be over. A crowd had gathered and she had to push through it to get to the room set aside for the models to change.

A lime-green dress she had hated on sight had been earmarked for her. She dragged it on, praying she would meet no one she knew in case it was thought to be hers. She met someone. Of all people, she met Shildon.

He was walking from the bar to the terrace with a glass in his hand and she nearly ran him down. 'What's going on over there?' he asked, nodding towards the pool.

'I'm afraid it's partly my fault.' She reminded him about the event, a source of much amusement in the office when it had been arranged. 'As you'd forgotten, you can't have come to lend support,' she chided. Neither had Oliver. He had gone to see a friend and planned to meet Rain later. The arrangement had been tentative: he had slept on her couch but was supposed to be arranging somewhere else to live.

'I came to see the Icelandic exhibition,' said Shildon. 'It sounded cooler than it was.'

When she stepped forward to pose, Rain's lime-green dress brought a hiss of distaste from onlookers. She could hear women's voices reverberating with 'that colour, colour, colour . . .' and it was very easy to follow the photographer's instructions and look put out.

Relieved that the performance was her last she accepted Shildon's offer of a drink before changing. He was not the person whose company she would have chosen, but she was desperately thirsty and he had a table in the shade. They did not refer to the disturbing episodes of the previous evening. He bought her a long cold drink and asked whether she had any news of the murder case.

'I've heard the net is closing,' she said. 'It sounds as though an arrest is imminent.'

She jiggled the ice cubes in her glass, letting the sun flash from them, while she tantalized him with her secret knowledge. Shildon put his glass down and said he was going inside and would be back in a few minutes. She was disappointed. She and Oliver had leaped at the police officer with cries of *'Who?'* when he had mentioned the case was nearing its end, and he'd had the fun of refusing them, either because he genuinely did not know the answer or because he dare not speak a name. Shildon had not even asked 'Who?'

The significance hit her like a blast of cold air. *He had not asked.* Since the killing he had repeatedly asked her about the case but the one time she appeared to have the answer to the mystery, he had not put the obvious question. Before realizing what she was doing, she was on her feet and halfway across the terrace. He had gone. Like a small child on a sandy beach he had been absorbed by the crowd.

She ran inside the building and recognized him in a dozen men who, closer, turned out to be other people. Useless to ask for him, he was unobtrusive and no description would help. She looked back to the terrace. Their table had been taken, he could not go back there.

Rain could think of no rational uncomplicated reasons for him leaving her the way he had, but on the other hand . . . She could think of a string of things on the other hand. He had hated MacQuillan, owned keys to the man's desk, worked slavishly to accumulate information to discredit him . . . And there was something else, something he had said earlier in the week which had puzzled her then and of which she had been reminded later. But on both those occasions there had been too many jokes and distractions and she had let the matter slide by . . .

She thought she spotted him on a higher level and ran for the lifts. They did not come or they were full. She raced up the stairs, frustrated by the people who paused on them to admire the view outside. She emerged at the wrong point and could not see a way to get across. Neither was she convinced it was Shildon she had seen. But if he were there, he would be able to see her: the lime-green dress made her as easy to trace as a cigarette burning in the dark.

She ran up more stairs, checked behind pillars, hung around at vantage points where she could look down on him — if he were there. She was still reciting the things that could be said against him.

When there was nowhere else to search inside — unless she talked her way into the concert hall or the theatre or the cinema — she went outside, not down to the terrace again but on the high-level sculpture court. Its pink brick expanse, cupped by the curving line of the university business school, concentrated heat like a crucible. An aeroplane wrote its slanting signature in the sky. Very few people were there: two sunbathers and Shildon.

He was sitting on a step in the only scanty shade and gazing at the vapour trail and did not stir until she was close. Then he said: 'I used to think there were new places, that you could buy a plane ticket to a fresh start if you were young enough and resilient enough.' He looked at her and laughed. 'You've never felt the need of that. I shouldn't think you've got a clue what I'm talking about.'

Before she could speak he said: 'I'm probably the only journalist who thinks improved communications the curse of the twentieth century! Have you ever thought that we are both the beneficiaries and the victims of them? We can get instant pictures and news from any part of the globe, but we can go across the world and find ourselves working for the same proprietor.'

She interrupted and he said: 'Oh yes, you don't want to hear all that stuff, you want to talk about MacQuillan. I don't know why: I've been telling you about him for days but you haven't been interested.'

'I'm listening now.' She felt a tingle of apprehension but children came running into the court, flung themselves on the steps near Rain and Shildon and played boisterous games for the minutes it took their parents to round them up and drag them away. When he spoke again Shildon did not refer to MacQuillan. He mentioned the police searching his flat and wondered whether she knew what they had been after and whether they had found it.

She owned up to her ignorance. He did not believe her, saying everyone knew about her and Wickham and that it was obvious she knew more about the case than anyone else. Ruefully, she remembered the times she had let Harbury and others exaggerate her knowledge. That, coupled with Wainfleet's rumours, had convinced Shildon. 'What could they have been looking for?' she asked.

'They didn't say. I left them to get on with it when I went to the Old Mitre. That's why I was late.' He got up, reading his watch. 'I've got to go now.'

The conviction which had sent Rain hurtling after him had dissipated. She could not bring herself to say outright: 'Did you kill MacQuillan?' And she ought to have known she could not, because previously she had not risked challenging him about searching her bag. The unasked question would not go away, but she knew that if it were voiced there would be only a sarcastic refusal to answer.

Frustratingly, she could still not recall what it was that almost alerted her days ago, but she was growing convinced it was something he had said. Despite the turmoil in her mind, she spoke casually: 'I must give this awful dress back.'

'And after that,' she thought, 'I ought to telephone Wickham.'

They went down in a crowded lift and parted. Rain was seized by *Metropolitan's* frantic fashion editor who all but accused her of stealing the dress. A public spectacle developed with Rain succinctly stating why the lime-green dress was the last garment in the world she would choose to steal, and the fashion editor spitting that the dress would have looked a lot better if Rain had shed the pounds she had promised.

After she re-emerged from the changing room Rain was bumped into by an enormous teddy bear which apologized from around the level of its chest that it was sorry but it was impossible to see where it was going. As it was actually in a line for a pane of glass, she offered to guide it to safety. And then she became aware of the unusually high proportion of bears on the loose. Each child carried one, some children had slipped bear masks over their faces and demanded constant astonishment from grownups, a sprinkling of adults had metamorphosed into bears. They were all heading in the same general direction, except for those whose peep-holes had become covered with fur, and she trundled her bear after them. Posters she had overlooked until then announced a teddy bears' picnic in the sculpture court. Bears and children floundered and as she was one of a minority confident of the route, she led her captive the whole way.

Bears were blundering up the stairs and clogging the lifts and comparing disguises. A brewery had sent along the massive bear from its television advertisements. Rupert Bear was there, but so were a number of cloned brothers. Paddington begged to be looked after. Pooh looked bereft without Piglet.

The sculpture court was transformed. Bears swarmed around tables where honey sandwiches were being given away. A band was playing the Teddy Bears' Picnic. Children's television personalities were mingling with the bears and one, Ramona Casey, who privately loathed children and was desperate for a change of job, ran up to say hello to Rain and gossip about her colleagues on the programme. They backed out of the court to find somewhere quieter to talk.

'Darling, it's totally unbearable,' said Ramona. 'They've found a nauseatingly precocious six-year-old and want her to do two or three of my interviews each week. Well, I told them: I've heard of job sharing, but this is ridiculous. And, Rain, you'll never guess whose daughter the little freak is.'

And Rain did not. Suddenly she knew what she had been trying to remember, what Shildon had said which hinted that he had special knowledge of one aspect of the MacQuillan case. She excused herself and darted away. She had recognized two men whose eyes were sweeping the crowds on the landing. They were detectives working with Wickham, and they did not deny they were looking for Shildon. One said they had seen him in the street outside as they drove up but he had run into the car park. They had not been able to find him again.

'He won't get out of this place, though,' he added. 'We've put men at the exits now.'

'How did you know he was here?' she wondered.

'We weren't sure but he'd ringed the Icelandic exhibition in today's paper in his flat.'

Back in the sculpture court the teddy bears were suffocating in their furs, the honey was getting runnier, the band was playing jauntily and children were lining their teddies up for the judging of Best Teddy. Assorted adult Ruperts and Paddingtons and more anonymous bears were supervising, and press photographers were milling around waiting for parents and others not in costume to be cleared out of camera range. Rain caught up with Ramona and made amends for her inattention. 'Come and talk over a drink by the pool once the teddies have got their prizes,' she whispered.

Ramona forgave her with a smile, but they never did meet by the pool and a piqued Ramona sold her story to Wainfleet instead. Rain did not mean to let her down, she was honestly prepared to wait through the judging for her. But a furious man with a Barbican security guard in tow appeared in the court repeating his claim that someone had stolen his teddy costume.

This outrage was greeted with sniggers from everyone except the guard who puckered his brow and asked whether the missing costume was to be seen. 'I mean to say,' said the guard, 'what would be the point of somebody taking it if he wasn't going to wear it? And if he wasn't going to wear it at the teddy bears' picnic, where *could* he wear it?'

A wag suggested the thief could have gone down to the woods. Rain asked where the man had been when the suit was taken. Another wag asked whether the man had been left in his bare skin. The man ignored the jokers and looked to authority in the shape of the security guard to answer Rain's question.

The guard said: 'He was going to change into it in the downstairs toilets and he put it on a shelf while he went into a cubicle. When he came out . . .' He pulled a face to indicate that he was sorry it was such a feeble story but some people's sense of security was just, well, feeble.

Rain cut out the guard and asked the man whether he recognized his suit in the arena. He said it was brown and shaggy. She singled out a few for him, different styles of teddy that might help identify the missing one. He couldn't say any of them were exactly like it, he really couldn't. But Rain knew what she was looking for, and it was no longer there.

Back on the landing she sought the detectives. She scurried about the building until she met up with one of them on the stairs. 'You want a teddy bear,' she said, cryptic and breathless. They flattened themselves against the glass walls as people pushed up and down beside them.

'In the sculpture court?' he asked.

She shook her head. 'Anywhere but there. He was there once but he's gone.'

'Are you sure of this?'

'Oh yes. Because I took him there.'

He retreated to a lower level and then radioed his message. It was the only time he ever suggested anyone arrest a teddy bear.

CHAPTER 25

Wickham had never charged a teddy bear before, either. He knew it was the sort of thing that would be remembered, a bit of nonsense to give the headline writers fun. The mundane story was that an arrest had become possible because the thread on the cupboard floor had matched Shildon's fraying trouser pocket, but without a flowing confession it might not have been enough. It had been a fumbling, unsatisfactory case.

'Guesswork,' Wickham criticized when Rain told him how she reached the conclusion that Shildon was the killer. She protested, but not much.

They had both been confused by the same thing: Shildon's detailed knowledge of MacQuillan and his affairs. Ordinarily it might have occurred to either of them that this bordered on obsession, but Eliot had unwittingly given Shildon the perfect cover when he asked his help. Not only did it mask the depth of Shildon's bitterness but it offered an excuse for secret movement.

Shildon had sat in the charge room, minus the sweltering bear skin, and explained in his normal quiet manner and meticulous way how he did it. He had bought a knife at a hardware shop three weeks earlier in another part of London so that the purchase could not easily be traced. He carried it to the office in a cardboard file containing papers on which he was working and it stayed like that in his drawer for days until circumstances were in his favour.

Then he transferred the knife to a library file of cuttings and carried that with him when he watched the printers' meeting in the yard. He had to watch because he needed to be sure the printers were going home as threatened and would not ask the chapel fathers to go back and negotiate with MacQuillan again.

When they had gone, Shildon tested whether MacQuillan was in his office by ringing the switchboard on an extension in the printers' room and asking to be put through. The telephonist said MacQuillan had gone to lunch and Mona was out too.

In readiness, he had also kept a thin pair of polythene gloves in his desk and these he put on while going up the back stairs to MacQuillan's office. The first thing he did was to use his duplicate set of keys to unlock the desk although this time he did not disturb anything in it: he had previously taken the list of computer codes and it was in the file along with the knife.

He went into the secretary's room to check that there was nothing which might upset his plan. The timed note from Pascoe seemed potentially dangerous because it might limit the period of the police inquiry, so he put it in his pocket. As he did so there were sounds on the landing and he retreated to MacQuillan's room.

No one entered and he proceeded with the next part of his plan. He laid the code list on the floor beside MacQuillan's chair, having gauged from the position of the furniture which way MacQuillan was likely to approach the desk. Then he went inside the cupboard and shut the door.

He calculated there was only a tiny risk that MacQuillan would go to the cupboard, because he had worked for him in Detroit in a hotter, more humid climate than a London heatwave and had never seen MacQuillan without his jacket.

If he had been wrong and MacQuillan discovered him, he would not have attacked.

But everything happened as he had hoped. MacQuillan came in, sat at his desk, saw the secret list on the floor and bent to get it. Noiselessly Shildon opened the cupboard door and as MacQuillan was bowed he brought the knife down with all his force.

'I always knew I wouldn't be able to get it out again,' he said in a matter-of-fact way. 'That's why I had been careful never to take the knife from its plastic wrapper until I was ready to use it. Once it was all over I put the computer list in the library file, the wrapper in my pocket and went to MacQuillan's cloakroom at the top of the back stairs. I tore up the gloves and wrapper and flushed them away.'

He ran downstairs and went, unnoticed, to the library for a time before braving the demonstrators and reaching his desk. The file had been returned to the library and the code list dropped into another file, one which had never been taken out in his name.

Shildon paused, as though expecting Wickham to applaud the skill with which the crime had been carried out. But when he next spoke he was not self-congratulatory. 'It went wrong,' he said. 'I'd been to all that trouble not to leave fingerprints or anything at the scene which could not belong there, and yet I'd left an enormous clue waiting, literally, to be picked up.'

'The keys?'

'Yes. The worst part wasn't stabbing him, it was realizing the keys were not in my pocket and I'd have to go back for them.'

He said he had killed MacQuillan before 2.30 and it was a full hour before the shock of missing the keys. He had checked the library in case he had dropped them there but his intuition was insistent that the keys had been left at the scene. And he was equally convinced that as soon as they were noticed they would be recognized as duplicates to

MacQuillan's desk and become the evidence that pointed to his guilt.

When he had bought the keys, at an office furniture suppliers shop near Fleet Street, he'd had no thought of killing and had paid by cheque. The keys were a gamble which had succeeded: he had seen Mona with the originals and bought some which looked similar. Shildon was confident the shop would remember the sale and his cheque would identify him as the purchaser.

Wickham asked what time he had returned to the second floor. Shildon said he did not know but after he realized he would have to go back there, he spent some time working out exactly where he might have dropped the keys. He knew he would not have time to search and that it was likely that he was already too late and the body had been discovered. Fearing the worst, he went up the back stairs again, heard footsteps running up behind him and hid in the cloakroom.

'It was Cecil Hunter-Blair,' he said. 'He saw MacQuillan dead, came out looking dazed, gathered his wits and ran. I watched through a chink of the cloakroom door.'

Shildon had not followed. 'I was expecting him to send people rushing up those stairs and thought I had a better chance of getting away through the secretary's room. There was no time to look for the keys.'

Wickham said he did not understand why Shildon had ever needed the keys, and why he had put the code list on the floor. 'MacQuillan would have picked up anything which was put on the floor by the desk.'

With polite patience Shildon explained that the keys and list had been of paramount importance because he originally set out to harass MacQuillan. It was common knowledge that he received hate mail in the States and was disturbed by it so Shildon sent him a death threat.

The decision to kill came later. 'I wanted to unsettle him, make him uneasy. He enjoyed manipulating and manoeuvring, undermining people so they didn't know who, if anybody, they could trust. I wanted him to experience something of the same thing. No, I don't mean he crept around desks at night snooping, he always got other people to do that kind of thing for him. If you wanted your work private you took it home, and then you found he'd got someone you thought was a friend to pursue you there.'

'But that was in another country?' suggested Wickham.

'He hadn't changed. I used those codes to get into the *Post* computer and check what he was up to, but my best sources of information were journalists in the States who've kept an eye on him for years because of his political links. They talked about him being stopped, but they only meant they wanted to publish stories that would embarrass him. Once they said there was proof he was paying for weapons for terrorists I felt the rules had changed. What did he think they were going to do with those guns? Petty harassments were no longer enough, he had reached new levels of destructiveness.'

Shildon's own aspirations to destroy had been fanned, he admitted, by changes at the *Post* which had cost many people their jobs and everyone the chance of a reasonably happy and productive working environment. 'I knew that what was happening was only the beginning. Some of them were optimistic that things would improve, some were willing to accommodate him but nobody was standing up to him. I knew they wouldn't. That's not the way people are made and that's why bullies like MacQuillan get their way.'

Repeating what Wickham had heard on his first day at the *Post*, Shildon stressed that MacQuillan's way was invariably underhand. Clear information or requests which could perhaps be overturned by rational discussion had never appealed to him. 'He employed rumour and veiled threat, and every kind of cunning. He used to joke about it, boast how he outsmarted his staff. But we weren't all outsmarted, not all the time. The trouble was no one knew what to do about him.'

Wickham drew him back to the events of Friday afternoon, to the point where he decided to hunt for the keys instead of fleeing. Shildon said he was entering MacQuillan's room from the rear lobby when he saw the door across the room start to open and withdrew. He thought he had been trapped by Hunter-Blair's dramatic news sending people dashing from both directions.

But what he saw was Tavett who burst into the room, staggered to a halt and then fled. Shildon crossed the room and closed the door behind Tavett. Since flushing away the gloves he had been meticulous about touching nothing directly, using a handkerchief to protect surfaces from his fingerprints.

He thought about staying in the room until someone else came, then pretending he had just discovered MacQuillan himself. The file he was carrying would have been a useful prop to that story, but in the end he preferred the lesser risk of a dash to the stairs. If challenged, he would have claimed he was running for help.

There was a moment when he thought he was sure to be discovered. Just as he touched MacQuillan's door handle, somebody walked quickly by on the way from the landing to the typists' room. He did not hesitate. He went as fast as he could to the landing, got into a waiting lift and rode to the ground floor. He walked upstairs to the newsroom without meeting anyone.

Compared to some stories Wickham had been obliged to sit through this was a model of calculation and execution. Had Shildon not dropped the keys and been forced to return, there would have been no glimpse by Rain of a running figure, no confusion with Tavett over doors shut or closed.

Shildon mentioned another mistake: he did not destroy Pascoe's note to Mona. He forgot to tear it and flush it away along with the plastic wrapper and gloves, and when he found it in his pocket later that afternoon he did no more than crumple it and toss it into Tavett's waste bin as he went up the room. He had only one reason for choosing that bin: it was conveniently in his path.

The choice later troubled him. He was afraid it might come to light and its discovery could be unhelpful to Tavett who was already in a miserable state. Shildon had sought a way of preventing the police concentrating on Tavett. 'He's not a bad sort. Irritating, perhaps, but harmless and he'd had a rotten time with MacQuillan. My purpose in dispatching MacQuillan was defeated if the innocent continued to suffer, wasn't it?'

Wickham grunted a vague agreement. Then said: 'You sent Tavett a knife to protect him?'

'Yes.'

'But you sent other knives, too. Why?'

'I thought Tavett might be alarmed if he were singled out but not if he were one of several recipients. The whole idea came because of the knife in Linley's pond. I don't know how it got there but that doesn't matter. Because MacQuillan was stabbed it *appeared* to be connected with the killing, to those who couldn't see it was nothing whatsoever to do with it,' said Shildon.

Wickham suspected he was being included in this. Shildon went on: 'I hadn't decided whether or not to emulate the Linley hoaxer and then I spotted a man selling knives similar to the MacQuillan one in Leather Lane. I got three, one for Tavett and two for people who I was sure would be tough enough to shrug off the incident. Eliot was an immediate choice but Rain Morgan didn't take long, either.'

After Shildon had been arrested in the Barbican, Rain told Wickham how the knives had led her to see that Shildon could be the killer. At the Marilyn Duxbody press reception Shildon had joked about three knives being sent to the office, whereas people only knew of two. Later, when she heard about the Eliot knife, recollection of his words had niggled, just out of reach on the edge of her memory. And it wasn't until Ramona Casey actually used the words 'two or three' that she had the trigger she needed. Wickham had pointed out to her that Shildon's slip while joking about the knives might only have hinted that he was a hoaxer. But she had laughingly countered that Wickham himself had persuaded her not to treat the knives too lightly.

Wickham thought it likely Shildon had been using Rain throughout the case, pretending to involve her in his work as an excuse for frequent contact with her so he could pump her for any information she had about the police investigation. Her news that an arrest was imminent had warned Shildon it was time to start running.

Wickham buried the question, telling himself that to put it would mean an unnecessary tangent. There was a submerged reason which he only acknowledged when he was driving home later. It would have exposed him in ways he did not welcome and which Shildon — and, for all he knew, Marshall the patient note-taker — might have enjoyed.

Wickham understood that Shildon believed his crime was different from others, that there were rare circumstances when it was permissible to break the law in such a serious matter as murder, and that Shildon had found himself in those circumstances. Wickham believed Shildon to be wrong. If he had indulged himself he could have argued the point, revealed how commonly murderers feel circumstances justify killing; and that when scapegoats were not to hand, circumstances invariably got the blame.

But it would have been a waste of time. Shildon had long ago shuttered his mind against plain common sense. He had lived with a gnawing urge for revenge ever since that trampling of ambition and career when he previously worked for a MacQuillan-owned paper. Towards the end of the afternoon's long session, Wickham had teased it all out of him. As the hours went by there was less talk of Shildon as a lone figure prepared to risk everything to snuff out the life of a man many people believed evil.

Shildon himself probably never saw the shift, but the final phases were devoted to Shildon as the man who took personal revenge for a personal wrong. MacQuillan had sacked him, damaged his reputation as a serious journalist, coerced a colleague to write the mendacious story which defeated Shildon's efforts and by ruining him professionally, had also destroyed his marriage. Shildon's American wife had refused to leave Washington and the divorce had been very expensive for him.

Marshall said, after the interview: 'MacQuillan was a bastard, wasn't he, sir?'

Wickham tried his admonishing look although, despite his initial expectations, he had never learned anything to MacQuillan's credit. The picture as it had appeared to him at the beginning of the case had been the complete one. Everything he had subsequently learned confirmed MacQuillan as a man unscrupulous in his treatment of people. Wickham had no doubt Shildon believed his story utterly but that did not make it all true, any more than his belief in the right to murder made it acceptable. He reminded Marshall about the library file: Shildon had told them which one it was and someone would have the task of going through its contents to look for an old cutting with a missing fragment which matched the snippet found in the cupboard. It was probable that Shildon had accidentally cut it off as he drew the knife out of the file just before he stabbed MacQuillan.

When the statement had been written and signed and the key had been turned, Wickham picked up the telephone to call Rain and let her know. He had promised as much when they spoke after the arrest. But then he thought he might call on her instead as he drove home. He dared not hope she would be free all evening, because everybody believes everybody else to be socially engaged on Saturday evenings, but he owed her an uninterrupted dinner and wanted to invite her for one next week. Quite simply, he wanted to see her, however briefly.

Traffic was heavy. The journey took much longer than usual, and he imagined himself being too late, ringing an unanswered doorbell because he had missed her by minutes. He pulled up near a callbox, shuffled change from his pocket as he rehearsed how he would persuade her to drop whatever plans she had for that evening and spend it with him. He got Oliver.

He had not been prepared for that. Oliver was meant to have left the flat, the office gossip had been quite explicit: Rain was supposed to have . . . or was it Oliver who was supposed to have . . . ? Wickham and Oliver exchanged the coolest of greetings, then Oliver was saying that Rain was out. He offered nothing more helpful and Wickham had to squeeze from him that she had not gone far and was expected back soon.

The only message Wickham left was that she was to be told he had rung. He was not confident she would get it. He drove on, remembering her speech about the absurd life of the newspaper office and feeling rash to have hoped he had meant any more to her than the other characters who had invaded her working life that week. It was depressing to bracket himself with Ruby Dobby, Zak Smythe and Sniffy Wilson.

CHAPTER 26

Oliver gave the message, coupling it with his own invention that Wickham had telephoned to say Shildon had been charged. This seemed the obvious reason to Oliver who had heard a veiled version of it on a radio news bulletin where all that could be reported was that a man had been charged with the murder of Hal MacQuillan and was expected to appear in court on Monday.

Rain picked up the telephone, but Oliver said: 'You can't ring him back. He was in a callbox, on his way to another case I think.'

She put the receiver down and went into the bedroom, stepping around Oliver's bag which was on the sitting room floor again. His things had begun creeping from the bag to their old corners in the flat. The toothbrush had re-established itself in the bathroom first, then the shaving tackle, then clothes ready for washing had worked their way into the linen basket. Neither of them had re-opened the subject, Rain choosing to ignore the situation rather than have an argument which would end with her relenting and letting him stay, and Oliver not daring say a word in case he was ordered out on the spot.

He was finding it extraordinarily difficult to arrange anywhere to move to, his closest friends being on holiday.

Even those who willingly lent him their spare beds or floors for odd nights jibbed at the idea of having him resident, however temporarily. He could not understand it. He commandeered the telephone and tried some more numbers, wishing Rain would go out again and not overhear the repetition of rejections.

Briefly, he had wondered whether she might not have sent out word that he was not to be helped because she secretly wanted him to stay at Kington Square. He rapidly dismissed the notion, although it was hard to know what to believe. He no longer understood how he had got into this mess, whether she had taken umbrage because he had been outraged about Brian Berg, or whether there was some other element which had escaped him. He shot her a sidelong glance as she went from the bedroom to the garden, and he wished he knew what she was thinking.

Rain was thinking about Holly. She had called her with the news about Shildon and, after the shock and the groping to take it in, Holly offered a minor but startling story of her own: she had just learned about MacQuillan's ridiculous plan for a three-page gossip column with herself editing it. Rain said: 'Would you have done it?'

'Don't worry, after the inadequate way I handled the Donaldson story, no one will ever ask me.' It was generously said, typical of Holly and cleared Rain's residual doubts: Holly had never been part of a MacQuillan plot.

Rain looked down over the parapet rail. Floors below, her neighbours were sitting around their pretty Victorian table and pouring out glasses of champagne. Laughter bubbled up to her. Mozart floated from somebody else's open window. She felt detached, denied companionship. If Oliver would get off her telephone she could call people, invite them round, arrange to meet them somewhere. But he began one call as he ended another, and her impatience erupted. She whisked up her bag and rushed out with only a word to him.

In the square she hesitated. If she walked to the wine bar she would certainly meet people she knew, but Oliver would equally certainly follow and the less they were seen together the more easily he would be offered somewhere else to live. She got into her car and opened her bag. From the welter of press invitations she received every week she chose a few which interested her. The most promising one that evening was a party on a boat on the Thames to celebrate the retirement of the head of a television company. Rain suddenly knew it would be a pity to miss it.

She did not get a word with the retiring television boss the whole evening but she met Crystal Daly who had acquired an equally young man to replace Georgie; Wainfleet; Linda Finch with Harbury; and Hunter-Blair with Maureen MacQuillan. Harbury saw her first and gave her news of Tavett, picked up by the Bristol police and sent home to rest. 'He won't go back to the features desk,' said Harbury with more foresight than knowledge. 'They'll move him to motoring, you'll see.'

Wainfleet hailed her with some noisy nonsense about teddy bears. She tried very hard to get him to admit he had guessed Shildon was guilty, but he would not have it. He said: 'Obsessed about MacQuillan, yes. But that was obvious, wasn't it?' She muttered something which did not reveal how the obvious had eluded her. He went on: 'The police were questioning him, your chum Wickham saw him several times. I didn't think it was up to me to interfere.'

Rain saw Wainfleet was caught between wanting to boast of his special knowledge and wanting to exonerate himself for not adding his penn'orth of information at the right time. She asked whether Shildon had been obsessive when they had worked together in Detroit. Wainfleet grabbed a fresh drink from a passing waiter before saying with a mock shudder: 'I'd probably be dead if he had been. MacQuillan got *me* to write the story which ruined Shildon's investigation into his political friends.'

'*You* did it? But why? I thought you were friends.'

Wainfleet defended himself. 'You make it sound as though I had a choice. When MacQuillan didn't get what he wanted, you were on the scrap heap. I didn't want to lose my job, I didn't want my reputation torn to shreds. He didn't just sack people, he destroyed them too. I did what was wanted and then saved up the fare to Fleet Street.'

Hunter-Blair wormed his way through the crowd to ask about Shildon. Wainfleet, overlooking what a regular source of copy the man had proved, thrust in a question of his own. Why, he demanded, had Hunter-Blair lied about being at the army camp demonstration?

Hunter-Blair blustered but Harbury came up and provided the answer. His police contacts had mentioned that Hunter-Blair had seen the body and run away. The MP looked shattered. Harbury challenged him to deny it: 'You were seen.' While they were all staring at Hunter-Blair and waiting for him to find words, Maureen MacQuillan appeared beside them.

She pushed her long loose hair back over her shoulder and stared at one face after another. 'What's going on here?' she asked. The atmosphere was unmistakably hostile. No one answered her, and she addressed Hunter-Blair. He looked at her and opened his mouth to speak, but snapped it shut and then tried to get away. Maureen stood squarely in front of him and he could not go. Maureen asked again what was happening.

Again, Harbury supplied the answer. Maureen was horrified, but the tension went out of her body and Hunter-Blair pushed past her and disappeared into the throng. 'Nobody could do that . . .' Maureen said in a broken voice. 'Why would he . . .'

'He lives by his reputation,' said Wainfleet. 'We all do. He didn't want to be involved.'

Maureen was blank, uncomprehending. Rain snatched a glass of wine for her from a tray being carried past shoulder high. Maureen's fingers bent around the stem but she never drank it. Linda came to fetch Harbury, Wainfleet took the chance to escape, too. Rain was left with Maureen.

Maureen said at last: 'I just don't understand. I thought he was a friend. He's been so helpful to me. How could he . . . ?'

Rain did not know how far the relationship between them had been professional, how far personal, and to which Maureen was referring. She had the cheek to ask, but did not. Instead, she used a catch-all question that Maureen could interpret any way she wished. 'What will you do now?'

'Sell the *Daily Post*,' said Maureen.

It was the last answer Rain had expected, the last she would have dared hope for. She held her breath, waiting for more. Maureen said: 'It's a luxury we can no longer afford. We have expensive trouble with the drinks carton business, and anyway the paper was very much my father's hobby. Ron Barron said when he died that we should consider pulling out of London. I thought I had a duty to my father to keep things going the way he would have wanted, and Cecil's been wonderful in trying to raise finance for it, but now . . .'

She put a hand to her face and turned away. Rain took the untouched glass from her hand and asked whether Maureen would like a cab to take her home. As she left the boat Maureen said to Rain: 'I know you thought I was a lousy reporter when I was on the column. But I gave you a good story in the end, didn't I?'

The drink ran out early and people were ferried ashore to find other venues to end the evening. There was no sign of Hunter-Blair. Harbury, Linda and Wainfleet were avid to know what Maureen had said to Rain but, in retaliation for being stranded, she declined to tell them. Once ashore she found a callbox and rang Eliot. Maureen could not be allowed to change her mind about the sale, word must be spread in the right quarters to attract a buyer.

Before leaving the callbox Rain rang her flat but the number was engaged. She pictured Oliver still phoning around, running up her bill and persuading no one to take him in. She walked towards her car, knowing she would be demoralized back at the flat and it was too early to go home, although she had refused several invitations from people intent on continuing the party elsewhere. The refusals seemed a mistake until she understood what she would rather do.

She ran back to the telephone box, cursing the ease with which she had accepted Oliver's message. She had lived for years with his garbled messages and had no right to be so trusting. Her change had all gone and she had to get the operator and ask for a transfer charge call. The wait was interminable but at last the telephone was answered and she heard the operator say: 'Rain Morgan is calling you from a Westminster callbox, will you accept the call?' Wickham did not refuse her.

As she drove to meet him she spared a thought for Oliver who would wonder what had become of her. She knew she ought to telephone him, but took pleasure in not doing so. She thought that, on the whole, it would serve him right.

THE END

THE JOFFE BOOKS STORY

We began in 2014 when Jasper agreed to publish his mum's much-rejected romance novel and it became a bestseller.

Since then we've grown into the largest independent publisher in the UK. We're extremely proud to publish some of the very best writers in the world, including Joy Ellis, Faith Martin, Caro Ramsay, Helen Forrester, Simon Brett and Robert Goddard. Everyone at Joffe Books loves reading and we never forget that it all begins with the magic of an author telling a story.

We are proud to publish talented first-time authors, as well as established writers whose books we love introducing to a new generation of readers.

We have been shortlisted for Independent Publisher of the Year at the British Book Awards three times, in 2020, 2021 and 2022, and for the Diversity and Inclusivity Award at the Independent Publishing Awards in 2022.

We built this company with your help, and we love to hear from you, so please email us about absolutely anything bookish at feedback@joffebooks.com

If you want to receive free books every Friday and hear about all our new releases, join our mailing list: www.joffebooks.com/contact

And when you tell your friends about us, just remember: it's pronounced Joffe as in coffee or toffee!

ALSO BY LESLEY GRANT-ADAMSON

RAIN MORGAN MYSTERIES

Book 1: DEATH ON WIDOW'S WALK

Book 2: DEATH IN THE SOUTH OF FRANCE

Book 3: DEATH OF AN EDITOR

Printed in Dunstable, United Kingdom

74728005R00139